Adventures of a Mad Scientist

by

Mike Bloemer

First Edition
First Printing 2017

SUMMARY: 13-year old Jesse Baxter and his 12-year old sister, Ororo, join forces with their mad scientist uncle, Mad Doc Xander, to save the world from an army of evil robots.

Printed in the United States of America

Hot Flash Entertainment
Copyright 2017

Other Books by Mike Bloemer

The School Bully Is My Brother

The Adventures Of Hairball & 'Hot-Flash' Granny

Renegade

Caution:

This novel contains action sequences that may be too intense for some readers under the age of 10. If this book were a movie, it would have a PG rating. Reader discretion is advised. (Intended for ages 10 and up.)

Chapter One: Birthday Blowout

At a refugee camp in Darfur, in the not-too-distant future...

"Ororo, get down!"

Jesse Baxter yanked his sister to the ground just as gunfire whizzed over their heads. Ororo's prosthetic arm slammed into his side, causing his eyes to tear up. Ororo started to say something, but all Jesse heard was *rat-a-tat-a-tat-a-tat-a-tat!*

As gunshots rattled Jesse's eardrums, he struggled to figure out what the heck was going on. He and his sister had been playing soccer when hot lead suddenly rained down upon their heads. He assumed Janjaweed militants were invading the refugee camp.

The gunfire suddenly stopped. Jesse and Ororo lay in the ditch for several nerve-wracking minutes.

They finally looked up when their mother, Mrs. Baxter, shouted, "Eat lasers, scumbags!"

Jesse watched in admiration as his mother ran out from behind a hut, wielding two laser blasters. She looked like Rambo in drag. The convoy of Janjaweed militants scattered like the cowards they were.

Ororo looked over at Jesse and grinned. "I bet this wasn't how you planned on spending your 13th birthday, huh?"

Jesse shrugged. "We spent your birthday battling wildlife traffickers in Malaysia. It's only fair my birthday sucks, too."

Ororo laughed and whipped out a laser blaster. "Let's get these bozos."

Jesse whipped out his own blaster. "Try and

save me some bad guys this time, alright?"

"I can't make any promises, bro."

Jesse and Ororo raced toward the Janjaweed militants at the front of the camp. Jesse fired lasers at on oncoming jeep. Two tires popped off, causing the jeep to skid to a halt. Five militants scrambled out of the vehicle, but they were immediately bombarded with lasers. The militants crumpled to the ground in unconscious heaps.

Jesse's hefty father, Mr. Baxter, ran over to check on him and his sister. His long, gray-streaked black hair fluttered in the hot African breeze, and his bulging belly shook as he weaved through gunfire.

"You guys okay?" Mr. Baxter asked, dragging Jesse and Ororo behind a hut.

"Yes, Dad," Jesse grumbled. His dad was always so overprotective.

"You guys need any more weapons?" Mr. Baxter emptied a burlap sack full of hi-tech weapons on the ground.

"Oh, I call the laser cannon," Jesse said, picking it out of the pile. This was one of the main reasons he loved traveling to the world's major hotspots; he got to play with dangerous, hi-tech gadgets.

"We must be the only humanitarian activists on the planet who carry more weapons than the United States Marines," observed Ororo, grabbing her own laser cannon. She aimed it at a Janjaweed helicopter up in the sky and pulled the trigger. A massive laser streaked through the air and slammed into the helicopter's propellers. Two militants jumped out just before the chopper crashed into the ground. It exploded on impact, raining flaming pieces of wreckage all over the countryside.

Jesse's 11-year old sister, Journey, ran out of a hut and shouted, "I wanna zap someone!" Her black hair hung over her face, indicating she had just awoken from a nap.

Journey grabbed Ororo's laser cannon and

crouched on the ground. She fired a laser at a jeep and blew it into the sky.

Mr. Baxter yanked the cannon out of Journey's hands.

"Hey! What's the big idea, Daddy?"

"Sorry, Princess, but I don't like you wielding weapons of mass destruction. It's like seeing Dora the Explorer with a grenade launcher, or Cookie Monster clutching a bazooka. It's just not right."

Journey chuckled. "That's funny. If Cookie Monster did have a bazooka, I'd probably watch more public broadcast television."

By now dozens of Janjaweed militants were pouring into the camp. Jesse and his family were vastly outnumbered.

"What should we do, Dad?" Jesse asked, peeking out from behind a hut. "We can't take all those bozos by ourselves."

Mr. Baxter opened his mouth to respond, but he was interrupted by the sound of whipping propellers. Jesse and his family looked up just in time to see a futuristic helicopter swoop overhead. Streams of tear gas and flash bombs rained down on the Janjaweed army. The militants dropped their guns and dashed out of the camp, gasping for air.

"We're not going to do anything," Mr. Baxter said with a smirk. "We're going to let your mad scientist uncle do all the dirty work."

Jesse grinned at the sight of his eccentric, middle-aged uncle poking his head out of the helicopter and shouting, "Where are you dirtbags going? The party's just getting started!" His shaggy, unkempt, gray-specked black hair swirled around in the gusting wind, as did his iconic white lab coat that he seemed to wear everywhere, even Walmart and McDonalds. (He liked everyone to know he was a world-famous scientist, even complete strangers he met on the street.)

Mad Doc Xander's helicopter hovered over Jesse and the gang like a monstrous bird protecting her newborn babies. The propellers sent Jesse's shaggy brown hair whipping around in a frenzy.

Mrs. Baxter fired the last of her lasers at the fleeing Janjaweed. "That's right, get out and don't come back! And tell your genocidal president we ain't gonna take it anymore, you hear?"

Ororo walked over and patted Mrs. Baxter on the back. "Calm down, Mom. You're gonna raise your blood pressure again."

"Sorry, dear. You know how much I hate those guys. They're the reason you…"

Mrs. Baxter gestured toward Ororo's eye-patch and prosthetic arm. Ororo nodded and blinked away the tears welling up in her good eye.

The terrified Darfurian refugees started emerging from their bullet-riddled huts. Upon realizing the Janjaweed invasion had been repelled, they all erupted in cheers.

"Aw shucks, I'm about to blush," Jesse cracked.

Doc landed his helicopter beside Jesse and hopped out. Mrs. Baxter rushed over and gave Doc a hug.

"Nice shooting, big brother," Mrs. Baxter said, rustling Doc's hirsute hair.

"You didn't do too bad yourself, sis," Doc replied.

"We can't ever seem to do any humanitarian work without running into warlords and militants," Mr. Baxter observed. He gestured to all the Janjaweed militants scattered throughout the camp, groaning in agony from their laser wounds.

"It's a good thing you always bring along your hi-tech gadgets," Mrs. Baxter said to Doc.

Doc walked over to Jesse and his sisters and gave them a smothering group hug. "You all acted heroically. Where did you learn to shoot like that, by the way?"

Jesse shrugged. "I guess from a lifetime of playing video games.

Several U.N. helicopters appeared over the horizon. They eventually landed in the center of the village to inspect the damage and arrest the wounded invaders.

One of the U.N. officials shook his head and smiled as he approached Jesse and his family. "I don't know what it is about you guys, but you always seem to attract trouble. Still, you've saved countless lives over the years. I'm glad you're on our side."

Jesse sighed and sat in the dirt. Ororo squatted beside him.

"What's wrong, bro?"

"Oh nothing. I was just hoping this summer would be little less dangerous and a whole lot more fun than all the others."

"But it was fun," Journey said. "We got to blast people."

Mr. Baxter wrung his hands. "Well, we wanted this to be a surprise, but... oh, what the heck. Your mother and I have decided it's about time we took a family vacation."

Jesse looked up and cocked an eyebrow. "Really?"

"Yep. We're going next week. And we're going on a cruise."

Jesse and his siblings stared at each other in shock.

"Seriously?" Journey blurted.

"Yep. Scout's honor." Mr. Baxter held up both hands to show he wasn't crossing any fingers. "We thought it might be nice to spend the summer somewhere nice... somewhere free of terrorists, warlords, drug lords, wildlife traffickers, slave traffickers, warlords...."

"You already said 'warlords', dear," Mrs. Baxter pointed out.

"Oh, sorry. Uh, warlords, terrorists...."

"Shut up, dear."

Jesse and his siblings erupted in cheers, frightening most of the refugees.

"Omigod, omigod, omigod!" Ororo cried, hopping around in circles. "I can't believe we're going on a cruise! Thank you, thank you, thank you!"

"Are you coming with us, Doc?" Jesse asked his uncle.

Doc shook his head. "Not this time, squirt. I have a... uh... top-secret project I'm working on."

Jesse rolled his eyes. His uncle was always working on top-secret projects. But he didn't care about that at the moment. For the first time in a long time, he was about to do something fun and non-life-threatening.

Jesse just hoped the good times lasted longer than a few hours this time.

Chapter Two: Fun In The Sun

One week later, off the coast of the Bahamas...

"So after we saved the refugee camp, my parents booked this cruise."

Jesse leaned back in his lounge chair and waited for a response. After a few seconds of awkward silence, with the notable exception of the Jamaican band playing a Bob Marley song and the kids splashing around in the pool, Jesse sat up and gave Alex Rodriguez a funny look.

"What's wrong? You don't believe me?"

Alex crossed her arms and shook her head, her shimmering black hair swinging back and forth. "Of course I don't believe you. That's the craziest story I ever heard!"

"Huh? No, seriously, I..."

"Look, Jesse, I think you're really cute. You could've won me over on your looks alone. You don't have to lie to me. I mean, we just met 20 minutes ago."

"But... I'm not... I mean..."

Alex stood up and started to walk away. "Goodbye, Jesse. I have to meet my family for dinner- AAHHH!"

Journey popped out of the pool and blasted Alex with a water gun.

"Journey, get out of here!" Jesse shouted.

"Why do you care about this dumb bimbo?" Journey asked. "Is she your *girlfriend?*"

"Bimbo?" Alex cried.

"Alex is not a bimbo," Jesse snapped. "She's the

finest woman I've ever met."

"Once again, we've only known each other for 20 minutes," Alex said. She then smirked and added, "But go on."

Jesse was about to say something, but Journey fired a stream of water into his mouth. Jesse gagged and spit it out.

Journey giggled and ran off, shouting, "Jesse's got a girlfriend, Jesse's got a girlfriend!"

Jesse rolled his eyes. "Sorry about that. My sister is off her Ritalin."

"Your sister?" Alex said. "But she looks so different from... wait a minute! That's the girl from your story? The one who reminds your dad of Dora the Explorer with a switchblade?"

"A grenade launcher," Jesse corrected. "I wish she only carried a switchblade. Journey prefers weapons that go 'BOOM'."

Alex stared at Jesse like he suddenly sprouted two heads.

"Journey was born in the Amazon," Jesse explained. "That's why she doesn't look like me. Her tribe was killed by illegal loggers, so my folks adopted her."

Alex put her hand over her heart. "The poor thing."

Jesse sensed an opening. Before he could capitalize, though, Ororo ran in front of them, kicking a soccer ball. The ball deflected off of a nearby lounge chair and flew straight toward Alex's face. Alex shrieked and covered her head. Jesse grabbed the ball right before it smashed into her nose.

Jesse laughed. "Relax, I saved you."

Alex uncovered her head. Ororo grabbed the ball away from Jesse and kicked it to the far end of the pool.

"Do you know her?" Alex asked.

"Yeah, that's my sister, Ororo. My folks adopted her from Darfur."

"Oh my gosh, she's real, too?" Alex cried.

"Jeez, I don't know if I like having all these weapon-wielding lunatics on the same boat as me and my family."

"Someone's stuck up," Jesse muttered.

Alex put her hands on her hips. "Excuse me?"

"Er, nothing," Jesse said quickly.

Jesse was interrupted by Journey's blood-curdling screams. He groaned at the sight of Journey being carried away by two burly security guards. He couldn't imagine the trouble she had gotten into in the two seconds he took his eyes off her.

Jesse held up his index finger. "I'll be right back. I need to save my sister from juvie."

Jesse hurried over to the security guards. "What seems to be the problem, officers?" His dad always said that whenever he got pulled over by the cops.

One of the guards gruffly replied, "This little girl was shooting passengers in the face with her aquatic firearm." He held up Journey's super soaker.

"We're at a freaking pool!" Journey hollered. "Who cares if people get wet?"

Ororo barged over and kicked one of the guards in the shin.

"Let my sister go, you jerks!"

Two other guards hurried over and grabbed Ororo. Ororo wriggled around like Journey, kicking her feet.

Jesse gently touched one of the guards on his shoulder. "Listen, I…"

The guard recoiled, like Jesse was about to hit him. Jesse suddenly realized it probably wasn't a good idea to make physical contact with the guards, especially after his sister nearly judo-tossed one of them into the pool.

Two other guards rushed over and grabbed Jesse. Now Jesse kicked his feet in the air.

As the guards carried Jesse and his siblings into the back, he shouted, "I'll see you later, Alex!"

Alex smirked and went back to working on her tan.

*

Fifty miles out to sea, a three-story high, 2,000-foot long airship floated over the tranquil Atlantic. A tall, pale man stood on the top deck, his brown ponytail whipping around in the brisk Caribbean breeze.

One of the man's lieutenants said, "We're about to overtake the cruise ship, Mr. Salazar. You should suit up."

Mr. Salazar flashed a grim smile… his first in many months. The Baxter family would be in his custody by night fall. And if they refused to come along peacefully… well, he wasn't called the 'Merchant of Death' for nothing.

Chapter Three: Mad Doc Xander and the Fountain of Youth

"I'm very disappointed with all of you," Mr. Baxter said as he ran his fingers through his long, graying hair.

"And I'm disappointed with your wardrobe," Jesse said. "It's embarrassing."

Mr. Baxter looked down at his unbuttoned Hawaiian shirt. His bulging, hairy belly hung over his 'daisy duke' shorts. "What do you mean? Your mother said I look nice. Right, Ariel?"

"Actually I lied, Hank," Mrs. Baxter replied bluntly as she helped Ororo don a new eye patch. "You look ridiculous."

"Oh." Mr. Baxter patted his belly. "Well, I think I look nice."

Journey hugged Mr. Baxter's leg. "I do, too, Daddy."

Mr. Baxter beamed. "Thanks, dear." He hugged her back.

"Don't you see what the kids are doing, Hank?" Mrs. Baxter said. "They're trying to make you forget they're in trouble."

Mr. Baxter slapped his forehead. "I always fall for that stuff."

Mrs. Baxter scoffed. "Unlike you, I don't fall for the kids' stupid tricks." She pointed at all of them. "You're all grounded."

"That's not a practical punishment, Mom," Jesse said, flipping through the channels on the flat- screen TV hanging from the wall.

"What do you mean?" Mrs. Baxter growled. "We're on a boat in the middle of the ocean. How are you going to ground us?"

"He's right, dear," Mr. Baxter said. "It's not very practical."

"Whose side are you on, Hank?" Mrs. Baxter snapped.

"I'm neutral, like Switzerland."

"Why are you guys so mad?" Ororo asked, checking out her new eye patch in the mirror. "We were just goofing around. Those security guards blew everything out of proportion."

Mrs. Baxter narrowed her eyes. "They showed us the security footage of you hoodlums harassing other passengers and threatening to beat up the guards. Do you have any idea how embarrassed I am? They probably think I'm a terrible mother."

"Worst of all, your mother and I were in the middle of a massage when they came to get us," Mr. Baxter lamented. "We wasted over 100 bucks!"

Mrs. Baxter sighed. "Look kids, your father and I decided to book this cruise because of everything we've been through. We thought it might be nice to spend a couple weeks in paradise instead of getting shot at. Can't you behave for the rest of the trip? Please?"

"We'll try," Jesse said.

"No, don't *try* to behave. Just behave, okay?"

Jesse and his sisters mumbled that they would be good, even though everyone in the room knew it was a lie.

"Okay, good." Mrs. Baxter grabbed the remote from Jesse and switched the channel to CNN.

"Hey, I was watching football," Jesse protested.

"Your uncle is supposed to be having some sort of press conference today about his top-secret project," Mrs. Baxter explained. "I want to see what he's been up to."

Jesse was surprised to see Uncle Xander on TV.

He was standing behind a podium, talking to a bunch of reporters.

"Aw man, we already missed some of it," Mrs. Baxter grumbled. She told Jesse and his siblings to shush and turned up the volume.

"...now I know there's a lot of skepticism out there, and rightly so," Doc said. "But you all know I'm not the sort of man who exaggerates. When I say I've created something that works, then by golly it works. That's why I'm thrilled to announce that after years of top-secret research, and millions of dollars in development, I have created... the Fountain of Youth."

Jesse and his family exchanged incredulous glances before staring back at the TV.

Reporters flashed their cameras and shouted questions. Doc raised his hands and said, "Please, I'll answer questions in a moment, but first allow me to elaborate. When I say I've created the Fountain of Youth, I mean I've developed a vaccine that inoculates the body against the effects of aging. This vaccine can be administered at any time... even moments before death.

"I'm sure most of you are curious as to how this works, so let me explain. Over the years scientists have made headway in the development of nano-technology. It's been theorized that scientists will one day be able to create billions of nano-bots that can be injected into a person's bloodstream. Those nano-bots will be able to locate and *destroy* cancerous cells, tumors, and pathogens. The nano-bots will also be able to clear arteries of cholesterol and plaque, repair brain aneurysms, and even perform surgery from *inside* the body."

Doc adjusted his microphone as the reporters mumbled amongst themselves. Once they quieted down, Doc said, "The nano-bots could also reverse the effects of old age. The reason people get old and die is because their cells are bombarded by free radicals, which decay and weaken the body. Free radicals are basically microscopic missiles chipping away at the walls of our cells. They're the reason elderly people get wrinkles, and why they die of organ failure and other causes of old age. It's thought that nano-bots would be able to repair the damage caused by free radicals. If that were to occur, then it would be possible to delay death indefinitely."

Jesse nodded in understanding. He knew all about free radicals. It was all Doc had been talking about for the past several months.

"So one day people will be able to live forever?" a reporter asked.

Doc Xander nodded. "Yes. But you are incorrect about one thing. You asked if it would be possible one day in the future."

Doc gripped the podium he was standing behind and looked out over the crowd.

"Ladies and gentlemen, those nano-bots are no longer a theory. They are a scientific fact."

Everyone at the news conference started talking again.

"This is not a hoax," Doc said. "Several months ago, my lab created the first batch of these nano-bots. In that time we've performed hundreds of tests. We injected hundreds of lab rats with the vaccine. And in recent weeks we began injecting humans."

Another reporter asked, "What was the success rate?"

Doc stared at the reporter. "I beg your pardon?"

"The success rate. How many rats were cured of their ailments?"

Doc paused a moment before replying, "The success rate was 100%. Every rat we vaccinated was cured of their disease, whether it was cancer, heart disease, or a virus."

"And what about the humans?" the reporter asked.

"The results were the same," Doc responded. "Every human we injected with the Fountain of Youth was quite literally brought back from the brink of death."

Now the reporters were talking so loud they

completely drowned Doc out.

CNN broke away from the taped conference and showed an African American reporter back at their Atlanta studio.

"This conference aired earlier this morning, and it's already the talk of the entire world," the reporter said. "Terminally ill people from all walks of life and all corners of the globe are hopeful that this invention... this 'elixir of life'... actually works. Now let's go to our panel of experts."

The reporter introduced the experts and asked one of them what she thought.

"If it turns out this immortality vaccine is the real deal, it will change the world," the expert replied. "People could live to be 200 or 300 years old. Some scientists I've talked to have said some people could live to be over 1,000!"

Another expert chimed in, "But that leads to an ethical question. Just because we *can* live forever, does that mean we *should*? I mean, look at all the problems facing the world. Overpopulation, climate change, dwindling natural resources... the list goes on and on. We can barely sustain the current human population. What happens when people stop dying? Can Earth carry a human population that numbers in the *tens of billions?*"

Mrs. Baxter turned down the volume.

Jesse looked around at his parents and siblings and grinned. "Uncle Xander created the Fountain of Youth? How cool is that!"

"I wonder if he'll give us a vial of the vaccine," wondered Mr. Baxter. "I'd like to live a couple hundred years."

"I don't care about that," Mrs. Baxter said. "I just want to get rid of my wrinkles."

Jesse's stomach suddenly growled, causing everyone to jump back in alarm.

Jesse grinned sheepishly and patted his belly. "I guess I'm hungry."

Mrs. Baxter looked at her watch and groaned. "It's getting late. Dinner starts in less than ten minutes. We need to hurry up and get dressed if we want good seats."

Mr. and Mrs. Baxter hurried to their rooms to change, as did Ororo and Journey. Jesse threw on his suit and tie and hurried into the hallway of the cruise ship.

*

Unbeknownst to Jesse and his family, a flying airship had just pulled up alongside their cruise ship. Only no one could see it. The airship had one of the world's first fully functioning cloaking devices. And it also carried one of the deadliest men the world had ever known.

Chapter Four: The 'Merchant Of Death' Comes To Dinner

When Jesse and the Baxters entered the dining hall, it was jam-packed. Only one table in the very back had six empty seats. To Jesse's pleasant surprise, it was occupied by Alex Rodriguez and her family.

Jesse ran over and said, "Hey Alex, what's up?"

Alex rolled her eyes, but Jesse noticed the faintest hint of a smile tugging at her lips.

"Would your family like to join us?" asked a heavyweight man sitting next to Alex.

"Yes, please do," said a woman who looked like an older, huskier version of Alex. "I'd love to talk to someone besides my flatulent husband and smart-alecky children."

"Hey," said a little kid with shaggy hair.

"I resemble that remark," Alex's dad said.

Mrs. Baxter walked over and asked, "Are you sure you guys don't mind?"

"Of course not," Alex's dad replied.

Jesse pulled out a chair and plopped down next to Alex. He cleared his throat and awkwardly said, "You look nice."

Jesse tried to act cool and collected whenever he talked to pretty girls, but on the inside he was always a nervous wreck. He really liked Alex and didn't want to come across as a creep.

Alex smiled at his compliment. "Thanks. You look good in a suit."

Jesse was pretty sure he was blushing. If Alex noticed, though, she never said anything.

After everyone settled down and ordered beverages, the Baxters and the Rodriguez family took turns introducing themselves. It turned out Alex's dad was Emanuel Rodriguez, the U.S. ambassador to Brazil, and her mom was Alyssa Rodriguez, a prominent Washington attorney.

Alex's brother, Jimmy, kept staring at Ororo's robotic arm. After a while, he blurted out, "Hey, where'd you get that cool arm?"

Mrs. Rodriguez pinched Jimmy, causing him to yelp. "That's not very nice, son."

She turned to Ororo and offered a sympathetic smile. "I'm sorry. He's still at that age where he doesn't know better."

"Don't worry about it, Mrs. Rodriguez. So Jimmy, you think my arm is cool?"

"Yeah!" Jimmy exclaimed. "Where can I get one?"

"Well, until they start selling them at Toys R Us, you kinda have to get your arm chopped off."

Jimmy made a face. "What?!"

Mr. Rodriguez choked on his water.

Mrs. Baxter gave Ororo a dirty look. "Come on, dear, I'm sure the Rodriguez's don't want to hear how you got your arm hacked off by Janjaweed militants when you were six years old."

Mr. Rodriguez choked on his water again.

"What's under your eye patch?" Jimmy asked excitedly.

Ororo took off her patch, revealing her glass eyeball. This time Mr. Rodriguez spit water all over the table.

"Cool!" Jimmy shouted.

Mrs. Baxter grabbed Ororo's patch and put it back over her eye. "My goodness, I can't take you kids anywhere."

Alex laughed and turned to Jesse. "I'm so glad you guys joined us. This is fun."

Jesse forced a smile, but he wasn't having fun at

all. His family was embarrassing him, like always.

The rest of the dinner was particularly torturous for Jesse. He tried to talk to Alex, but he kept getting interrupted by his wacky family. His parents whipped out baby photos from their wallets and passed them around the table. Alex nearly snorted water out of her nose when she saw the photo of Jesse in the bathtub. Journey and Jimmy ran around the table, playing tag. Ororo kept taking off her eye patch to freak out little kids. And Alex's mom attempted to talk to him about legal issues. Jesse tried to feign interest, but he secretly couldn't think of anything more boring than the United States legal system.

Jesse was thankful when the waiters brought out their food. At least now he had something to do.

As Jesse tore into his steak and garlic mashed potatoes, he tried to look out the large glass windows overlooking the ship's balcony. It was hard to see the water because the dining hall was so bright. All he could make out was his own bored reflection.

Jesse had started day-dreaming about making out with Alex when the window exploded in a shower of glass.

Everyone in the dining hall stopped what they were doing and turned around.

Mrs. Baxter shouted, "Everyone under the table, now!"

All the Baxters jumped under the table. The Rodriguez's stayed put, stunned by what was happening. Jesse and his family yanked them to the floor just as six men flew into the dining hall on what appeared to be giant flying pizza pans. All the men wore black, metallic suits and clutched hi-tech blasters. Five of them wore helmets.

The last man didn't have a helmet. He had a ghostly pale face, piercing blue eyes, and a brown ponytail that fluttered in the cool breeze. The man looked familiar to Jesse, but he couldn't remember why.

"What in the world," Mrs. Baxter muttered.

"Hank, is that Aladdin Salazar?"

"My God... it is!" Mr. Baxter exclaimed.

Jesse now knew why he recognized the man. He was the Merchant of Death.

Aladdin Salazar was wanted by nearly every government on Earth. He provided hi-tech weapons to terrorist organizations, drug cartels, warlords, human slave traffickers, and brutal dictators. He was the exact opposite of Uncle Xander. Whereas Doc developed armaments for the U.S. and her allies, Aladdin helped weaponize the scum of the Earth. He was considered by many to be the most dangerous person alive.

Everyone in the dining hall was now in full-fledged panic mode. People screamed and ran for the exits. Aladdin's armored mercenaries fired off several shots. Balls of crackling electricity exploded into the wall, raining debris on crying women and children.

In a clunky Russian accent, Aladdin said, "If anyone leaves this room, my men will kill you all."

The hundreds of terrified passengers huddled under their tables.

Jesse turned to find Alex staring at him, her eyes wide with fear.

"Why did you guys grab your silverware?" she whispered.

Jesse glanced down and realized he was clutching a knife and fork. His family was as well.

"When you've been to as many hotspots as we have, you learn to be armed at all times." Jesse tried to smile reassuringly, but it didn't work. If anything, Alex appeared more terrified.

Jesse looked back out at Aladdin and his mercenaries. He now realized the men were not, in fact, standing on flying pizza pans. They were actually hovercrafts. He had heard scientists were working on them, but he didn't realize they had actually been built.

One of the waiters stepped forward and said, "What do you think you're doing?"

Aladdin aimed his blaster at the waiter and fired. Electricity slammed into the waiter's chest, sending him flying across the room. He landed on top of a table with a thud, knocking over glasses and plates. Gasps and screams echoed throughout the dining hall.

"Don't worry, he's not dead. Not yet, at least," Aladdin said in a cold, emotionless voice. "But people will start dying if I don't get what I came for."

A brave, old man on the far side of the room called out, "What do you want?"

"Ah, a man who likes to get straight to the point. I like that."

Aladdin flew to the center of the room so everyone could see him. "I know everyone's time is valuable, and I apologize for interrupting what appears to be a splendid dinner. However, I have a serious problem, a problem that must be solved without the slightest delay. And that problem can only be solved by a certain group of people... a family, to be exact."

Mr. and Mrs. Baxter lowered their heads and groaned. Jesse groaned, too. He knew what the world's most wanted terrorist was about to say before he even opened his mouth.

"I'm looking for the Baxters. If they come along peacefully, everyone will live. If they do not... then this ship will become the world's largest floating *tomb*."

Chapter Five: The Brave Are Always The First To Die

Alex continued staring at Jesse, her body quaking with fear. "Why does he want you guys?" she whispered.

"I have no clue," Jesse said. He clutched his utensils so hard that his knuckles had turned white.

Unlike Alex, her brother, Jimmy, stared at Jesse with excitement. "Wow, you guys are the coolest people I've ever met! You have robot arms, glass eyeballs, and now evil dudes on flying pizza pans want to kill you!"

Mrs. Rodriguez threw her hand over Jimmy's mouth and whispered, "Be quiet, son. You're going to get us killed."

Aladdin slowly rotated on his hovercraft. After the third rotation, he said, "I must say I am severely disappointed. I was told the Baxters were an honorable family. It would appear my sources were mistaken."

The same old man who spoke before said, "Maybe this 'Baxter family' you speak of isn't here. Maybe you have the wrong ship."

Aladdin's cold, emotionless face showed the first signs of anger. "I do not make mistakes, old man."

The man snorted. "Well, there's a first time for everything."

Aladdin chuckled.

"You have an abundance of courage. I guess it's true what they say; the brave are always the first to die."

The old man's face turned white. "Wait, what?"

Aladdin whipped up his energy blaster and fired off several shots. Shimmering blue balls of electricity exploded into the man's chest. The man flew through the window on the far side of the ship and plummeted into the dark abyss of the Caribbean. His family cried out in grief.

Aladdin once again spun around on his hovercraft. "You fools are bending my patience to the breaking point. I'm only going to ask one more time. Where are the Baxters?"

Jesse and his siblings glanced at their parents.

Mrs. Baxter mouthed, "Stay put."

Aladdin gritted his teeth. "I really didn't want to have to do this, but…"

Aladdin gestured toward his men. All the passengers gasped as Aladdin's men reached underneath tables and grabbed little children. The children screamed as they were lifted into the air.

Just when Jesse thought things couldn't get any worse, Jimmy disappeared.

Mrs. Rodriguez jumped up and screamed, "No, not my son!"

Jesse peeked out over the side of the table. Aladdin clutched Jimmy to his chest, his energy blaster planted against his head.

"We have to do something, Mom," Jesse said, preparing to stand up.

Mrs. Baxter clutched his shoulder and said, "Not yet… but get ready."

Aladdin floated out a shattered window on his hovercraft and dangled Jimmy over the side of the ship.

Jimmy squirmed and shouted, "Let me go, you big doo-doo head!"

"Are you sure you want me to do that?" Aladdin sneered. He turned Jimmy upside down and held him up by his left ankle. Jimmy's shaggy hair now wriggled liked thousands of little worms, blowing in the crisp Bahaman breeze.

"No, I changed my mind! I forgot I can't swim!"

Mrs. Rodriguez staggered toward Aladdin. Her husband followed.

"Please, I beg of you, release my son! Take me

hostage if you want to, but leave my son alone!"

Aladdin pointed his energy blaster at the Rodriguez's and barked, "Back off!"

Mr. Rodriguez grabbed Mrs. Rodriguez's shoulders and pulled her back to the table.

Still dangling Jimmy over the side of the ship, Aladdin shouted, "I was told by legitimate sources that the Baxter family would be on this cruise ship, in this dining hall, at this precise time. *Where are they?!*"

Alex's eyes welled up with tears. "I'm sorry, Jesse, but I have to save my brother."

Jesse's heart thumped against his chest.

"Alex, wait!"

Jesse tried to grab her arm, but she had already stood up.

Alex pointed down and shouted, "They're under this table!"

The table instantly flipped over and six forks and knives went air-borne. The utensils clattered against the helmets of two of Aladdin's mercenaries. The mercenaries dropped their hostages and instinctively covered their heads. The kids scrambled to their feet and ran to their sobbing, horrified parents.

Before the mercenaries could regain their bearings, Mr. and Mrs. Baxter charged toward them. Mr. Baxter grabbed a chair and swung it at one of the mercenaries, knocking him off his hovercraft. Mrs. Baxter shocked everyone by leaping onto a table and drop-kicking the other mercenary square in the chest. The mercenary flew into the wall, shattering a framed picture. He slid to the ground as shards of glass rained down on top of him.

Jesse and Ororo grabbed the fallen mercenaries' energy blasters and aimed them at Aladdin's remaining men, who were still clutching hostages.

Mrs. Baxter landed softly on her feet and lowered into a karate stance. "Whew! I bet that was the first time anyone here has seen a 200-plus pound woman do a drop-kick."

Jesse crouched beside her and cocked his blaster. "That was pretty impressive, Mom. Your black belt in karate is finally paying off."

Aladdin threw Jimmy back into the dining hall. Jimmy landed on his butt and crawled toward his sobbing mother.

Aladdin flew toward the Baxters and barked, "Stop them! But make sure your weapons are set to stun! I need them alive!"

The three other mercenaries released their hostages and whizzed toward Jesse and the gang, their blasters a-blazing.

"Look out, kids!" Mrs. Baxter shouted as she flipped backwards to avoid an energy blast.

Jesse and Ororo rolled onto the floor and fired off several of their own shots. The mercenaries zoomed around like giant insects, narrowly avoiding the balls of electricity. The blasts blew holes in the ceiling, sending chucks of debris crashing to the floor.

Mr. Baxter continued to grab silverware and chuck it at the flying mercenaries. It didn't knock any of them off their hovercrafts, but it distracted one of the mercenaries long enough for Jesse to blast him in the back. The mercenary fell off his hovercraft and landed in front of Mrs. Baxter. Mrs. Baxter kicked the mercenary twice in the neck. She then tore off his helmet, revealing a young-looking guy with long blonde hair and a nose ring.

"You should be in college getting an education, not running around with these clowns," Mrs. Baxter said as she smashed the guy over the head with his own helmet. The mercenary collapsed into an unmoving heap.

Jesse fired off several more energy bolts, sending the last two helmeted mercenaries scrambling. One of his shots shattered the crystal chandelier hanging from the ceiling. Shards of glass and crystal fell to the ground like daggers, imbedding into the floor.

Journey snatched a crystal glass and hurled it at

one of the mercenaries, distracting him long enough for Jesse to zap him in the chest. The mercenary flew off his hovercraft and smashed into another framed picture. He slid to the ground just like his buddy and slumped over.

Jesse and Ororo twirled around and zapped the last mercenary at the same time. The mercenary flipped around in mid-air and crashed through a window on the far side of the room.

Jesse and his family turned their attention to Aladdin, who continued hovering in the front.

Doing his best to sound brave, Jesse said, "You wanted the Baxters? Well, now you got us."

Journey crossed two forks in front of her face. "Come get you some, scumbag," she snarled.

Much to Jesse's surprise, Aladdin burst out in laughter.

"This turned out to be a lot more entertaining than I expected. I really have missed you, Ariel. You too, Hank. We used to have so much fun together. But alas, that was a long time ago. How things have changed."

Jesse slowly turned toward his parents.

"Mom… Dad… what is the world's most wanted terrorist talking about?"

Mrs. Baxter continued glaring at Aladdin, but her pale face betrayed her emotions.

"Don't listen to him, son. He's a madman."

"Madman?" Aladdin cried. "Is that anyway to talk to an old friend?"

"Friend?" Ororo shouted.

"Yes," Aladdin sneered. "Is it really that hard to believe your parents would be friends with the world's most wanted fugitive?"

"Enough, Aladdin!" Mrs. Baxter snapped. "What do you want?"

Aladdin narrowed his icy eyes and inched closer to the Baxters. "It should be obvious what I want. I want your mad scientist brother. More specifically, I want his immortality vaccine."

"Why?" Mr. Baxter asked. "Are you dying? Or are we not that lucky?"

Aladdin continued chuckling. "We're obviously not getting anywhere, and I'm assuming you guys won't come along peacefully."

"Wow, you're not as dumb as you look," Jesse retorted.

Aladdin smirked and pressed a button on his arm. Six writhing, glowing cables popped out of his back. At the end of each cable were snarling, robotic snakeheads. The snakeheads resembled vipers.

The electric, robotic vipers opened their mouths and bared their gleaming fangs. Their forked tongues flickered, creating a horrifying hissing sound. It was hands down the most terrifying thing Jesse had ever seen, and he had seen lots of terrifying things.

The electric vipers zoomed toward Jesse and the Baxters and wrapped around their bodies, constricting them like pythons. Jesse and his family screamed as electricity coursed through their flailing bodies. Jesse's viper slithered right up to his left earlobe and hissed, adding even more horror to the torturous assault. The dining hall was bathed in a bright, blue light, and the crackling electricity drowned out all the screams from the passengers. Jesse was on the verge of passing out.

"No!"

Jesse watched through blurred vision as Alex grabbed his fallen blaster and aimed it at Aladdin.

Aladdin's eyes widened in surprise.

"Don't even think about it, you little…"

A ball of electricity slammed into Aladdin's chest, cutting him off. His electric vipers immediately unraveled, sending Jesse and his family tumbling to the floor.

Jesse glanced up just in time to see Aladdin fly out of the already shattered window and plummet overboard. His viper cables wriggled in the air before disappearing from view.

Chapter Six: Back From The Dead

Alex knelt beside Jesse and cradled his head in her arms.

"Are you okay?" she whispered. Tears streaked down her cheeks and plopped onto Jesse's face.

Jesse groaned and cracked open his eyes. His head felt like it was on fire.

"I've seen better days..." he muttered. He then rolled onto his stomach and vomited.

Alex stumbled backwards. "Ew, gross." She grabbed a pitcher of water from a nearby table and handed it to him. Jesse downed half the pitcher in one gulp.

Mr. Rodriguez, Mrs. Rodriguez, and Jimmy rushed over to help the rest of the Baxters. They were all smoking from their mild electrocution. Aladdin didn't discharge enough electricity to kill them, but to Jesse it sure felt like he did.

"Oh my gosh, Mr. Baxter is on fire!" Mrs. Rodriguez exclaimed, pointing at Mr. Baxter's smoldering tie. Flames lapped around the singed edges.

Mr. Rodriguez grabbed a vase, yanked out the flowers, and dumped water all over Mr. Baxter's body. Mr. Baxter shook his head like a dog that had just gotten a bath.

By now all the Baxters were either sitting up or leaning against chairs. Most of the other passengers walked around in a daze, like they had just survived a war zone. And in many ways they had.

"This is the worst vacation ever," Journey grumbled, running her fingers through her singed hair.

"I'm sorry, baby," Mrs. Baxter said, hugging Journey to her chest. "Next time we'll go to Disney World."

"You can count me out on that vacation," Jesse said in between gulps of water. "Knowing our luck, Mickey Mouse and Goofy will try to assassinate us."

"So I guess I owe you an apology, Jesse," Alex said, staring at her feet.

"You mean for ratting us out to the Merchant of Death?" he asked.

Alex glanced up and said, "Actually, I was going to apologize for not believing you when you said you were shot at in Darfur. This pretty much proves you weren't lying. But I guess I should apologize for that, too."

Jesse wiped his mouth with his smoldering tie. "Don't sweat it. You were just trying to protect your brother. To be honest, I probably would have done the same thing if Journey had been taken hostage."

"I wouldn't have been taken hostage," Journey said. She gave Jimmy a dirty look. "I would have fought back."

Jimmy raised his hands in the air and shouted, "Are you kidding me? I'm ten! What was I supposed to do?"

Journey shook her head and sighed. "Boys. You always have excuses."

Jesse chuckled, which ended up hurting his sides.

Alex helped Jesse to his feet. Jesse staggered back and bumped into an overturned table. An elderly man helped him regain his footing. He patted Jesse on the back and said, "You did real good, kid. Your whole family did. Thanks for saving our lives."

An old lady who Jesse assumed was the man's wife bitterly remarked, "They may have saved our lives, but they're also the ones who put us in danger. If they had never come on this blasted cruise, then that psychopath never would have come here."

Jesse felt his face turn red. The old woman was right. His family had endangered the lives of thousands of people. But it wasn't like they *knew* the Merchant of Death was after them. Although his parents apparently used to be on good terms with him…

Using Alex as a crutch, Jesse made his way over to his mom.

"So what's this about you and Aladdin Salazar being old pals?"

Mrs. Baxter avoided eye contact. "Now is not the time, Jesse. We'll talk about this later."

"How about we talk about it now?"

Mr. Baxter sternly said, "Hey, don't talk to your mother that way."

"Why don't you guys quit hiding secrets from us?" Jesse shouted. Even he was surprised at how angry he sounded.

Jesse expected his parents to scold him, but instead they stared at the ground, like they were ashamed.

"I thought we told each other everything," Ororo said, adjusting her lopsided eye patch. "It would've been nice if you mentioned you were friends with a psychotic terrorist."

"We're not friends with him," Mrs. Baxter said. "We just used to know him, back before he turned… bad."

"He was our classmate at Harvard," Mr. Baxter said. "Your Uncle Xander was our professor."

"Wait, what?" Jesse said. "Isn't Doc only a few years older than you? How could he have been your teacher in college?"

"Your uncle is a brilliant man," explained Mrs. Baxter. "He graduated from college while he was still a teenager. He got a job at Harvard shortly before your father and I went there."

Jesse was about to ask another question when a loud clanking noise interrupted him. Everyone in the dining hall turned around just in time to see a glowing, metallic viper cable wrap around the ship's railing. Then another viper appeared, then another and another. Finally Aladdin Salazar levitated into the sky, his vipers pulling him from the depths of the Caribbean. His long hair now hung over his face like sopping wet seaweed, and his teeth were gnashed together like a rabid pit bull.

"Oh no, doo-doo head is back from the dead!" Jimmy hollered, hiding behind his mom.

Most of the ship passengers screamed and stampeded toward the exit. A few people got knocked over. Jesse hoped they survived being trampled.

The Baxters and the Rodriguez family were the only ones to stand their ground. Jesse and Ororo grabbed their energy blasters and aimed them at Aladdin. The rest of the family armed themselves with food-stained silverware and shattered glasses.

Jesse pointed toward the exits. "Alex, take your family and get out of here!"

"But---"

"No buts!" he snapped. "We can handle ourselves. But you guys need to leave, now!"

Mrs. Rodriguez picked up Jimmy and ran toward the exit. Mr. Rodriguez grabbed Alex's shoulders and practically had to drag her with him.

"Be careful guys!" Alex cried.

"Don't worry, we won't," Jesse replied.

Aladdin cracked his knuckles and growled, "That's it, no more Mr. Nice Guy."

"Nice guy?" Jesse cried. "Are you freaking kidding me?"

Aladdin pressed a button on his arm. His hovercraft shot off the ground and flew under his feet. Aladdin's electric viper cables retracted back inside his armored, robotic suit, and he landed on the hovercraft with a thud. He then held out his hands, which began to emit a soft red glow.

A split-second later, ten ruby-red lasers ejected from Aladdin's fingertips. Jesse and his family dived for cover. Jesse rolled under a table and fired his blaster.

The energy bolt narrowly missed Aladdin's head, passing by so closely that some of his hair stood up. Aladdin aimed his entire right hand at Jesse and blew his table to bits.

Jesse rolled around on the floor, narrowly avoiding the barrage of lasers. One laser did eventually strike his leg. Jesse cried out in pain and grabbed his knee. It felt like being stung by twenty bumblebees.

Aladdin flew around the room to avoid the silverware the rest of the family chucked at him.

"Surrender and I'll show mercy. Resist and you will die."

"You sure do play up your 'bad guy' image," Jesse grunted, hopping around on one leg while firing off a salvo of electricity.

Jesse was relieved when six security guards barged into the dining hall. All six of the guards pulled out their guns and pointed them at Aladdin.

"Freeze! You're under arre... what in the world?"

Jesse could tell the guards were surprised to see an armored nutjob whizzing around on a flying pizza tray.

While Aladdin focused his attention on the security guards, Jesse and his family jumped through a shattered window and ran out on deck.

Gasping for air, Mrs. Baxter said, "I'm getting way too old for this stuff."

"And I'm too fat," Mr. Baxter said, clutching his love-handles.

"What do we do now?" Ororo asked breathlessly.

Before anyone could respond, Journey shouted, "Look at that!"

Jesse and his family turned to where Journey was pointing and gasped. Right next to the cruise ship was a gigantic, 3-story high aircraft carrier. Except the aircraft carrier wasn't on the water... it was floating in the air!

Mrs. Baxter shook her head in disbelief. "I heard that thing existed, but I thought... I hoped... it was a rumor."

Blinding blue light suddenly lit up the dining hall. One of the guards flew out the window and plummeted into the ocean. Then another guard flew out the window, then another, then another, then another, then another. Once all of the guards were disposed of, Aladdin zoomed outside on his hovercraft, his metallic vipers swinging erratically over his head.

Aladdin zoomed down and grabbed Journey by her arm. He started to carry her into the sky when Journey slashed him across his cheek with a fork. Aladdin screamed and dropped her. Jesse caught Journey while Ororo zapped Aladdin in the chest, sending him crashing through another dining hall window.

"Move, move, move, move!" Mrs. Baxter screamed.

Jesse and his family took off toward the rear of the ship.

Chapter Seven: Cruise Ship Guerilla Warfare

As Jesse's feet pounded the deck, he noticed dozens of hovercrafts zooming toward him. They all seemed to be coming from the flying aircraft carrier.

"Aw man, Aladdin's sending a whole freaking army after us!"

"What should we do, Mom?" Ororo huffed, firing shots over her shoulder

"Well, they certainly have us outnumbered," Mrs. Baxter said as she ran through the pool area, which was now deserted. "So we'll just do what every underdog army has done throughout history: wage guerilla warfare."

"Guerilla warfare?" Jesse repeated.

"Yes. Out in the open we're sitting ducks. So let's go inside the cramped interior of the ship. It'll be harder for his men to snatch us."

"Sounds like a plan to me," Jesse said, continuing to fire energy bolts.

Jesse and his family ran into a side door and barged down a flight of stairs to the top floor of the pavilion. The pavilion was basically a three-story shopping mall. Each floor was constructed in the shape of a horseshoe, with dozens of stores. There was a massive rail-encircled opening in the center of each floor, allowing passengers to see the entire shopping area. Of course, there were no passengers in the pavilion at the moment. Jesse assumed most of them were hiding in their rooms. The ship looked like a ghost town.

Six of Aladdin's mercenaries burst into the pavilion and fired their energy guns. Some of their shots sparked fires in the stores. Water began pouring from the sprinklers.

A mercenary popped up next to Ororo and fired a grappling hook. The grappling hook wrapped around Ororo's leg, knocking her flat on her face. Ororo's energy blaster clattered to the floor. The mercenary then took off toward the front of the ship, with Ororo dangling in the air.

"Ororo!" Jesse shouted. He zapped another mercenary zooming toward him. The mercenary flew backwards like a bomb had exploded and fell over the side of the pavilion. His hovercraft crashed into the wall and fell to the ground, spinning in circles before finally coming to a stop.

Jesse took a deep breath and hopped onto the hovercraft. It levitated into the air, nearly knocking him off balance.

Out of the corner of his eye, Jesse saw his dad pick up Ororo's fallen blaster and start zapping the other mercenaries. His mom dropkicked a mercenary zooming toward her while Journey rooted them on. Relieved that his parents and little sister were holding their own, Jesse decided to rescue Ororo. He leaned over the edge of the hovercraft, causing it to shoot forward like a cannonball.

It only took Jesse a few seconds to figure out how to work the flying pizza pan. It was sort of like a segway scooter, accelerating in whichever direction he leaned. Jesse soon caught up with Ororo and fired energy bolts at the mercenary dragging her through the air.

Ororo raised her upper body and grabbed a blade strapped to her thigh. She then hacked through the grappling hook. Jesse caught her just as she started to fall.

"Thanks, bro," Ororo said, hopping onto the hovercraft. She grabbed his energy blaster and fired at two mercenaries riding their butts.

Mrs. Baxter zoomed past Jesse and Ororo,

piloting her own stolen hovercraft. Mr. Baxter popped up behind her, carrying Journey.

"Now that we all have hovercrafts, we can fly to safety," Mrs. Baxter said.

Mrs. Baxter led Jesse, Ororo, and the rest of the family into the ship's sprawling weight room. The room had dozens of treadmills, elliptical machines, and free weights. Flat-screen TVs hung from the ceilings. The room was U-shaped and completely enclosed behind full-plate glass windows, which looked out over the sparkling ocean.

Mrs. Baxter was just about to blast through one of the windows when several of them shattered, blowing glass shards everywhere. Six mercenaries flew inside.

A powerful gust of wind blew in from the sea and nearly knocked Jesse off his hovercraft. He watched in horror as one of the mercenaries blasted his mother in the chest. She flew off her hovercraft and crumpled to the ground. Jesse's dad landed to check on her.

Jesse landed his hovercraft as well so he and Ororo could draw the mercenaries away from their parents. Ororo exchanged shots with the mercenaries, illuminating the gym in an eerie, electric blue light. One of her energy bolts blasted a mercenary out to sea. His blaster fell to the ground, which Jesse promptly grabbed.

As Jesse and Ororo traded energy bolts with Aladdin's mercenaries, errant blasts blew apart flat-screen TVs, short-circuited treadmills, and shattered windows and mirrors. Every time a window blew out, even more wind swooped in, transforming the gym into a giant wind tunnel. Sparks from the demolished TVs and treadmills rained down all over the place, swirling around in the wind.

Mr. Baxter picked up a barbell with two 45-pound weights attached to the ends.

"This was a lot easier when I was younger," he grunted.

Mr. Baxter turned and heaved the barbell at a mercenary just as he lit up the room with an energy blast. The barbell knocked the mercenary off his hovercraft. The hovercraft slammed into a mirror and clattered to the ground, inches from where Mr. Baxter was standing.

Mr. Baxter slung Mrs. Baxter's semi-conscious body over his shoulder and stepped onto the hovercraft. He immediately levitated into the air. "Let's move, kids!"

Jesse handed Journey a fallen mercenary's blaster and yanked her aboard his hovercraft. Ororo hopped onto an abandoned hovercraft that lay off to the side.

Mr. Baxter barreled out of one of the shattered windows, dodging several mercenaries. Jesse and his siblings followed suit.

Mr. Baxter tried to lead Jesse and the gang to the front of the ship, but they were forced to change course when a phalanx of 25 mercenaries zoomed around the corner, firing a relentless onslaught of electricity.

"Okay kids, back inside the ship!" Mr. Baxter hollered, banking sharply to the left.

Mr. Baxter flew through a glass-plated door, shattering it into thousands of pieces. Jesse and his sisters squeezed through the shattered door unscathed.

Jesse and the gang whizzed through a narrow hallway and burst into the ship's auditorium. Hundreds of people were huddled near the stage, seeking safety.

"Jesse!"

Jesse looked down to see Alex standing on stage, wildly flailing her arms. Jimmy was next to her, jumping around excitedly. The kid looked like he was having the time of his life.

"Hey Alex, glad to see you're okay!" Jesse shouted.

Still jumping around like a maniac, Jimmy yelled, "Hey Journey, do you wanna go out sometime?! We can go to Chuck E Cheese!"

"Sorry, I don't date boys shorter than me!" Journey replied.

A dozen mercenaries whooshed into the auditorium, firing their energy blasters. The curtains hanging from the stage almost immediately caught fire. The cruise passengers screamed and ran for the exits.

Jesse turned up the voltage on his blaster, aimed it at the wall, and fired several energy bolts. The wall exploded outward, leaving behind a gaping hole. This enabled all the passengers to flee at once, reducing the risk of anyone getting trampled.

"Good thinking, son!" Mr. Baxter shouted, zipping toward the new exit. He led Jesse and his siblings back through the demolished pavilion. Most of the shop windows were cracked and shattered, and several were still on fire. The sprinklers had released so much water that the bottom floor was flooded.

Jesse and his sisters were flying a good twenty yards behind their parents. Jesse got a clear view of a mercenary on the third floor of the pavilion, crouched like a sniper, his energy blaster aimed directly at Mr. Baxter's head.

"Dad, look out!" Jesse shouted.

He was too late. An energy blast smashed into the side of Mr. Baxter's head. Mr. Baxter flew off his hovercraft and plummeted toward the water-covered floor, his face white from shock, his body crackling with electricity. Mrs. Baxter tumbled after him. For Jesse the traumatic event seemed to unfold in slow motion.

Jesse was too far away to catch his parents. All he could do was watch in horror as his mom and dad fell three stories and slammed onto the floor.

Mr. and Mrs. Baxter both landed spread-eagle, like fallen angels, partially submerged in a pool of water. They did not move. They did not open their eyes. For all Jesse knew, his parents were dead.

Journey's ear-splitting scream snapped Jesse back to reality. And the energy bolts whizzing past his head got him moving. He desperately wanted to check on his parents, but half a dozen mercenaries were already hovering over their unmoving bodies, like vultures surveying a carcass. And dozens of other mercenaries barreled straight toward him and his sisters, like mosquitoes drawn to a bright light. Without looking back, Jesse zoomed toward the pavilion exit.

"We have to go back and get Mom and Dad!" Journey screamed, tears streaking down her cheeks.

Blinking away his own tears, Jesse said, "It's too late for them. If we go back, we're dead."

Journey pounded on Jesse's chest. "No! We can't leave them! They would never leave us! Go back! Go back!!"

Jesse ignored his hysterical sister. He had enough trouble weaving through criss-crossing energy blasts. He glanced behind him and was relieved to see Ororo hot on his trail. He knew it was killing her to leave their parents behind.

Jesse and his sisters finally exited the pavilion and flew back on deck. There were now so many mercenaries buzzing around in the sky that they looked like a swarm of giant locusts. Their armor reflected the moonlight in such a way that some of them resembled fire flies.

Dozens of mercenaries dived toward him. Jesse flew to the only place left to go… the miniature replica of New York's Central Park, right next to the pool.

The cruise ship was one of the biggest ever built. It had a climbing wall, ice-skating rink, movie theater, bowling alley, and most impressive of all, a mini forest on the top deck. Jesse and his family didn't go on vacation often, but when they did, they splurged. And it was a good thing they did, because it gave Jesse and his siblings a great place to hide.

Jesse flew deep into the forest, past several artificial ponds. He knew Aladdin's mercenaries were hot on his trail. He could hear dozens of hovercrafts zipping past trees.

Jesse landed the hovercraft next to one of the ponds. He grabbed Journey's hand and pulled her even further into the forest. Ororo landed and ran after them.

They had just crouched behind several bushes when three mercenaries flew by on their hovercrafts.

"We can't hide here forever," Ororo whispered, peeking through the bushes.

Jesse knew that. He just hoped to hide long enough to formulate a plan. Unfortunately, he couldn't even do that. They had only been hiding for a few minutes when four mercenaries landed 100 feet away and began searching behind all the trees.

Jesse grabbed Journey's hand and ran in the opposite direction. Jesse glanced behind him, expecting Ororo to be right there. He was horrified to find her lying on the ground, tied up with a grappling hook.

Ororo lifted her head and shouted, "Don't worry about me, go get help! Get-ARRGGH!"

A mercenary zapped Ororo with an energy gun. She now lay in an unconscious heap.

"Ororo!" Journey screamed. She tried to run toward her, but Jesse quickly slung his feisty little sister over his shoulder. Journey struggled to get down, but Jesse held her tight.

Jesse had just started running when six mercenaries flew overheard.

"There they are!" shouted one of the mercenaries. "Zap 'em!"

Jesse twirled around and took off down a faded path. Energy bolts detonated inches from his feet, sending clumps of dirt into the air. The combined weight of Journey and both of their blasters was wearing him down. He didn't know how much farther he could run before collapsing from exhaustion.

Six more mercenaries suddenly popped up in front of him. Jesse turned to his right and nearly ran into another six mercenaries. He turned to his left just in time to see six more mercenaries appear.

One of the mercenaries hopped off his hovercraft and slowly approached Jesse. "Give it up, kid. There's no way out. We can do this the easy way or the hard way."

Jesse lowered Journey to the ground and aimed his blaster at the mercenary. "Oh yeah? What's the hard way?"

"We beat you and your sister to a bloody pulp. Mr. Salazar said we couldn't kill you, but that doesn't mean we can't break a couple bones."

Jesse calmly replied, "Okay, so what's the easy way?"

"This." The mercenary zapped Jesse in the chest. Jesse flew backwards and slammed into a tree trunk. The force of the impact nearly knocked him out. He slid to the ground and struggled to stay conscious.

"Jesse!"

Jesse cracked open his eyes and groggily watched as Journey blasted the mercenary off his feet. She then twirled around in circles, firing a steady stream of electricity. All of the mercenaries backed away.

Journey continued spinning until her gun stopped spitting out electricity.

"What the---"

The mercenaries flew back toward Journey.

"You drained the battery, kid," one of the mercenaries said with a demented chuckle.

The remaining mercenaries all pointed their blasters at Journey.

"Put your hands over your head, girlie," another mercenary commanded. "We don't want to hurt you, but we will if you force us to."

"Do your worst," Journey snarled. She yanked a fork out of her blouse and held it in front of her face.

The mercenary chuckled. "This is why I never had kids."

"Oh, is that why?" Journey snapped. "Are you sure it's not because you're a loser and no girl would ever go out with you?"

The mercenary zapped Journey in the stomach. She slammed into a tree trunk like Jesse, then slid to the ground in a crumpled heap. She did not get back up.

Two mercenaries lowered to the ground to retrieve Journey's unmoving body. Jesse took that opportunity to stagger to his feet. All the mercenaries twirled around and stared at him in shock, like they couldn't believe he was still fighting. Jesse hopped onto a hovercraft a mercenary had foolishly left nearby and shot into the sky.

Jesse planned on flying to the Bahamas to get help, but Aladdin's men cut him off. Over fifty mercenaries revolved around him in a giant circle.

Aladdin Salazar hovered in front of Jesse, his ponytail fluttering in the breeze. Three fresh scars lined his right cheek, the result of Journey slashing him with a fork.

"Hello, Jesse. I haven't seen you since you were a baby."

"Wait, you knew me as a baby?" Jesse stammered, struggling to stay calm.

"Yes. I wasn't lying when I said your parents and I used to be close."

Jesse narrowed his eyes. "Yes, it's a shame they decided to quit hanging out with a mass-murdering lunatic."

Aladdin simply smirked. "You are brave, child. Stupid, but brave."

Jesse mustered up all his remaining courage and barked, "Now let us go or…"

"Or what?" Aladdin snapped. "What are you going to do, child? You're vastly outnumbered. Escape is impossible."

"Maybe," Jesse acknowledged, doing his best to keep his voice from trembling. "But I'm not going down without a fight. My mom always said if you're surrounded by a bunch of bullies, you should take out the leader. The rest will run scared."

Aladdin's men burst out in hysterical laughter.

Aladdin grinned. "Your mother is a smart woman."

"The smartest I've ever known," Jesse said. He

then leaped off his hovercraft and hurtled toward Aladdin.

Jesse intended to tackle Aladdin off his hovercraft. That didn't quite work out. Aladdin moved at the last possible nano-second and caught Jesse by his neck. Jesse dangled high in the air, Aladdin's armored hand clutched firmly around his throat.

Aladdin whispered into Jesse's ear, "Do you surrender now?"

"Go... to... Hell...," Jesse gagged.

"Oh, I plan to. Most of my favorite people are already there."

Aladdin tightened his chokehold. Jesse's eyes rolled into the back of his head and his world went black.

Chapter Eight: Mad Doc Xander & The President Of The United States

Inside a military base on the outskirts of Los Angeles...

"Ladies and gentlemen, I present to you the world's first invisibility suit."

Mad Doc Xander stepped back and gestured toward... nothing.

After a moment of awkward silence, Secretary of Defense Robert Paternus said, "I don't see anything."

"Well duh, Robert," Doc replied. "It's invisible. You wanted me to develop an invisibility suit for the military, so I made one."

Most of the people in the room chuckled. The Secretary of Defense scowled and mumbled under his breath. He wasn't the world's biggest Mad Doc Xander fan, but he did realize he was extremely talented at what he did... which, in the case of the U.S. military, meant providing hi-tech, futuristic weapons. With Aladdin Salazar helping arm America's enemies, the U.S. was desperate for her own hi-tech arms dealer. Mad Doc Xander may have been eccentric, but he was America's best deterrent against Aladdin's illegal weapons trade.

While Paternus may not have been particularly fond of Doctor Xander, the president certainly was. President Barry Robinson folded his dark hands over his mouth so no one could see him smile. Unfortunately, the crinkles near his eyes gave him away.

Secretary of Defense Paternus ran his fingers through his thinning white hair and gruffly said, "Listen

Xander, we are giving you hundreds of millions of dollars a year to create weapons that allow America to defend herself. So hopefully you can understand why I get slightly agitated when you play practical jokes on us. My time is valuable, and so is the president's time."

"Actually, all I have going on later is a Hollywood fundraiser," President Robinson replied.

"Well, my time is valuable!" Paternus groused. "We're waging several counter-insurgencies throughout Africa and the Middle East. I don't have time to... *AHHHH!!!*"

Secretary of Defense Paternus clutched his chest and toppled out of his chair. The president looked alarmed as well. And for good reason; a floating head materialized out of thin air.

"Whew, it's getting mighty hot in this suit, Doc," the floating head said. The head was rather good-looking, with long blonde hair that covered bright green eyes.

"Martin, put your helmet back on," Doc ordered. "You nearly gave the Secretary of Defense a heart attack."

Paternus was still on the floor, breathing heavily. President Robinson helped him to his feet. He then waved at the floating head and said, "Hey Martin, how you been?"

"Eh, I've been better, Mr. President," the floating head replied. "Stupid Doc here made me wear this terrible invisibility suit all day long."

Doc chuckled nervously. "Shut up, Martin. The suit is not terrible. It's a technological marvel."

"That's what you said about the jet-pack you invented two years ago," Martin said. "Your old assistant hasn't been the same since his pack exploded 1,000-feet in the air. And remember when---mmmmm!"

Doc threw his hand over Martin's mouth and smiled at their high-profile guests. By now the president wasn't even trying to hide his amusement. Paternus, on the other hand, looked more infuriated than ever. He wasn't too fond of people capable of nearly short-circuiting his pacemaker.

Doc continued giving Martin Carter a dirty look, but he didn't berate him. He didn't want Martin to get mad and storm out. It's not like he could put an ad in the paper and get another assistant. He had tried that many times, and it never worked. All of Doc's previous assistants nearly died in horrific accidents, so there weren't too many people eager to work for him.

Martin was only 19, but he was one of the most brilliant teenage prodigies Doc had ever met. He was able to type up lines of complex computer codes, and he was one of the few people on the planet who comprehended quantum mechanics and string theory. He graduated from high school by the age of 14 and graduated from Harvard just last year. And for the past two years he had been Doc's part-time assistant.

Martin may have been incredibly intelligent, but he was also very clumsy. He was so clumsy, in fact, that no other lab in the country wanted anything to do with him. That was probably one of the reasons he agreed to work for Doc, a job other scientists privately referred to as suicide.

"So how does this contraption work?" Paternus barked, pointing at Martin's floating head.

"Great question," Doc said. He whipped out a remote and pointed it at Martin. A split-second later, his entire body came into view.

Martin wore an armored exoskeleton covered with a shiny, reflective material. He also carried a helmet. Paternus walked over and stared at the invisibility suit in shock.

"This computerized exoskeleton is covered in a thin layer of 'Metaflex'," Doc explained. "Metaflex is composed of metamaterials, which are a bunch of microscopic structures that have the ability to control light. These metamaterials are what render the exoskeleton invisible. It's based on the same sonar-cloaking technology used on subs, aircraft carriers, and stealth fighter jets. And, best of all, you can control the invisibility function at will."

Doc pressed another button, and Martin's body vanished. Only his head remained visible.

"Amazing," Paternus muttered. "If our troops wear this out in the field, they'll be virtually unstoppable."

"Once again you've outdone yourself, Doc," President Robinson said. "When do you think these suits will be ready for mass production?"

"Right now I only have a few prototypes, but if you guys like them, I could probably have a couple hundred ready for you by the end of the year."

"We'll take 'em!" Paternus blurted.

"Now hold on, Robert, we need to make sure this will be worth the cost." The president turned to Doc and asked, "How much will this cost us, Zach?"

"Normally I'd say a billion…"

"A billion?!" Paternus cried, once again clutching his chest.

"…but since I like you all, I'll cut you a deal. Does $500 million sound good?"

President Robinson shrugged. "Eh, the national debt isn't going down anytime soon. What's a few extra hundred million dollars?"

Martin nodded. "That's what I like to hear, fiscal irresponsibility."

"I'll also throw in a few of these cool laser blasters I invented." Doc grabbed a blaster off the table and fired a red laser through the wall, leaving a gaping hole

"Nice," Paternus said.

The president swatted at two giant flies buzzing above his head.

"Hey, don't hit those robotic locusts," Doc commanded. "They cost me a fortune."

"Why on tarnation would you make robotic locusts?" Paternus cried.

"Why wouldn't I? These robotic locusts are

amazing. They fire lasers, project holographic maps and images, and have tiny cameras. You can program them to follow your enemies and record top-secret meetings."

Paternus' eyes began to glaze over. "Wow! I want 'em!"

"Are you prepared to fork over another half a billion dollars?"

The president spit out the water he was drinking. "Why would two robotic bugs cost $500 million dollars?"

"Because these 'bugs' are a couple of the most destructive weapons ever created."

"Oh yeah?" Paternus said, sounding highly skeptical. "Prove it."

Doc cupped his hands around his mouth and shouted, "Goldie, get in here!"

A robot that looked like a trash can with blinking lights rolled into the room. Goldie had an upside-down fishbowl on top of her 'garbage can' body. Inside the fishbowl was a giant goldfish. Goldie also had metallic arms, mechanical hands, wheels on the bottom that allowed her to move around, and a small TV screen on the front. Inside her body she housed various weapons, including laser guns, tasers, miniature heat-seeking missiles, metallic tentacles, and a ventilation shaft that released knock-out gas. Goldie was basically a futuristic mobile Swiss army knife… with an attitude.

In a voice that could have belonged to any girl from New Jersey, Goldie said, "Whadda ya want, Doc? I was watchin' my soaps."

"You programmed your robot slave to like soap operas?" Paternus asked incredulously.

"Who ya callin' a slave, ya yutz?" Goldie snapped. The lights on her body began blinking like a malfunctioning Christmas tree. "This ain't the 1800s, pal. I'm compensated for my services. Doc pays me by the kilowatt hour."

The Secretary of Defense had no response to smart-alecky robot one-liners, so he simply stared at Doc with a dumbfounded look on his face.

"Goldie isn't just some dumb robot," Doc explained. "She's one of the first robots ever installed with human-like artificial intelligence. She learned to like soap operas all on her own. She also likes lusty romance novels."

Paternus cocked an eyebrow. "The robot with the fishbowl head reads?"

"Of course I read, ya yutz!" Goldie retorted. "Do I look like an idiot ta ya?"

Paternus continued shaking his head in disbelief. "Why on Earth does she have a fishbowl on her head?"

Doc shrugged. "I like goldfish."

Goldie wheeled toward Doc. "The Secretary of Defense keeps insultin' me. I don't need this. I'm goin' back ta my soaps."

"No Goldie, I need you to help me with something."

Goldie pointed at Martin's floating head. "Why can't junior help ya? He never does any work."

"I need your help because... uh... Martin's not as smart as you."

"Hey," Martin said.

If robots could blush, Goldie would have been as red as a fire truck.

"Jeez Doc, you're embarrassin' me. Okay, whadda ya want me ta do?"

"Just... uh... stand there and look pretty."

Goldie flapped her mechanical hand. "Oh hush."

Doc pointed at Goldie and said, "Okay boys, sic her!"

The robotic locusts zoomed toward Goldie and began tearing off pieces of her body.

"AHHHHH!!! I'm being violated!!!"

Goldie wheeled around in circles, waving her hands in the air. Martin's floating head burst out in hysterical laughter. Everyone else in the room gawked in horror at the disturbing sight of Goldie being assaulted by robot locusts.

"Help! Get 'em offa me! Get 'em off! This is above my pay grade!"

The robotic locusts stopped tearing off pieces of Goldie's trash can body and hovered in the air.

Goldie stopped wheeling around in circles and said, "Thank goodness. That was the scariest thing that ever happened ta me."

The locusts made a weird grinding noise, then their bellies opened and two more locusts popped out.

"Ahhh, they're reproducing!" Goldie cried, spinning around in circles.

The four locusts went back to tearing off pieces of Goldie's body.

"Um, aren't you going to do something, Doc?" the president asked, shouting to be heard over Goldie's ear-splitting screams.

Doc waved his hands and shouted, "Okay boys, stop!"

The locusts spit out pieces of Goldie's body and hovered in the air.

Sparks shot out of the inside of Goldie's body as her repair mechanism kicked on. "Would ya mind tellin' me what the heck that was all about?!" Goldie hollered.

Doc turned to Paternus. "These locusts are the first robots to be installed with a self-replicating mechanism. They're programmed to take organic material and use it to create clones."

Paternus shook his head. "I'm afraid I don't follow you, son."

"Think of the locusts as having a miniature factory inside their bodies," Doc explained. "They take bits of metal and other organic material and break them down to their subatomic level. The locusts then reassemble those microscopic particles and build replicas of themselves. The clones then take bits of organic material and make their own clones."

Doc could tell by Paternus' blank stares that he still had no idea what he was talking about.

"Think of it this way," Doc elaborated. "If you

start with two locusts and program them to attack a tank, for instance, they will use the tank's material to make two more locusts. Then those four locusts will create four more locusts. Then those eight locusts will make sixteen locusts, then those locusts will make thirty-two locusts, and so on and so forth. Eventually you will have a giant swarm of tiny, flying robots tearing apart buildings, planes, tanks, aircraft carriers, rogue nuclear reactors, you name it. Within a matter of hours, two of these robotic locusts will become thousands of destructive parasites. You could drop two locusts on top of an aircraft carrier, and within an hour it'll have completely vanished. It's like having self-replicating piranhas. "

Paternus smiled as he finally understood what Doc was talking about.

"You sold me. I want 'em!"

Doc returned the grin. "I truly think the locusts are my greatest creation."

"No, I'm your greatest creation, and you nearly killed me," Goldie said as she put the finishing touches on her reconstructive surgery. She now looked brand new.

"Actually, your greatest creation is your Fountain of Youth," Martin said.

President Robinson beamed. "That's right. I've been meaning to ask you about your immorality vaccine. I can't tell you how many heads of state have called me up asking about it. You have the hopes of the entire human race on your shoulders."

Doc gave a nervous chuckle. He himself had been blown away by the response. He clearly underestimated how badly people wanted to live forever.

One of Paternus' aides, a middle-aged woman with gray-streaked black hair and glasses, leaned forward. "So does it really work, Doctor Xander?" she asked eagerly.

Doc hesitated a moment, then said, "Er, yes, Maggie. It really does work. Even I was astonished by the results. I expected it to work maybe half the time. I certainly didn't expect it to have a 100% success rate. It truly is a miracle drug."

"So when will it be ready for the market? My sister is very sick." Maggie removed her glasses and rubbed her moist eyes. "She has stage-four pancreatic cancer. She could really use a miracle."

Doc's heart almost cleaved in two. He lowered his head and quietly said, "I'm very sorry to hear that, Maggie. The FDA hasn't approved it for the market yet, but…"

Maggie looked up. Her tear-filled eyes expressed the faintest glimmer of hope.

"…maybe I could set your sister up for a test trial."

Maggie threw her hands over her mouth and gasped. "Oh my goodness, could you really, Doc?"

Doc nodded. "Yeah, I don't see why not."

Maggie ran up to Doc and hugged him. "Oh thank you! Thank you!"

There wasn't a dry eye in the room (with the notable exception of Goldie, who didn't exactly have an eye). Even Paternus had to discreetly wipe away a tear.

After Maggie sat back down, Doc cleared his throat and said, "You guys seem more interested in my Fountain of Youth than the laser blasters and invisibility suits. I find that somewhat ironic, considering you're paying me for the weapons."

"You really shouldn't be surprised," Maggie said. "This cure you've created, this vaccine that quite literally eradicates death, changes everything."

"Maggie's got a point," President Robinson said. "If people begin living hundreds of years, our society will drastically change. This is bigger than the creation of the light bulb, the computer, the atom bomb, and the moon landing *combined*. I wouldn't be surprised if you replaced Einstein as the most influential scientist of all time."

Doc blushed. "Oh stop. I may be more

influential than Isaac Newton, but not Einstein." ·

"Way to be humble, Doc," grumbled Martin's floating head.

"I am concerned about the national security aspects of Xander's vaccine," Paternus grunted.

"What do you mean?" the president asked.

"Think about it, sir. Xander here has created a vaccine that cures every disease known to man. How many millions of people out there are suffering from some sort of ailment? Am I the only one worried that some of those sick people will become desperate and do whatever it takes to secure a vial of the vaccine?"

The mood in the room changed instantaneously. Nobody but Paternus had thought about the potential dangers of advertising a cure for all diseases.

President Robinson massaged his head and sighed. "You bring up a somber point, Robert. We very well may see a global outbreak in violence as desperate people utilize desperate measures to ensure their immortality."

A young female military officer burst into the room and rushed over to the president. She whispered something in his ear, then stepped back. The president's normally dark face turned ghostly pale.

After a moment of awkward silence, the president said, "Bring up the video."

"What's wrong, Mr. President?" Paternus asked.

President Robinson glanced at Doc. "Zach, when's the last time you spoke with your family?"

Now Doc's face turned pale. "Just a few days ago, Mr. President. Right now they should be in the Bahamas. I'm supposed to pick them up at the airport next week."

The aide turned on a massive television screen hanging from the wall.

"The Pentagon was informed of this video about 20 minutes ago, Mr. President," the aide said as she pressed the play button. "The CIA director thought Mr. Xander should know about it immediately."

Everyone watched in horror as the Baxter family popped up on screen. All five of them sat huddled in a dark room, their hands bound behind their backs and gags placed over their mouths. Several armored mercenaries towered over them.

Doc gritted his teeth. "Who has them?"

Doc's question was answered seconds later when Aladdin Salazar appeared. His hair was tied in a ponytail and three scratches ran up and down his cheek.

"Good evening, Doctor Xander. Long time no see. I apologize for posting this video on the internet, but it's not like I could send it to you personally. You never did send me your new e-mail address."

Doc growled.

"You're probably wondering why I kidnapped your family. Heck, you're probably wondering how I found them in the first place. I will explain everything once we reunite."

Aladdin stepped back, and his entire body came into view.

"If you ever want to see your beloved family again, I strongly suggest you come to the Greenland ice sheet... *alone*. And while you're at it, bring along a vial of your newest invention... your Fountain of Youth."

"Son of a witch," Martin cursed.

Aladdin narrowed his icy blue eyes. "If you bring anyone with you, Xander, your family will perish. I am not in the mood for any of your tricks. You have 48 hours."

Aladdin walked off screen and the TV went black.

Chapter Nine: The Fountain Of Death

Mad Doc Xander quivered with rage.

"Martin, Goldie, let's go. We're going to Greenland."

Paternus blocked Doc's path. "You're not going anywhere, Xander. We're not letting you throw your life away."

"Robert, I have nothing but the utmost respect for you and your distinguished career. But if you don't get out of my way, I will deck you."

Paternus rolled up his sleeves. "Oh yeah? You and what army?"

"This army," Goldie said. A propeller popped out of her back and she flew into the air. Laser blasters ejected from her mechanical hands.

Paternus gulped and stepped back. "That's a good army."

President Robinson marched in between the flying trashcan and his secretary of defense. "All right, that's enough! Everyone calm down for just a minute!"

Goldie lowered to the ground but kept her guns out.

"See, this is what I was talking about," Paternus said. "Xander's Fountain of Youth is gonna make the world go nuts. We've already got the Merchant of Death kidnapping people over it. How are we gonna stop other nut jobs from imitating him?"

The president continued massaging his head. "One problem at a time, Robert. Let's figure out a way to avert this crisis first."

"Why would Aladdin want the vaccine in the

first place?" Martin asked. "Is he sick?"

"I have no clue," Doc said. "I haven't seen or talked to Aladdin in years. But he was always very health conscious. I doubt he's ill."

"Maybe he wants ta sell it on the black market?" Goldie proposed.

"Maybe. But I don't think…"

Doc's face suddenly turned sickly green.

"What is it, Doc?" the president asked.

Doc gulped. "I think I know why Aladdin wants the vaccine. And it's not a good reason."

"Be up front with us, Doc. What does Aladdin plan to do with your Fountain of Youth?"

Doc paced back and forth, which he always did whenever he was nervous. "Well you see, there's a teensy, weensy little glitch with the vaccine. The nano-bots are basically tiny computers. So theoretically you could hack into the nano-bots, recalibrate their circuitry, and program them to *attack* a person's body instead of healing it."

"So the nano-bots would essentially act like a virus?" Paternus asked.

Doc nodded. "And not just any virus. An *incurable* virus. Nothing inside the human body would be able to stop the nano-bots as they ripped people apart from the inside out. It would be a slow, painful death. Think of it as cancer on steroids.

"Even worse, the nano-bots can be programmed to behave like my robotic locusts," Doc rattled on. "That means they'd be able to take organic material, use it to create clones, and self-replicate exponentially. It would be the fastest spreading virus the world has ever seen. No one… and I mean *NO ONE*… would survive."

Martin shook his floating head, his long hair flipping back and forth. "So basically what you're saying, Doc, is that your Fountain of Youth can be used as a 'Fountain of Death'?"

Doc grimaced. "I suppose you could say that. But I'd rather you didn't."

"Why must you create things that threaten the free world?" the president asked.

Doc shrugged. "Hey, you guys give me taxpayer money to do it."

"None of this makes any sense," Paternus said, scratching his head. "How would Aladdin know your nano-bots can be used to kill people? I mean, goodness gracious, the world didn't know about your vaccine until this morning."

Doc lowered his head and continued pacing. "Well, as most of you know, Aladdin used to be one of my students. He took all of my courses, including one where I talked extensively about futuristic technology."

Paternus cocked a bushy eyebrow. "What kind of futuristic technology?"

"All kinds," Doc said, quickening his pace. "Laser weapons, artificial intelligence, faster than light starships, time machines... and yes, nano-bots that could make a person immortal."

Everyone in the room groaned and threw their hands in the air.

"Granted this was all 20 years ago," Doc continued, wringing his hands. "I had no idea two decades later I would be the architect of an immortality vaccine, and my star pupil would be a mass-murdering madman."

"Funny how life turns out," said Martin's floating head. "In high school, kids said I was most likely to end up in a psych ward."

"You may end up there yet," Goldie cracked.

"Hey Goldie, why don't you do everyone a favor and stick your arm in a toilet so you short-circuit?" Martin snapped.

"*Anyway,*" Doc said, interrupting his bickering sidekicks. "I discussed the pros of an immortality vaccine... and the cons."

"Surely Aladdin doesn't remember a lesson from 20 years ago," the president said.

"I wouldn't be so sure," Doc said, stepping in

front of Goldie because she had just pointed a laser blaster at Martin's head. "Aladdin may be a heartless monster, but he's vastly intelligent. He would remember anything that greatly intrigued him. And if I'm not mistaken, he did find that particular lesson fascinating."

"I was thinking about just giving Aladdin a vial of your vaccine, but we can't do that if he's planning on turning it into a virus," the president said.

"Even if he wanted it for his dying kid, I still wouldn't care," Paternus said. "We don't negotiate with terrorists, not now, not ever."

"Aladdin has no children," Doc gloomily replied. "I'm positive he wants to weaponize the vaccine."

"Why would Aladdin want to unleash an incurable pathogen?" Maggie asked. "What purpose would it serve to kill everyone on Earth? Is he really that mentally unstable?"

"He probably wants to blackmail world leaders," Martin said. "Basically *'do what I want or everyone dies'*."

Doc rubbed his chin. "But that doesn't sound like Aladdin. He never cared for world domination."

"Why is he at war with us, then?" Paternus growled.

"It is true Aladdin hates western culture," Doc explained. "But he never aspired to rule the planet. He just wanted to change things, loosen our 'imperialistic stranglehold' on the world." Doc made quote marks with his fingers.

"How about we all stop pretending to be psychiatrists?" Paternus snapped. "Aladdin is a genocidal lunatic and must be stopped at all costs. So let's get him!"

"No. You heard Aladdin's ultimatum. If anyone goes with me, my... my family will die."

Doc's voice cracked. He struggled to fight back tears.

"Let's be realistic, though, Xander," Paternus

said, his voice sounding less gruff than usual. "Letting you go to Greenland by yourself would be insane. How do we know Aladdin won't kidnap you, too?"

Doc stared at the floor. "Trust me, he won't. My former student may be a psychopath, but he is a man of his word. He'll release my family as long as I give him what he wants. But if he suspects I'm being followed... if he sees special-forces hiding out on the Greenland ice sheet... he will kill them all."

After a lengthy silence, the president said, "I'm sorry, Doc, but I cannot in good conscience send you off to die alone."

"But..."

The president interrupted Doc. "You will be accompanied by special forces. If you resist my order, I'll have no choice but to put you into holding until the rescue operation is complete."

Doc realized if he wanted to be involved in the rescue mission, he would have to obey the president's order. Or at least *pretend* to.

"Okay, Mr. President. You win."

The president and secretary of defense breathed simultaneous sighs of relief.

Paternus patted Doc on the back. "Don't worry, Xander. We'll get that jerk and make him pay."

Doc flashed a grim smile. The secretary of defense had a tough exterior, but deep down inside he had a sympathetic heart. Well, a sympathetic pacemaker.

"Before we do anything, though, I need to head back to my lab and get the vaccine," Doc said.

"Why?" the president sputtered. "Didn't we just establish letting Aladdin have the vaccine would be extraordinarily dangerous?"

"I'm going to deactivate the nano-bots first," Doc explained. "I just think it'll be good to have it with me in case things go horribly wrong. Think of it as a harmless bargaining chip."

President Robinson paused for a moment, deep in thought. He finally said, "Okay, Doc. We'll do it your way. But you better hurry. And you're not going to your lab alone."

"What, you don't trust me? I promise I'll be right back." Doc crossed his fingers inside his pockets.

"Of course we don't trust you," the president said. "You're the most reckless mad scientist the world has ever known."

Paternus puffed out his chest. "I'll go with Xander. He won't be able to pull anything past me."

Doc struggled not to smirk. He loved a challenge.

The president glanced at his watch. "I'm late for my fundraiser. Robert, keep me updated. Doctor Xander, good luck."

Secret service agents escorted the president out of the room.

"Alright, let's go kick some butt!" Goldie exclaimed.

"That's what I'm talking about!" Paternus said, thrusting his fist into the air.

The secretary of defense led Doc, Martin, and Goldie to his armored SUV. The flying locusts followed them.

Martin leaned toward Doc and whispered, "So I take it we're ditching Paternus the first chance we get?"

"Absolutely," Doc replied. "Enjoy your last few minutes of freedom. We're about to become fugitives on the run from the United States of America."

Chapter Ten: Fugitives On The Lam

Secretary of Defense Paternus hopped into the driver's seat of his armored SUV. A young aide climbed into the passenger's side.

Doc opened the back door. "Martin, help me get Goldie in here."

"I don't want that smart-alecky garbage can in my car," Paternus snapped.

"I'm not too fond of you, either, grandpa, but I don't air my grievances in front of everybody," Goldie shot back.

"Settle down, Robert, Goldie will behave," Doc grunted as he and Martin hoisted his robot sidekick into the back seat. Martin's floating head turned bright red and sweat poured down his cheeks.

"Jeez, how much do you weigh?" Martin grumbled.

Goldie's body started blinking like crazy. "That's a terrible thing ta say ta a full-figured woman. You're gonna cause me ta have an eatin' disorder."

After everyone buckled in, Paternus floored the car and zoomed off. He rolled through a stop sign, nearly hitting a truck, and sped through a stoplight that just turned red.

"Don't you think you should obey at least a couple traffic laws?" Martin said.

"I've been driving since before you were born, sissy," Paternus said, weaving in and out of traffic, nearly hitting pedestrians and parked cars. "I know what I'm doing."

Goldie cackled and flashed her lights. "Yeah,

quit being such a wuss!"

"So where's your lab, Doc?" Paternus asked, fiddling with his GPS.

"It's 314 Einstein-Newton Lane," Doc replied. His robotic locusts buzzed above his head. Goldie scooted as far away from them as she possibly could.

Paternus punched in Doc's address. The GPS showed a route that lead to a sprawling estate up in the mountains.

As he navigated through a traffic jam, Paternus said, "Let's go over the battle plan so we're all on the same page."

"Um... okay," Doc said.

"What we'll do is drop you off on the Greenland ice sheet by yourself. Unbeknownst to Aladdin, a fleet of Blackhawk helicopters will be waiting several miles out to sea, well out of sight. After Aladdin swaps your family for the vaccine, special forces will sweep in and take out the son of a gun."

Doc saw so many things wrong with Paternus' plan that it was almost funny, but he refrained from saying what he really thought. Instead, he said, "Uh... great plan."

"Are you kidding?!" Martin cried. "That's a horrible plan! In fact, I---mmmm!"

Doc threw his hand over Martin's mouth. He agreed with his junior lab assistant, but he also didn't want to create a scene. None of it would matter in a few minutes anyway.

Paternus gave Martin a dirty look in the rear-view mirror and mumbled, "No good rotten kids." He then started fiddling with the radio.

Doc tapped Goldie on her fishbowl head and whispered, "Now."

Two gas masks popped out of a concealed compartment on Goldie's side and fell to the floor. Doc and Martin strapped them on.

Seconds later, green gas shot out of Goldie's body, filling up the entire car. Paternus and his aide gagged. The SUV swerved up on the sidewalk and crashed into a fire hydrant. A column of water exploded into the air and rained back down. People sitting at a nearby café stared at the accident in horror.

Paternus and his aide tried to roll down their windows, but it was too late. Within seconds they slumped over, victims of Goldie's highly concentrated knock-out gas. Once they were incapacitated, a hose protruded from Goldie's side and sucked all the gas back inside her body.

Breathing heavily through the mask, Doc said, "Good job, Goldie. Knock-out gas is expensive. You should always recycle."

"Yeah, ya never know when I'll have ta use it on Martin," Goldie chortled.

Martin punched Goldie in the side with his invisible hand. Goldie smacked Martin upside the back of his floating head.

"Quit fooling around and let's move," Doc snapped. He and Martin tore off their masks, handed them back to Goldie, and jumped out of the car. The robotic locusts continued buzzing around Doc's head.

Doc and Martin were about to help Goldie out of the car when she blew a hole through the roof with a heat-seeking missile. A ball of flame shot out of the top, and the windows shattered. Doc and Martin flattened on the ground and covered their heads.

Goldie floated out of the smoldering car with her whipping propeller.

"Was that really necessary?" Doc shouted, wiping dirt off his lab coat.

"No, but it was fun. Now quit your bellyachin' and let's go!"

By now dozens of people had gathered around Paternus' demolished SUV, snapping pictures and pointing fingers.

"You're right, we need to get to the lab immediately," Doc said, sidestepping glass and flaming wreckage. "The police will be after us soon enough."

Goldie hovered over Doc and Martin and dropped a rope ladder. Doc climbed it first, then Martin hopped onto the bottom half. Goldie then floated high into the sky, with Doc and Martin hanging on for dear life. Flashing police cruisers could be seen off in the distance, speeding toward the accident.

Goldie flew over a wooded area, then descended toward a sprawling mansion enclosed behind a barbed-wire, electrified fence. Laser guns and cameras popped out of the manicured lawn and followed Goldie. Silver robotic 'hawks' flew overhead, their glowing red eyes ready to fire lasers at the first sign of danger. Once the cameras registered what the 'unidentified flying object' was, they lowered back into the ground, along with the guns. The robotic hawks went back to circling the mansion.

Goldie hovered in front of the steel-plated front door so Doc and Martin could hop off the ladder. She then retracted her propellers and landed beside them.

"That was fun," Goldie said. "We should take out prominent government officials more often."

Doc ignored his wacky robot and pressed his finger against a sensor near the door. The steel door slid into the wall, and Doc, Martin, and Goldie hurried inside.

The trio dashed through the massive, chandelier-lit dining room and slipped behind a revolving bookcase. They then took an elevator down to the dungeon. Fluorescent lights popped on, nearly blinding them. Doc led his assistants into his gigantic lab, which was stacked to the ceiling with all sorts of hi-tech inventions.

Doc yanked open a refrigerator and withdrew a transparent canister of grayish, metallic-looking liquid. Swimming in the liquid were literally millions of microscopic nano-bots. Doc grabbed a small pistol off the wall and aimed it at the canister. A bright, green light emitted from the barrel, illuminating the entire canister.

"What's he doing?" Martin asked.

"That's an electromagnetic pulse gun," Goldie

replied. "He's deactivating all the nano-bots. Jeez, didn't they teach ya anything at Harvard?"

Martin glanced at Goldie's back for an 'off' switch, but unfortunately could not find one.

Doc stuffed the canister inside his lab coat. "All right, let's go to Greenland."

Goldie and Martin followed Doc to his massive, underground hangar. The hangar contained dozens of hi-tech vehicles, including flying cars, flying boats, flying motorcycles, and spaceships. One of his most versatile aerial vehicles was a helicopter-plane. It flew several times faster than the speed of sound, and was capable of landing and taking off like a helicopter. That was what Doc decided to fly to Greenland.

Once everyone climbed aboard, Doc pressed a button and the helipad lifted into the air. A hole opened in the ceiling and the helicopter-plane floated into the sky. Doc's locusts and two of his robotic hawks flew inside the helicopter-plane just before the hatch door swung shut.

Doc glanced down at his sprawling estate. Several cop cars had just pulled up to the front entrance.

"Perfect timing," Martin said.

"Everyone strap in. We're on a non-stop flight to one of the coldest places on Earth." Doc pressed another button and his helicopter-plane shot forward, breaking the sound barrier several times over.

Chapter Eleven: Guests Of The Devil

Jesse and his sisters were being held in a brightly-lit jail cell. Inside the cell were a couple toilets, a sink, and several cots protruding from the wall. Thick iron bars prohibited their escape. A tiny glass window overlooked the Arctic Ocean.

Outside the cell were two armed guards, marching in lock-step. Numerous cameras hung from the ceiling. As far as jail cells went, it was actually quite comfortable, but there was no privacy. Still, Jesse and his siblings did the best they could.

Speaking so low that his sisters could barely hear him, Jesse said, "Just to make sure we're on the same page, let's go over the plan again."

Ororo and Journey groaned. Jesse figured it was because they had already gone over the plan a dozen times; he was a stickler for perfection when it came to elaborate jail breaks.

"In a few minutes, Journey will pretend to fall deathly ill. The guards will rush in to check on her. That's when we'll strike. I'll dropkick one of the guards into the sink while one of you grabs his energy blaster and stuns the other guard. Then we'll dash up to the top deck and steal a plane. If we happen to pass the infirmary on the way, we'll look for Mom and Dad. If we can't find them, though, we'll just have to leave."

"But we can't leave Mommy and Daddy!" Journey protested.

Journey meant to talk quietly, but it came out as a shout.

One of the guards banged his energy gun against

the bars. "Shut up in there, you blasted kids!"

Journey wiped her moist eyes and whispered, "We already left Mommy and Daddy once." She gave Jesse a dirty look. "We're not leaving them again."

"Jesse did what he needed to do to keep us safe," Ororo said. "Don't you ever make him feel guilty about that."

Jesse smiled warmly at Ororo. They may have bickered like normal siblings, but she always had his back when it mattered most.

Jesse patted Journey on the shoulder and soothingly said, "We're not leaving Mom and Dad behind. We're just getting help. If we can reach Uncle Xander, he'll help us bust them out of here."

Journey blinked away her tears and nodded.

The guard banged on the bars again. "Hey, what did I just say? Stop talking!"

"Let's do it now so I can shut that idiot up," Jesse whispered.

Journey clutched her stomach and staggered toward the front of the cell. "Ohhhh... I don't feel so good."

Journey coughed and fell to the floor. Jesse and Ororo rushed over, feigning concern.

"Please, help my sister!" Ororo pleaded. "Something's wrong with her!"

Jesse struggled not to smirk. His sisters were great actresses.

One of the guards looked at the other and said, "You think she's faking? The boss said not to let them out no matter what."

"Only one way to find out," the other guard said, pointing his gun into the cell.

Jesse jumped back. "Wait, what are you doing?!"

The guard fired an energy bolt mere inches from Journey's head. Journey yelped and jumped to her feet.

"You bonehead! I'm dying over here and you nearly killed me!"

"You sure move fast for a dying girl," the guard sneered.

Journey clutched her stomach. "What I meant to say was, *Ohhhh... my tummy....*"

The guard fired another shot, sending Jesse and his siblings scrambling to the back.

"That didn't work out like I planned," Jesse grumbled, plopping down on a cot.

Jesse and his sisters were just beginning to devise another plan when four more guards brought their parents to the cell.

"Mommy! Daddy!" Journey cried.

"Hi Pumpkin," Mr. Baxter groaned, leaning against a guard as he hopped on one leg. His right ankle was wrapped in a bandage. He was still wearing his tuxedo, but his shirt was unbuttoned, revealing even more bandages. He looked to be in agonizing pain. Mrs. Baxter was wrapped in bandages as well and appeared to be in a daze.

Two of the guards raised their energy blasters.

"Step back!" one of them shouted.

Jesse and his sisters backed up against the wall.

One guard swung open the door and shoved Jesse's parents inside.

Jesse and his siblings rushed over to their parents and smothered them with hugs. Mr. and Mrs. Baxter groaned in pain, but they didn't push anyone away. They were just thrilled to be reunited with their kids.

"Let's give Mom and Dad some breathing room," Jesse said, leading his parents to the cots in the back of the cell.

Journey and Ororo backed up. Mr. and Mrs. Baxter plopped down on the cots. Mr. Baxter propped up his injured foot.

"Are you okay, Daddy?" Journey asked, resting her head against his chest.

"I've been better, Princess, but I'll live. The doctor gave me a couple painkillers."

"Is anything broken?" Jesse asked.

"I've got a couple cracked ribs and a sprained ankle," Mr. Baxter said. "And the doctor says I suffered a mild concussion. But it could've been a lot worse."

"I'll be okay, too, kids," Mrs. Baxter said, kissing Ororo on her forehead. She then pulled Jesse to her chest and hugged him so tightly that he could barely breathe.

"I'm so proud of you guys," she whispered, her tears plopping on Jesse's head.

A long shadow descended far into the cell. Jesse and the rest of the Baxters looked up to find Aladdin Salazar towering in the doorway, wearing a black suit and navy blue tie.

"Sorry to interrupt your family meeting," Aladdin said, not sounding sorry at all. "I was wondering if you wanted to join me for a late night snack."

"A snack?" Ororo cried. "First you tried to kill us, and now you're offering us something to eat? Are you mental?"

Aladdin simply smiled. "I never tried to kill you. In fact, none of you would have been hurt if you surrendered peacefully. But I don't hold grudges. Since you are my guests, it is my duty to be a courteous host. I truly do feel horrible for interrupting your dinner, and I can only imagine how hungry you are."

Jesse patted his grumbling belly. "I suppose I could go for a bite to eat."

"Good," Aladdin said. "Oh, by the way, this dinner isn't optional. You're all coming whether you like it or not."

"Well, that makes things a lot easier," Mr. Baxter said, staggering to his good foot. He leaned against Jesse and Ororo to maintain his balance.

One of the guards opened the door while six other guards raised their energy blasters. Jesse and his family slowly filed out of the cell.

As soon as they were free, Journey ran up to

Aladdin and kicked him in his shin.

Aladdin grabbed his leg and shouted, "Why you insufferable little snot!"

Journey lowered into a karate stance. "Come on, guys, let's get him!"

Mrs. Baxter rushed over to Journey and pinched her on the neck.

Journey yelped and twirled around. "What was that for?"

Mrs. Baxter pinched her again. "Behave yourself, Journey. I know you're only 11, but even you must realize this is a battle we can't possibly win."

Journey mumbled under her breath, but she didn't kick anyone else.

Aladdin turned his back on the Baxters and took off down the hall at a brisk pace. Talking over his shoulder, he said, "I trust you won't attempt to escape. We're several thousand feet in the air, just above the Arctic Circle. There are nearly 100 armed mercenaries all throughout the ship. You would do well to enjoy your stay until the Mad Doctor arrives."

"How do you know my brother will come?" Mrs. Baxter asked, struggling to keep up.

Aladdin turned his head. "Oh, I'm certain he will. Dr. Xander won't leave his family to die. You of all people should know that, old friend."

Mrs. Baxter gritted her teeth, but didn't say anything else.

Still walking at a quick pace, Aladdin said, "Don't think of yourselves as prisoners during your stay aboard my floating citadel. Think of yourselves as my guests."

"Guests of the Devil," Jesse muttered under his breath.

Aladdin led Jesse and the gang into a sprawling dining room. A long, rectangular table sat in the middle, covered with a ruby red table cloth. The chairs surrounding the table were solid wood, with padded seats. Crystal chandeliers hung from the high ceiling.

Marble statues of animals stood all over the room. Exquisite, golden-framed paintings of exotic landscapes hung from the walls. Glass-plated windows were everywhere, revealing the star-covered Arctic sky. Soft jazz filtered through speakers on the walls and ceiling. Jesse had no idea the Merchant of Death was such a classy dude.

Aladdin sat at the far end of the table. Jesse, his mom, and his sisters sat on one side. A guard led Mr. Baxter to the other end. Several of Aladdin's mercenaries sat at the table as well. The men wore suits and ties, and the girls wore sparking dresses.

Jesse stared at the gorgeous young women in stunned silence. He was especially attracted to the stunning blonde teen sitting right across from him.

Aladdin chucked. "I see you're surprised I have women under my employment."

Jesse snapped out of his trance.

"Uh, no," Jesse quickly said. "I... um..."

Aladdin simply chuckled. "The fair blonde you seem infatuated with is one of my highest-ranked commanders, Annabeth Ferdinand. Annabeth is a distant relative of Archduke Franz Ferdinand, whose assassination in 1914 thrust the globe into the First World War."

"That's... cool.... I guess," Jesse said. He knew all about World War One. He knew about pretty much every major event in history. His mom homeschooled him and his sisters during their travels around the world, and she treated them like college students. He was currently doing Calculus Mathematics when other kids his age hadn't even mastered Algebra yet.

"Annabeth was unfairly labeled a far-right extremist in her home country of Austria," Aladdin elaborated. "I liked her... ruthless style... so I busted her out of prison."

In a thick, Austrian accent Annabeth said, "Herr Salazar is my savior. I owe him my life... my freedom... everything."

Aladdin blushed, as if Annabeth's words truly moved him.

"My large family of arms traffickers consists of pirates, runaways, so-called terrorists, the homeless, and other ostracized youngsters seeking a safe haven and a purpose. I take them in, provide food and shelter, and help rehabilitate their shattered lives. In essence, I provide them safe refuge from a brutish, callous world that has turned its back on them."

Aladdin's mercenaries all nodded and smiled. They seemed to adore their 'savior'.

"Yeah, you're a real Mother Teresa," Jesse grumbled.

Aladdin scowled at Jesse, but did not offer a rebuttal. It was probably because a guard wheeled out a sick-looking boy in a wheelchair. The boy was bald and pale. His eyes were red and puffy, and he was covered in thick wool blankets. Every few seconds he coughed, a loud, hacking cough that seemed to come from the very depths of his lungs.

Aladdin rushed over to the boy and kissed him on his forehead. "Hello, Mikhail. Are you feeling better today?"

Mikhail nodded, but his frail, shivering body told another story.

"My goodness, Aladdin, is he alright?" Mrs. Baxter asked, her voice full of concern.

Aladdin sat down and stared at his empty plate. "No, Ariel, he is not. My son is a very sick boy."

Mrs. Baxter's mouth dropped open in shock. "I never knew you had a son."

"How could you know?" Aladdin said quietly, his pale blue eyes ablaze with malice and deep-seeded fury. "Your government has hunted me to the ends of the Earth. I have kept my son's existence a secret to protect him from my many enemies."

"What's wrong with him?" Journey asked.

Jesse nudged his little sister in the side and whispered, "That's not a polite thing to ask."

If Aladdin was insulted by the question, he never let on. "Mikhail has an aggressive form of cancer, my dear. We've tried every treatment known to man, but nothing seems to work. Our doctor says Mikhail has only weeks to live."

"So that's why you want Xander's Fountain of Youth," Mr. Baxter replied with a grimace, still clutching his cracked ribs.

Aladdin gave Mr. Baxter a peculiar look. "But of course. Why else would I want it?"

"How old is he?" Mrs. Baxter asked, her eyes beginning to tear up. Jesse understood why she was so upset. During their travels around the world, nothing upset his mother more than the sight of a child about to be robbed of a full life.

Aladdin twirled a glass in his hand. "Mikhail is 12. His mother passed away from the same disease several years ago. And now it's about to take my only son."

"If you wanted to cure Mikhail, why didn't you just tell Uncle Xander?" Jesse asked. "Why go through the trouble of kidnapping us?"

Aladdin burst out in laughter. "Ahhh, that's what I love about children. They have such idealistic views of how the world works."

Jesse narrowed his eyes. He hated grownups who acted like kids were stupid.

"In case you haven't heard, child, I am the most wanted man on Earth. It's not like I can stroll into the United Nations and say, *'Hey, how about we forget our little feud for the moment and you hand over one of the most miraculous medications ever created.'* I don't think it would have worked out the way you apparently imagine. I need your uncle's immortality vaccine *now*, and the best way to do that is by kidnapping the people he holds dearest to his heart."

Aladdin was about to say something else, but several servers brought out platters of food. All conversation stopped as everyone dug into the hearty feast. The platters were overflowing with various fruit cobblers, pastries, salads, spinach lasagna, and finger sandwiches stacked with fresh cheeses and vegetables.

Picking through the food, Jesse asked, "Hey, where's the meat?"

Aladdin narrowed his eyes. "Only a barbarian slaughters animals for food. Everyone on my ship is a vegetarian, either by choice or force."

Jesse couldn't believe Aladdin was so concerned about the plight of animals when he had such little regard for people.

As Jesse and his family dined, Aladdin cut his son's food into tiny pieces. Mikhail tried to eat what he could, but his weak stomach had trouble keeping it down. He took a few bites before pushing his plate away.

"I'm sorry, Dad, but I can't eat anymore," Mikhail muttered.

"It's okay, son. I just wanted you to eat something solid. You're wasting away on Jell-O and broth."

Jesse felt terrible watching Mikhail grimace in pain. During his travels around the world, he had seen thousands of sick and dying children. One would think he'd be used to it by now, but he wasn't.

"So, Aladdin, how did you find us?" Mrs. Baxter asked, eager for more information.

"I've always known where you were. I have spies in government agencies all over the world. I can find anyone."

Aladdin took a sip of sparkling water before continuing. "This morning I, like everyone else, heard about Xander's Fountain of Youth. I immediately called up one of my spies and asked for your current whereabouts. He informed me you had just booked a cruise. I waited to invade the ship until you were out to sea, eating dinner in the dining hall. I assumed you would come along peacefully to avoid civilian casualties." Aladdin smiled. "I was obviously mistaken."

"So you and my parents used to hang out?" Jesse asked casually, doing his best to hide his revulsion at the very thought of his parents associating with a terrorist.

Mrs. Baxter choked on her water. "I don't think we should be talking about…"

"Yes we did," Aladdin said, cutting Mrs. Baxter off.

Aladdin glanced at Jesse's parents and frowned. "I frequently think back to our days at Harvard. Things were much simpler then. I remember how we used to assist Xander with his lesson plans. We even accompanied him on some of his top-secret missions. He taught me everything I know about robotics and futuristic technology.

"Xander is truly one of the smartest men I've ever known," Aladdin continued. "I thought of him as a father figure, despite the fact we are only a few years apart. I considered all of you to be family. It's a shame things fell apart as we got older."

Aladdin glanced at Mrs. Baxter. "Things weren't supposed to turn out this way. We were supposed to get married, raise a family, save the world. How cruel fate has mocked us."

Jesse choked on his pastry.

"Do what?" he hollered.

"I take it your mother never told you we used to date?" Aladdin asked, his thin lips curled up in amusement.

"No, she never did," Jesse said, giving his mother a funny look. Mrs. Baxter put her head in her hands and groaned.

"Our dad could have been the Merchant of Death," Journey muttered. Her face was ghostly pale, as if the very thought sickened her.

"Merchant of Death," Aladdin snarled. "You have no idea how much I despise that nickname. The U.S. is full of 'Merchants of Death'. Why does everyone think that title applies specifically to me?"

It never occurred to Jesse that Aladdin hated his

nickname. Then again, he supposed he wouldn't like it, either.

"So what happened between you guys?" Jesse asked.

"Let's just say your mother and I fell out of love," Aladdin replied darkly. "She fell for your father… my best friend."

Mr. Baxter gulped and yanked at his tie. "Is it hot in here or is it just me?"

"It's you, dear," Mrs. Baxter said. "You're probably having hot flashes."

Aladdin turned toward Ororo. "So my sources tell me you were adopted from a Darfuri refugee camp?"

"Yeah, my family was killed by Janjaweed militants," Ororo replied quietly.

"I'm terribly sorry to hear that." Aladdin turned to Journey. "I take it your family was robbed from you as well, my dear?"

Journey simply stared at the floor and nodded.

"The world is full of cruel and evil people."

Jesse continued to note the irony in Aladdin's seemingly compassionate statements.

"Ororo. What a beautiful name," Aladdin continued. "It means 'Beauty', correct?"

"Yeah," said Ororo, sounding impressed. "How do you know that?"

Aladdin smirked. "I've traveled all over the world, child. I speak dozens of languages. I have forgotten more than you will ever know."

"Well okay then, Mr. Cocky," Ororo replied.

Mrs. Baxter took a sip of water and tepidly asked, "Aren't the Janjaweed one of your biggest clients, Aladdin?"

Aladdin pursed his lips. "The Sudanese government does purchase weapons from us. And the Janjaweed are the militant arm of the Sudanese government. So I suppose in a roundabout way that would be correct."

"You also give weapons to illegal loggers and

ranchers in Brazil," Mrs. Baxter added.

Aladdin scowled. "We have done business from time to time."

"So basically you're responsible for my parents' deaths," Ororo snarled through gritted teeth.

"Mine, too," Journey said, her eyes narrowing into tiny slivers of hate.

"That's like blaming the NRA for all the firearm deaths in America," Aladdin snapped.

Jesse noticed Ororo clutching a knife. He reached under the table and gently squeezed her thigh. In a quiet whisper, he said, "He's not worth it, sis."

Ororo relinquished her hold on the knife, sending it clattering to the table. She then blinked away the tears trickling down her left eye.

Mikhail suddenly started coughing. Aladdin leaned over to check on him.

Jesse nudged his mom in the side and whispered, "Should we try to escape? I'm sure we can take these guys."

Mrs. Baxter thought for a moment, then said, "No. Let's wait for my brother. That way he can give Aladdin's son the vaccine."

Jesse nodded. His mother really did have a good heart.

In the middle of Mikhail's coughing fit, a guard rushed in and whispered something in Aladdin's ear.

Aladdin looked up and said, "Our sensors on the Greenland ice sheet have detected an approaching aircraft. It's probably Doctor Xander. I'm sorry to cut this dinner short, but I think it would be best if you all waited in your cell."

Aladdin's mercenaries stood up from the table and pointed their energy blasters at Jesse and his family.

Mrs. Baxter raised her hands. "Hey, there's no need to get violent.

"Just a safety precaution, Mrs. Baxter," Annabeth said. She jabbed her energy blaster into Mrs. Baxter's back. "Please head back to your cell."

Jesse and his family filed out of the dining hall. On their way out, Jesse overheard Aladdin say, "Take my son back to the infirmary. It's time I reunited with an old friend."

Jesse closed his eyes and prayed Doc knew what he was getting himself into.

Chapter Twelve: The Mad Doctor & His Pupil

Doc had just finished telling Martin and Goldie how he planned on rescuing his family.

"Well? What do you think?"

"Your plan is insane," Martin replied.

"That's why I love it," Goldie said.

Doc groaned. If Goldie liked it, then it was probably a bad idea. But he didn't just want to rescue his family. He also wanted to take down his psychopathic student. And this was the only way he knew how.

Doc landed the plane near the edge of the Greenland ice sheet. Martin put his helmet on, becoming completely invisible. Doc placed the fake vaccine in his pocket and jumped onto the ice. Martin followed him. The only thing that gave Martin away were his footprints in the snow.

Doc leaned into the plane and said, "Stay out of sight, but don't go too far."

"Aye aye, Captain," Goldie said. "Good luck. Make sure you leave some bad guys for me."

"Trust me, there will be plenty."

Goldie blasted into the sky and took off toward the western horizon.

The Arctic was cold even in the summer, and with it being the dead of winter, it was even more frigid than usual. Making matters worse, all Doc had on was his lab coat, a pair of slacks, and a bulletproof vest. He probably should have grabbed a coat, but he was in such a hurry that it slipped his mind. There was one good thing about standing on the Greenland ice sheet, though. There were no lights. He could look up and see thousands of stars. He rarely got to enjoy the Milky Way in Los Angeles.

Doc and Martin waited for what felt like hours, but in actuality was only a few minutes. Just when Doc had lost all feeling in his arms and legs, the sound of whipping propellers cut through the arctic air. Doc looked up into the sky, but didn't see anything but twinkling stars.

"Do you hear that?" Martin asked.

"Yes," Doc said. "It sounds like dozens of helicopters. I don't know---- jumping Jupiter!"

Doc staggered backwards, and for good reason. A massive airship materialized out of thin air and hovered directly over them.

Doc had backed up so far that he was now teetering over the edge of the ice sheet. He was just about to topple over when an invisible hand grabbed his arm and yanked him back onto firm ice.

"Gotcha Doc," Martin said.

"Thanks," Doc mumbled. He clutched the canister of deactivated nano-bots to make sure he didn't drop it.

A dozen mercenaries flew toward the glacier on hovercrafts, armed with energy blasters. Doc looked up to see another hovercraft floating toward him. A tall, slender man in an armored suit straddled the center of the levitating platform. His brown ponytail fluttered in the breeze. Three fresh scars lined his right cheek. His thin, red lips curled into the faintest hint of a smile.

Aladdin Salazar hopped off his hovercraft and landed on the ice with a soft 'crunch'. His faint smile transformed into a full-fledged grin.

"Hello, Doctor. You look well."

"You do as well, Aladdin," Doc replied in an icy tone.

Aladdin held out his hand. "Do you have the immortality vaccine?"

Doc held up the transparent canister of grayish liquid. It glistened in the starlight.

Aladdin reached for the canister, but Doc yanked it back to his chest. "Do you have my family?"

"But of course. They are aboard my ship."

"Are they okay?"

Aladdin scoffed. "Of course they're okay. You didn't think I'd hurt them, did you?"

Aladdin once again reached for the vaccine. Doc stepped backwards, nearly stepping on Martin's invisible foot.

"I'd like to see them first."

"Suit yourself."

Aladdin snapped his fingers at his mercenaries. Three of them landed on the ice and checked Doc for weapons.

One of the mercenaries said, "He's wearing a bulletproof vest, Mr. Salazar."

Aladdin waved a dismissive hand.

"Doc always wore Kevlar. I can't say I blame him. He's made himself quite the target over the years."

"Much like yourself," Doc pointed out.

"Touché, Doctor."

Aladdin gestured toward his hovercraft, which was floating two feet off the ice. It was large enough for two average-sized people, but not many more than that.

"Hop aboard, Xander. I'd like to give you a tour of my floating castle."

Doc shot a fleeting glance behind him, hoping Martin would be smart enough to follow. He then jumped onto the hovercraft. Aladdin hopped on next to him.

The hovercraft had just started to levitate into the air when Aladdin bumped into Doc, nearly knocking him off. Aladdin grasped Doc's arm and held him steady.

"Sorry about that, Doctor. It felt like someone bumped into me."

Doc grinned. Martin was on the hovercraft as well, most likely standing on the very edge. He just hoped Aladdin didn't widen his stance and knock him off. Thankfully Aladdin stayed perfectly still.

As they floated toward the airship, Doc was astonished by its immense size. It was nearly half a mile long and three stories high. Dozens of propellers jutted out of the bottom and the sides, keeping the mammoth structure afloat. When they flew over the top deck, Doc was stunned to see dozens of hi-tech aircrafts. It looked like something from the future.

Aladdin's hovercraft landed on the airship's deck with a thud. Doc stepped off and stared at the airship in stunned silence.

"Impressive, isn't it?" Aladdin said, standing beside him.

"How did you make your airship invisible?" Doc asked. "I poured millions of dollars into creating an invisibility suit for the U.S. military, and..."

Doc immediately threw his hands over his mouth. He had a nasty habit of accidentally mentioning top-secret government projects.

"My airship is covered in metamaterials," Aladdin responded. "I assume your invisibility suit works the same way?"

"As a matter of fact, it does." For a moment Doc was almost proud of his former student.

Aladdin patted Doc on the back. "You taught me everything I know."

Doc grimaced. "Yes, I know. Don't remind me."

Doc followed Aladdin to the rear of the airship. On the way they passed two giant, ten-foot tall silver robots. The robots had glowing red eyes and a bluish orb in the center of their chests. Two gleaming, metallic wings protruded from their backs, making them resemble sinister angels.

"When did you build these things?" Doc asked.

"A few weeks ago," Aladdin replied casually. He said it as if he had built a ham radio. "They're self-thinking robotic mercenaries equipped with laser eyes, tear gas cannons, rocket-powered wings, and electric tentacles that pop out of their chests. I call them 'archangels'… robotic winged harbingers of death."

"How many have you built?"

"Just a few. But I'm about to mass-produce them. Dictators and rebel groups all over the world are interested in my archangels. These prototypes cost me a pretty penny, but I stand to make billions off of them once they go into mass production."

Doc realized he picked a terrific time to take Aladdin out. If his robot army ever came to fruition, no military force on Earth would be capable of stopping him.

"So why do you want my vaccine?" Doc asked as they headed below deck.

"It's for my son," Aladdin replied.

Doc stopped abruptly. A mercenary nearly ran into him.

"You have a son?"

Aladdin sighed. "I'm having déjà vu. I just had this conversation with your family."

Aladdin led Doc into the infirmary. Mikhail was back in bed, covered in thick wool blankets.

"What's wrong with the poor lad?" Doc asked.

"He has cancer," Aladdin replied somberly. "It's pretty far along. We fear he won't last the month. That's why I kidnapped your family, to get you to hand over your vaccine. Hopefully you understand."

"Why didn't you just tell me?" Doc asked, shaking his head in confusion. "I would have gladly given you the vaccine if I knew it was for your terminally ill son."

"And the déjà vu just keeps on coming. Like I told your sister, my reputation makes it impossible for me to get in touch with you or your government. I did what I had to do to get the vaccine in a timely manner."

Aladdin held out his hand. "Can I have it now? My son's life depends on it."

Doc continued clutching the vaccine to his chest. "Not until I see my family."

"I'll take you to them after Mikhail is injected with the vaccine," Aladdin said in a stern voice. His guards surrounded Doc and pointed their energy blasters at his head.

Aladdin thrust his hand in Doc's face. "This is not negotiable, Doctor. Don't make me take it by force."

Doc reluctantly handed over the canister.

Aladdin turned to Mikhail. "I hold in my hands the key to your salvation, son. Pretty soon all your pain will go away."

Doc nervously twiddled his thumbs. He wasn't sure how Mikhail would react to the deactivated nano-bots. He was afraid his body would treat the nano-bots as foreign invaders and fight them like a virus. That, of course, would make Mikhail even sicker than he already was. But he couldn't come out and admit that the vaccine was a fake. If he wanted to save his family... if he wanted to stop his psychopathic student once and for all... he would have to play along.

Aladdin grabbed a syringe and sucked out about a quarter of the vaccine. He then attached a needle and injected it into Mikhail's arm. Mikhail groaned and squirmed, then rolled over and went back to sleep.

Aladdin grasped Doc's shoulder. "If this works... if my son becomes healthy again... I will forever be indebted to you, Xander."

"Can I see my family now?" Doc asked bluntly.

"But of course." Aladdin pointed to his guards. "Put the Doctor into holding with his family."

"What?" Doc cried.

Aladdin cocked his head to the side. "You didn't think I was going to release you right away, did you?"

"We had a deal, Salazar!" Doc snapped, jabbing Aladdin in the chest. Aladdin's guards brought their energy blasters even closer to Doc's head.

Aladdin stepped back. "I'm a man of my word. Once my son shows signs of improvement, you and your family will be released. Until then, you will remain aboard my airship. Don't consider yourself a prisoner... consider yourself my guest."

Doc gritted his teeth, but didn't bother wasting his breath on a retort. Instead, he followed Aladdin's guards to the prison block.

On the way to his cell, Doc felt a pinch on his arm. He turned his head but didn't see anyone. He assumed it was Martin, letting him know he was there. Doc glanced up and noticed his robotic locusts flying around near the ceiling. All of his weapons were in place.

The locusts latched onto two cameras hanging from the ceiling. Goldie controlled the locusts from a laptop on the plane. She typed in several complex lines of computer code and had the locusts hack into the airship's computer database. The ship's surveillance system was now under her control.

The great jail break was about to begin.

Chapter Thirteen: The Great Jail Break

Jesse had just dozed off to sleep when the clanging of the cell door jolted him away. He was shocked to see two mercenaries shove Doc into the cell. The mercenaries promptly locked the cell door and stormed off, leaving the two guards to keep watch.

"Doc!" Journey shouted. She rushed over and hugged his leg.

Doc grinned and patted her head. "I've missed you, sweetheart. I know it's only been a few days, but it's felt like weeks."

"Did you bring presents?" Journey asked.

Mrs. Baxter limped over and crossed her arms. "Why would your uncle bring presents? We're imprisoned on a flying aircraft carrier!"

"He just usually brings presents whenever he visits," Journey grumbled.

Doc chuckled.

Jesse, Ororo, and Mr. Baxter hurried over to give Doc hugs. Once they were done, Mrs. Baxter leaned toward Doc's ear and whispered, "So how are we getting out of here?"

"Watch," he whispered back.

Doc pointed to the two guards pacing in front of the jail cell.

Jesse stood next to Doc and said, "Watch what?"

Doc patted Jesse on the head. "You'll see, nephew. You'll see."

Jesse and the Baxters all stared at the guards, waiting for something to happen.

One of the guards finally snapped, "What are

you freaks looking at?!"

A locust suddenly landed on the guard's head. The guard shook violently as electricity cascaded all over his body. The guard then slumped to the ground in an unmoving, smoking heap.

"What the---" stammered the other guard.

The other locust swooped down and blasted the guard with a burst of electricity. The guard flew to the other side of the hallway and slammed into the wall.

Jesse and the rest of the Baxters stared at the robotic locusts in sheer amazement.

"Whoa, what the heck are those things?" Jesse shouted.

"One of my finest creations," Doc proudly proclaimed.

Mrs. Baxter pointed to the cameras hanging from the ceiling.

"That was pretty neat, big brother, but we have eyes in the sky. Aladdin and his mercenaries will be down here any second."

"No they won't," Doc said. "My locusts have already hacked into the ship's computer database and hijacked the surveillance system. Right now all the cameras are replaying snippets of footage they've already captured. It'll be at least a few minutes before the guards in the control room notice anything unusual."

The locusts flew inside the jail cell and hovered above Doc's head.

"Okay, now what?" Jesse asked.

"Now we wait for Martin," Doc replied.

Ororo and Journey both got googly-eyed.

"You brought Martin?" Ororo asked, sounding like a love-struck tween.

"He's so dreamy," Journey giggled.

Jesse rolled his eyes. "Jeez, he's not even that cute. Heck, I'm cuter!"

"The heck you are," Journey protested. "Martin is super hot."

Mrs. Baxter pinched Journey's neck, causing her

to yelp. "You're too young to talk like that. You're not allowed to date until you're 16."

"Preferably 30," Mr. Baxter said.

Ororo jabbed Jesse in the chest. "And don't act all holier-than-thou. We all watched as you slobbered over Annabeth. And remember your girlfriend, Alex Rodriguez? You embarrassed yourself by the pool."

"Alex is not my girlfriend," Jesse grumbled. "At least, not yet."

Journey shoved Ororo. "Why were you acting all giddy when Doc said Martin was here? You do realize he's *my* future husband, right? Not yours, but mine!"

"Oh lord," Mrs. Baxter grumbled, massaging her head. "I don't need this right now."

Ororo shoved Journey back. "Please, Martin doesn't like immature 11-year olds. He wants a mature woman, like me."

"You're 12!" Journey hollered.

"I'll be 13 next month!" Ororo said.

Jesse grinned as his dad banged his head against the wall. Apparently his pops found bickering tween girls as annoying as he did.

"Girls, girls, don't fight over me," said a voice out of thin air.

Jesse and his family looked around the cell in flabbergasted astonishment.

"Who said that?" Ororo asked.

"Martin, you bonehead, you're still invisible," Doc said.

"Oh, sorry Doc. I forgot."

Martin's floating head popped up next to Journey.

Everyone but Doc screamed bloody murder and ran to the back of the cell. Journey jumped into Jesse's arms, knocking him to the floor. Martin screamed, too, and hid behind Doc.

Doc smirked and shook his head in mild amusement.

Jesse and the gang continued staring at Martin's floating head in horror.

Jesse finally mustered up the courage to ask, "Where's the rest of Martin's body, Doc?"

"His body's still there," Doc replied nonchalantly. "It's just hidden beneath an invisibility suit. Now let's get out of here."

The locusts fired lasers at the cell bars, slicing them in half. The bars clattered to the ground and rolled down the hall. Jesse, Doc, Martin's floating head, and the rest of the Baxters rushed out of the cell and dashed toward the stairs leading to the top deck. Jesse watched as the locusts flew away from them.

"Where are your bugs going, Doc?" Jesse asked.

"You'll find out soon enough," Doc said as they thundered up the stairs.

*

Aladdin remained in the infirmary, keeping watch over his son. He fully planned on releasing Doctor Xander and the Baxters. He just needed to make sure his former professor's immortality vaccine actually worked.

At first Aladdin was hopeful. But after several minutes had passed with no noticeable improvement, he began to grow concerned. The concern escalated when Mikhail's condition began to deteriorate.

Mikhail looked even paler than usual, and he was pretty pale to begin with. He also started moaning in discomfort. When Mikhail rolled to the side of the bed and vomited into a bed pan, Aladdin knew something was horribly wrong.

Aladdin pounded his fists against a table and barked, "I thought this blasted vaccine was supposed to cure my son, not make him worse!"

Aladdin grabbed a moist rag and dabbed Mikhail's sweating face.

Mikhail cracked open his puffy eyes. "Dad, I don't feel so good…"

He then leaned over the side of the bed and vomited again.

Aladdin pointed at a guard by the door. "Bring me Xander, *NOW!!!*"

The guard pressed a button on his arm and nervously said, "Derek, this is Tim. Mr. Salazar wants Xander ASAP."

There were several seconds of static, followed by the guard shouting, "Derek? Are you there? Derek?"

Aladdin growled and grabbed a remote off the night stand. He aimed it at a flat-screen TV hanging from the wall, bringing up the ship's surveillance system. He flipped through all the security cameras until he reached the ones in front of the prison.

Aladdin leaned forward and scrutinized the footage. He saw Xander being shoved into the cell. Then all the Baxters rushed over to hug him. Then Xander pointed toward the cameras. Then Xander patted Jesse on the head. Then the screen went black. Then two guards shoved Xander into the cell. Then all the Baxters rushed over to hug him. Then Xander pointed at the cameras.

Aladdin's face turned as pale as his dying son's.

"No... NO!"

Aladdin pressed a button on his arm. Red lights flashed and ear-splitting sirens blared throughout the entire ship.

"This is Aladdin," he shouted into his arm. His voice echoed everywhere. "The prisoners are on the loose! I repeat, the prisoners are on the loose!"

Chapter Fourteen: Over The Edge

Jesse and the gang ran up on deck just as the sirens went off.

"Where's Goldie?" Doc shouted.

"I told you she's a worthless piece of junk," Martin said.

Several mercenaries rushed over, firing their energy blasters. Jesse and the gang all dove for cover, ducking under planes and helicopters. Martin put his helmet on, becoming completely invisible.

One mercenary was just about to blast Ororo when he fell flat on his face, like he had been punched by a ghost. The mercenary's energy blaster floated in the air and zapped his friends. Three more mercenaries keeled over and dropped their weapons. Jesse, Ororo, and Journey grabbed the blasters and started zapping away, knocking out even more mercenaries.

"Good job, Martin," Doc said, giving two thumbs up to his invisible assistant.

By now all the Baxters were armed, including Mr. and Mrs. Baxter. They all dashed behind planes and exchanged shots with Aladdin's army. Columns of heavily armed and armored mercenaries spilled onto the deck. Jesse was doing his best not to panic, but it was becoming increasingly difficult.

"Dang it, Goldie, where the heck are you?" Doc shouted, unloading his energy blaster.

Aladdin appeared seconds later in his armored exoskeleton, his mechanical vipers whipping around like real ravenous snakes. He was flanked by two archangels.

"Resistance is futile, Xander! Surrender now or

face certain death!" Aladdin roared.

Doc responded by blasting his former student in the chest. Aladdin flew all the way to the other side of the ship and slammed into a guardrail, the only thing protecting him from the freezing, churning Arctic.

"Woo-hoo! Nice shot, Doc!" Jesse exclaimed, weaving through a crossfire of electricity. It was times like this that he was grateful his parents taught him karate, tae kwon do, martial arts, gymnastics, and every other athletic endeavor known to man.

Jesse watched out of the corners of his eyes as Aladdin slowly pushed himself off the ground and pressed a button on his arm. His silver robots marched over to Doc and towered over him.

Doc looked up and gulped. "Oh boy, this isn't good."

Four red-hot lasers ejected from the archangels' glowing eyes. Doc dropped his blaster and ran like mad to the other side of the ship. The lasers followed Doc the entire way, burning holes through the steel floor.

The archangels marched toward Jesse, their footsteps echoing against the steel deck.

Jesse dropped his blaster and made the peace sign with his quivering right hand.

"Uh… peace, dudes?"

The archangel on the left thundered, "We were programmed to reject peace."

The other archangel aimed his massive right hand at Jesse. "Prepare for imminent incineration."

"Mom! Dad! Help!!!" Jesse screamed, ducking for cover.

An energy beam ejected from the archangel's hand and whizzed over Jesse's head. The beam slammed into one of Aladdin's planes, detonating it into a million flaming pieces. The explosion rocked the entire ship. Jesse was thrown into the ship's guardrail, the top of his shaggy hair singed to a black crisp.

"Hold on, son, we're coming!" Mr. Baxter shouted, hobbling toward the archangels on his good leg.

He fired off several shots, but they barely fazed the ginormous robots.

Martin and the rest of the Baxters rushed over to gang up on the archangels. Martin was still invisible, but his energy blaster hovered in the air, giving away his location. Jesse grabbed a blaster lying on the ground and joined the assault.

Everyone ran around the archangels in a giant circle, firing at them from all angles. Doc made his way over and blasted a couple mercenaries off their hovercrafts.

The archangels suddenly released dozens of metallic tentacles from the glowing orbs on their chests. The tentacles snatched everyone up, including Martin, and dangled them in the air.

"I... can't... breathe..." Jesse gagged, clawing at a tentacle wrapped around his neck. The archangels squeezed Martin so hard that his invisibility suit short-circuited, leaving him fully visible.

Aladdin used his electric vipers to lift himself into the air. He surveyed his gagging prisoners, grinning like a sadistic madman. Just when Jesse's world started to turn dark, Aladdin waved his hand. The archangels loosened their tentacles, allowing everyone to breathe.

"I should have you all killed," Aladdin snarled. "But I have decided to grant mercy... under one condition."

"And... what's... that...?" Doc gasped.

Aladdin grabbed Doc by his throat.

"GIVE ME YOUR BLASTED VACCINE!"

Before Doc could respond, his helicopter-plane descended from the sky.

Aladdin released his stranglehold. "What the devil?"

The hatch door swung open and out flew Goldie, her propeller slicing through the Arctic wind.

"Sorry I'm late, Doc!" Goldie shouted. "I lost track of time watching Netflix. *Fuller House* is like the greatest show ever created. I laughed my metallic butt off."

Aladdin burst out in laughter. "What is that ridiculous piece of junk, Xander? It looks like a trash can with an upside-down fishbowl."

Goldie's body began blinking like an out-of-control police cruiser. "Trash can?! Can a trash can do this?!!"

Ten laser blasters popped out of Goldie's body and began mowing down Aladdin's mercenaries. A concealed panel on her belly popped open and two miniature cruise missiles zoomed toward the archangels. The missiles detonated on impact, sending the towering robots crashing into a plane. The archangels released their tentacled death grip on Jesse and the gang, sending them all plunging to the ground. Jesse landed hard on his right ankle and cried out in pain. It felt like he cracked it.

"Stop that thing before it blows this ship to kingdom-come!" Aladdin screamed, pointing a quivering finger at Goldie.

Goldie cackled maniacally as cruise missiles and lasers rained down on the airship. A few of her missiles landed on Aladdin's hi-tech planes. The planes exploded in spectacular fireballs that shook the entire ship. The thick, black smoke from the explosions seared Jesse's lungs, making it hard to breathe. His eyes watered and his nose dripped snot from all the carcinogens. A flaming piece of wreckage narrowly whizzed over his head, nearly decapitating him.

Goldie landed next to Doc and dropped five laser blasters on deck.

"Oh, I love these things," Journey exclaimed, grabbing one of the blasters.

"Hey, I want one!" Ororo hollered, shoving Journey out of the way.

Jesse and his parents grabbed the last three blasters.

Doc pointed to his hovering plane. "Let's roll!"

A ramp extended from the hatch door and clanked against the deck. Doc was just about to run onto the ramp when an explosion knocked him backwards, sending him colliding into Jesse. Several anti-aircraft guns popped up out of the side of Aladdin's airship and bombarded the helicopter-plane with lasers. The plane immediately shot into the air to avoid being obliterated.

"Hey, where's it going?" Jesse cried.

"The stupid autopilot is in defense mode," Doc grumbled.

Aladdin and his mercenaries circled Jesse and his family. There were well over 50 of them. They were soon joined by the archangels. Goldie's cruise missiles didn't destroy the robots, but they severely damaged them. Giant chunks of armor had fallen off, exposing wires and gears. Sparks flew out of their necks. One of the archangels was missing a wing, and the other was missing an eye.

"Lay down your arms or risk immediate execution," Aladdin snarled.

"I don't think so, bub." Goldie blasted into the air and released a dazzling bombardment of laser beams, taser darts, and tear gas. Aladdin and his mercenaries covered their faces and ran for safety.

"Die, robot," said the archangel with the missing wing. He raised his hand and blasted Goldie with a laser.

Goldie flew to the other side of the ship and landed with a thud. "Great, a self-hating robot," she grumbled. "That's the worst kind of prejudice."

By now almost every mercenary on the airship had spilled out on deck. Jesse estimated there were well over 100 of them.

Jesse and his family ducked behind planes and helicopters and exchanged fire with Aladdin's massive army. Streams of blue electricity and red lasers darted back and forth, blowing up planes, hovercrafts, and everything in between. Shards of glass and flaming pieces of wreckage flew all over the place. And the noise... the noise rattled Jesse's eardrums so much that he feared they were about to burst.

Jesse watched his parents and siblings with

admiration. They behaved like superheroes, running from plane to plane, knocking out mercenary after mercenary. His mom continued to resemble Rambo, leaping through streams of electricity. Ororo and Journey went after mercenaries like mindless robots. His dad hobbled around on one leg, zapping mercenaries out of the sky like they were birds. Doc and Martin blasted more mercenaries than anybody. And of course Goldie was a beast. She knocked out half of Aladdin's army by herself. If it wasn't for her, Jesse and his family would have been overwhelmed, just like they were back on the cruise ship.

Inspired by his family, Jesse took a deep breath and jumped out into no-man's land. Electricity streaked past his head, but he stood his ground, unloading his laser blaster.

The archangel with the missing eye turned toward Jesse and raised his hand. Jesse aimed his blaster at the archangel's other eye and zapped it, leaving him blind. He then fired at the archangel's damaged neck. After the seventh shot the head severed completely. A column of flame shot out of the archangel's decapitated neck, and he toppled backwards in a crumpled heap.

Goldie whizzed by and said, "Good job, kiddo!" She then went after the rest of Aladdin's forces.

Doc dashed over and said, "I've got your back, Jesse. Let's take out the other bucket of bolts."

Jesse and Doctor Xander started blasting the other archangel. The archangel spun around and raised his right arm. Jesse and Doc bombarded the archangel's cracked shoulder with lasers. The arm suddenly fell off and thudded against the deck. Sparks flew out of the giant robot's hacked-off shoulder.

Jesse and Doc had just started blasting the archangel in the face when glowing cables wrapped around their ankles, sending them crashing head-first onto the steel deck. Their laser blasters flew out of their hands and slid overboard. Stars floated across Jesse's eyes, followed by Aladdin's scowling face.

"I hope you two have enjoyed your health over the years, because you're both about to become cripples."

Aladdin was about to pull Doc up by his hair when a 'death hawk' whizzed by and fired a volley of lasers. The lasers blasted Aladdin into a guardrail.

Aladdin had just staggered to his feet when Doc tackled him from behind. Jesse pushed himself off the ground and watched as his uncle engaged in a fist-fight with the Merchant of Death. Doc delivered a few good licks before Aladdin struck back. His armored hand slammed into Doc's mouth, further bloodying his lip. The two old friends rolled around on deck like a couple of high school wrestlers.

"Why didn't you just give me the vaccine?" Aladdin demanded.

"I didn't know it was for your son!" Doc exclaimed, smashing his knuckles into Aladdin's crooked nose.

Aladdin rolled onto his back, tucked his legs under Doc's chest, and kicked outward. Doc slammed into the guardrail.

"Why else would I want it, you idiot?" Aladdin bellowed, his vipers whipping around over his head.

"I thought you wanted to weaponize it," Doc said, clinging to the guardrail.

Aladdin cocked his head to the side. "What do you mean 'weaponize' it?"

"The nano-bots can be programmed to heal... and to kill."

Aladdin arched his eyebrows. "So it can be engineered to become a virus?"

Doc nodded.

Aladdin smirked. "So your 'Fountain of Youth' can be used as a 'Fountain of Death'?"

Doc rolled his eyes. "Can everyone please stop saying that?"

Aladdin resumed his scowl. "Why would you think I'd know how to weaponize your vaccine? I didn't even know it existed until this morning!"

Doc grimaced. "I thought you might have remembered our lessons at Harvard."

"What?!" Aladdin exploded. "Why would I remember a lesson plan from over 20 years ago?!"

"What was I supposed to think?" Doc snapped, clutching his injured gut. "You don't exactly have the world's greatest reputation."

Before Aladdin could respond, the airship started quivering. Jesse jumped to his feet and clung to a guardrail. A gaping hole opened up in the middle of the deck, swallowing an entire plane. Seconds later, a massive column of locusts exploded out of the hole. The locusts arched high into the air before plunging back into the hull of the ship. The sound of screeching metal was deafening.

Aladdin turned back toward Doc and whispered, "What have you done, Xander?"

Doc smirked. "Meet my newest creation: self-replicating locusts. Soon your entire airship will be nothing but scrap metal on the bottom of the Arctic Ocean."

Aladdin gritted his teeth and clenched his fists. He looked like he was about to pop a blood vessel.

Aladdin grabbed Doc by his hair and delivered a vicious upper-cut. Doc collapsed to his knees and clutched his bleeding mouth.

Jesse charged toward Aladdin and dropkicked him in the chest. Aladdin fell flat on his back. Jesse was about to stomp on Aladdin's head when a viper wrapped around his waist and hoisted him into the air.

"Let me go, douche bag!" Jesse shouted, kicking his feet. He leaned his head to the left to get as far away from the viper's hissing mouth as he possibly could.

Aladdin cackled. "You and your siblings are admirably brave. Stupid, but brave. As I stated back in the Bahamas, the brave have a much lower life expectancy than the general population."

Aladdin used his viper cables to fling Jesse to

the other side of the airship. Jesse slid across the deck and came to a stop right beside Ororo, who was firing her laser blaster at mercenaries flying around in the sky.

Ororo glanced down and said, "Are you gonna lay there all day, or are you gonna help me?"

Jesse grabbed an energy blaster from an unconscious mercenary and joined in the firefight.

The airship continued shaking. Cracks appeared everywhere. Locusts were now all over the place, tearing into planes, gnawing on energy guns, ripping apart hovercrafts, and dismantling armor. A whole swarm of them devoured the last archangel in a matter of seconds. Goldie remained airborne, which kept her out of harm's way.

Jesse and Ororo stood back-to-back, firing energy bolts at the last few mercenaries. Most of the other mercenaries had already evacuated the airship.

"Aladdin's goons have the right idea," Ororo said. "We need to get out of here, and fast!"

Out of the corner of his eye, Jesse saw a stray energy blast detonate next to his mother. She flipped over the guardrail, grabbing the railing with her right hand.

"Mom!"

Jesse started dashing toward her, but a bombardment of energy blasts sent him scrambling for cover.

Thankfully Mr. Baxter was nearby. He hobbled over on his bad leg and grabbed his wife's hand.

"I've got you, hon," Mr. Baxter grunted, clutching Mrs. Baxter's arm. Her long hair whipped around in the fierce Arctic wind.

Jesse had just clambered to his feet when an energy bolt slammed into Mr. Baxter's back, knocking him overboard.

"Mom! Dad! No!!!!"

Jesse dashed toward the railing and looked over the side. All he saw were dark, churning waves.

His parents were gone.

Chapter Fifteen: A Thousand Knives

The lights on the airship flickered on and off for several seconds before finally fizzling out for good. The entire ship was now plunged in darkness, save for energy blasts and flaming wreckage. Jesse didn't notice; he continued leaning over the guardrail, staring into the dark abyss of the Arctic Ocean.

Ororo ran up to Jesse, flicking locusts off her prosthetic arm.

"What are you doing, bro? We gotta get out of here!"

Jesse turned to Ororo, his eyes welled up with tears.

She grasped his shoulder. "What's wrong, Jess?"

Jesse wiped his eyes and sobbed, "They're gone, Ororo. Mom and Dad... they fell off the ship."

"What?!"

Ororo spun around and looked over the guardrail. "No!"

"We need to get Doc's plane," Jesse said, grabbing Ororo's artificial arm. "Maybe we can still save them."

Jesse and Ororo ran toward Doc, sidestepping all the cracks and gaping holes. On the way they ran into Journey and Martin, who were exchanging shots with the last few remaining mercenaries.

Ororo ran up to one of the mercenaries and socked him in the face. Her robotic arm crashed through his helmet. She then tore off the cracked helmet and kicked the mercenary in the side of the head. The mercenary flew sideways and plummeted into a hole.

Jesse was even more ruthless. He tackled a mercenary to the ground, tore off his helmet, and proceeded to beat the holy snot out of him. He only stopped when Martin yanked him off.

The mercenary staggered to his feet, blood dripping from his mouth. Ororo delivered a savage roundhouse kick to the side of his head, sending him sprawling to the floor.

"Dang, Jesse, I've never seen you like this before," Journey observed. "I've seen Ororo go crazy, but not you!"

Jesse looked up at Journey, tears streaming down his cheeks.

Journey's face turned pale. "Whoa, what's wrong?"

Ororo wiped tears from her left eye. "Jesse saw Mom and Dad fall off the ship."

"What?!" Journey ran to the guardrail and peered into the ocean.

"It happened on the other side," Jesse said, pointing to the opposite end of the ship. "We need to look for them. They might still be alive."

Martin rubbed the back of his head and awkwardly said, "I hate to be a pessimist, kids, but I doubt anyone could survive a fall into the freezing Arctic. They probably…"

Martin shut up when Jesse and his siblings gawked at him in horror. He gulped and said, "You're right, let's go look for them."

Jesse and the gang ran over to Doc, who was still clinging to the guardrail, bickering with Aladdin. Goldie joined them. They all surrounded Aladdin and pointed their blasters at his chest.

"Give it up, Aladdin!" Doc shouted. "You're surrounded. All of your mercenaries have fled. If you surrender, I will give your son the vaccine."

Aladdin's face turned ghostly pale. "My son! I completely forgot about him!"

Aladdin pressed a button on his arm. "This is

Aladdin. Who has my son?"

One of Aladdin's lieutenants replied, "I evacuated him moments ago, sir. We're up in the air. Where are you?"

"Don't worry about me. I'll be there shortly."

"You're not going anywhere," Doc said.

"Oh yes I am. Because you know you're not taking me alive. And if I go down, I'm taking you and everyone else down with me."

Aladdin's electric vipers wriggled in the air, causing everyone to back up.

Doc sighed and pointed to the sky. "Go. If you want your son to die, then go."

Aladdin scowled and pressed a button on his arm. A hovercraft shot toward him. Aladdin jumped onto the hovercraft and zoomed toward one of his planes.

Goldie started blinking her lights. "We had that lunatic on the ropes! Why are you lettin' him go?"

"Aladdin will never go down without a fight," Doc said. "And I don't have the heart to kill him."

"I don't care about any of this!" Jesse hollered. "We have to save Mom and Dad!"

"Where are they?" Doc asked, glancing around.

"They fell overboard!" Jesse cried.

Doc's eyes widened in horror. "No! Goldie, go get our plane!"

Goldie flew toward the plane, which was circling the airship several thousand feet in the air.

The deafening sound of screeching metal caused Jesse to jump back in alarm. He twirled around and gasped at the horrifying sight of the airship literally splitting in half. It reminded him of the Titanic after it hit an iceberg. Locusts now covered the deck like termites on a rotted tree stump.

"Goldie, hurry up!" Doc hollered.

The plane finally lowered toward the deck. The hatch door swung open and a ramp thudded against the ground. Locusts immediately latched on.

Martin shoved everyone out of the way and

barged inside.

"Martin isn't much of a gentleman," Journey grumbled, running aboard the ship "This might mess up our wedding plans."

Ororo followed her.

Jesse and Doc were just about to run onboard when the airship finally split in half. Jesse and his uncle clung to one of the ship's many holes so they wouldn't plunge into the icy water.

When the ship slammed into the Arctic, ice-cold water sprayed into the air, soaking Jesse from head to toe. The water was so cold it felt like dozens of daggers had penetrated his skin. It was one of the most painful experiences of Jesse's entire life. He opened his mouth to scream, but no sound came out. He could barely catch his breath.

Jesse and Doc continued clinging to the side of the hole. The ship bounced around in the water before tilting into the air. Once the bowhead became completely submerged, the ship tilted vertically, at a 90-degree angle, and continued its descent into the Arctic. Jesse and Doc held onto the side of the ship for dear life, ignoring all the locusts dancing around their bodies. The ocean sped toward them at an incredible speed.

"Take a deep breath!" Doc shouted. "We're going to sink pretty deep. Kick your feet as fast as you can and swim toward the stars."

Jesse nodded and inhaled as much oxygen as he possibly could. A split-second before hitting the water, he clenched his mouth shut. Then he plunged into the icy abyss.

The instant he hit the water, Jesse nearly opened his mouth to scream. It now felt like he was being stabbed with a thousand daggers.

Jesse fought through the mind-numbing pain and kicked his legs, swimming toward the stars twinkling above the surface. Just when his lungs were about to burst, Jesse popped his head out of the freezing water.

Jesse gasped for air and continued kicking his

legs, struggling to stay afloat. It became increasingly harder to move his limbs. Most of the blood in his extremities had moved to his core.

Jesse was glad to see Doc's head burst forth from the ocean. He tried to swim toward his uncle, but he couldn't get his frozen limbs to work properly.

"I... I can't.... I can't...."

Jesse couldn't handle the pain any longer. It was too much. He stopped kicking his legs and his head sunk back into the water.

Jesse looked up and watched as the twinkling stars grew fainter and fainter. He was now on his way to the bottom of the ocean. He was about to open his mouth to end it all when blinking lights floated toward him. At first he thought he was seeing things. That changed when a robotic hand grabbed his arm and dragged him toward the surface. The stars reappeared and grew brighter and brighter with each passing second. Jesse finally burst forth from the ocean, only this time he continued flying into the air. The fierce wind almost felt warm compared to the water below.

Jesse wiped his eyes with his one free hand. With his vision finally clear, he could see Goldie holding his arm, her propeller slicing through the wind. The Northern Icecap glistened off on the horizon. Icebergs were everywhere.

Goldie flew over to Doctor Xander and grabbed him by the back of his lab coat. She then carried both of them to the hovering helicopter-plane. Ororo and Journey peered out of the hatch door, clapping and cheering like crazy.

Goldie brought Jesse and Doc inside the ship and closed the hatch door. She then plopped them on the ground.

"T...t...t...thank...y...y...you....," Jesse chattered, shivering uncontrollably.

"Don't mention it, kid," Goldie said. She actually sounded concerned. She wheeled over to a closet and grabbed several thick wool blankets.

Ororo and Martin helped Jesse and Doc strip out of their wet clothes. Normally Jesse would have freaked being naked in front of people. He was so cold, though, that nothing like that mattered at the moment. All he wanted was to warm up.

Jesse wasn't naked for long. Immediately after he and Doc were dried off with towels, they were covered in blankets and led to cots in the back of the plane.

Journey gave Jesse a hug. "I'm so glad you're okay."

Jesse hugged her back. "I'm...g...g...glad you're o...o...okay, too."

Jesse suddenly started crying. He wasn't crying because he was in agonizing pain. He cried because he now realized what Martin was trying to tell them... that his parents were dead. There was no way they could have survived a plunge into the icy Arctic. He had only been in the water for 30 seconds and it nearly killed him.

Jesse had just started to accept that his mom and dad were gone when Martin ran into the cockpit and said, "Let's find your parents."

Ororo and Journey dashed into the cockpit to join Martin. As exhausted as Jesse was, even he rolled out of the cot and trudged to the front of the plane.

They spent several minutes flying low over the ocean, shining a spotlight over the churning water. Just when Jesse had given up all hope, Ororo pointed out the window and shouted, "Is that them?"

Martin lowered the plane over a massive iceberg. The spotlight revealed two people clinging to the ice. Martin pressed a button and the hatch door swung open. Goldie flew outside to investigate. A moment later, Goldie returned with Mr. and Mrs. Baxter dangling from her robotic arms, both of them dripping wet and freezing cold, but miraculously still alive. Their skin was so blue that they resembled Smurfs, and they were shivering so hard it looked like they were having seizures.

Jesse and his sisters showered their parents with hugs and kisses. Mr. and Mrs. Baxter hugged them back, nearly getting them as cold and wet as they were.

"We need to get you guys out of your clothes," Martin said.

Goldie and Martin helped Mr. and Mrs. Baxter disrobe. They were then given towels to dry off and thick, wool blankets to cover up in.

Chattering incessantly, Mr. Baxter mumbled. "T…t…t…thanks…."

"Shhh, keep quiet," Goldie said. "You're wastin' valuable energy."

"We need to get them to a hospital immediately," Doc said, shivering under his own blankets.

"You and Jesse need to get checked out, too," Ororo said, rubbing Jesse's back. Jesse smiled appreciatively.

Martin went into the cockpit and chartered a new course for America.

Jesse plopped down on a cot and continued shivering under his blankets. He should have been happy that his parents were rescued, but he couldn't help feeling angry… angry at *them*. Things didn't have to be like this. Things *shouldn't* be like this.

As Jesse looked down at the icebergs floating in the sea below, he continued simmering in anger. He didn't want to come across as an ungrateful brat, but he was tired of his life of nonstop action and adventure. He was tired of always traveling, always tangling with evil super villains. Aladdin may have been one of the most formidable foes he ever encountered, but he certainly wasn't the first.

Jesse couldn't even say he wanted to go home, because he had no home. His parents were like gypsies, dragging him and his siblings to dangerous, exotic locations. He knew his parents had big hearts, that they were trying to make the world a better place, but he was starting to wonder why. What had the world ever done for them, besides try to kill them?

Jesse knew he sounded bitter, but he didn't care. He was tired… tired of traveling… tired of running… tired of fighting… tired of caring. He was just so tired.

Jesse finally closed his eyes and drifted off to sleep.

Chapter Sixteen: The World's Gone Mad

Jesse woke up just as their plane landed in the parking lot of a New York City hospital. Jesse could tell the hospital security guards weren't too thrilled when Martin landed the helicopter-plane in the parking lot, but they kept quiet when they saw Goldie and all her laser blasters. Jesse figured they didn't want to make her mad.

Paramedics rushed out and placed Jesse's parents on stretchers. They then wheeled them into the emergency room. Jesse and his siblings tried to follow but were forced to wait in the waiting room. Initially Goldie wasn't allowed in because she set off the metal detector, but after she threatened to blow up the maternity ward, security reluctantly allowed her inside.

Jesse and his siblings were finally allowed to see their parents several hours later. It turned out Mr. and Mrs. Baxter had the beginning stages of hypothermia, but they would pull through with enough rest and medicine. While Jesse and his sisters showered their parents with hugs and kisses, Martin went out to buy everyone new clothes. Ororo and Journey were still wearing their torn and tattered cruise dresses, and Jesse and Doc were still covered in blankets. Jesse, Doc, and the Baxter girls were thankful for the change in attire.

Ororo and Journey remained with their mom and dad while Jesse, Doc, Martin, and Goldie played poker in the waiting room. (Goldie always carried a deck of cards in her body.) They were in the middle of a particularly thrilling game when President Robinson and Secretary of Defense Paternus barged into the room, flanked by secret service agents.

Jesse was the first one to notice the president's presence.

"Um, Doc? We have company."

Without looking up from his hand, Doc said, "They can wait. I'm about to win $100 dollars from Goldie."

President Robinson crossed his arms and said, "Doctor Xander, I never thought of you as a compulsive gambler. It would seem even the most intelligent among us have their vices."

Doc looked up and gasped.

"Uh… hello, Mr. President. I… um…"

Doc suddenly jumped up and ran into the Baxter's room. President Robinson and Paternus dashed after him. Jesse, Goldie, and Martin brought up the rear.

Jesse walked in to find Doc cowering behind Mrs. Baxter's bed. President Robinson stood on the other side of the bed with his arms crossed.

"Zach, this is ridiculous," the president said.

Doc clasped his hands in front of his face and begged, "Please don't arrest me for attacking the secretary of defense."

"You attacked the secretary of defense?" Mrs. Baxter hollered.

The nurse ran over and grabbed Doc by the back of his shirt.

"You all need to get out of here. Mr. and Mrs. Baxter need their rest."

The nurse turned around to berate the president, but stopped when she realized who he was.

The nurse clapped her hands and giddily said, "Oh, Mr. President! What a pleasure to meet you! I almost voted for you, but I decided to go with the other guy because I saw a commercial on TV that said you hate America… and babies!"

President Robinson forced a painful-looking smile. "Thank you, ma'am. You do realize, though, that most campaign ads are misleading, right?"

The nurse blew raspberries. "Oh Mr. President,

don't be silly. Television doesn't lie."

The nurse then scurried out of the room and hollered, "I have to call my mother and tell her I met the president she hates!"

The president shook his head and muttered, "Everyone's so partisan nowadays."

Paternus marched up to Doc and jabbed him in the chest. "You've gotta lot of nerve blasting me in the face with knock-out gas and blowing up my car, Xander!"

"Actually, sir, Goldie did all that. I was merely an accomplice."

Goldie wheeled over to Paternus and started blinking her lights. "Yeah, I knocked ya out and blew up your car, and I'd do it again in a heartbeat. You got a problem with that, bozo?"

President Robinson stepped in between Paternus and Goldie. "We didn't come here to argue." He turned to Doc. "While I'm disappointed you misled us, I am glad you and your family managed to escape relatively unscathed."

The president glanced at Mr. and Mrs. Baxter, who were hooked up to IVs.

Mrs. Baxter waved and said, "Hello, Mr. President. I'm so embarrassed you're seeing me like this. My hair's a hot mess."

Mr. Baxter jumped out of bed and shook the president's hand. "Hey Barry! I can call you Barry, right?"

"Actually, Mr. President is fine."

Mr. Baxter guffawed and slapped the president on the back. "You're such a joker, Barry. So I want you to know I was so planning on voting for you, but I haven't voted since, well, ever, and I figured '*Why start now?*'"

The president grimaced. Jesse figured it was because his dad's robe was wide open.

Jesse ran over and helped his goofy dad climb back in bed.

Doc wrung his hands. "So you're not mad at me, Mr. President?"

"Of course I'm mad!" hollered the president. "But I learned long ago you don't get far in life by holding grudges. So I'm willing to forgive you for your deceit."

"So to what do we owe the pleasure of your visit?" Doc asked, eager to change the subject.

"Besides checking on you guys, I'm here to attend an emergency meeting at the United Nations tomorrow morning."

Doc cocked an eyebrow. "What's the meeting about?"

"Let me show you." President Robinson pointed a remote at the flat-screen TV hanging from the wall and changed the channel from ESPN to CNN.

"Aw man, I was watching football," Mr. Baxter whined.

"It was a blow-out, dear," Mrs. Baxter said. "Quit complaining."

Jesse and everyone in the room watched as the CNN anchor rattled on about an explosion in kidnappings, terrorist attacks, and threats of war between major nations. From North and South America to Europe, Africa, and Asia, the entire world had gone completely mad. According to the anchor, all the attacks and kidnappings were copy-cat versions of Aladdin's brazen assault on a cruise liner. People wanted Doc's immortality vaccine, either for themselves or dying loved ones, and they were willing to do whatever it took to secure it.

"When did all this craziness start?" Doc asked.

"Shortly after Aladdin went viral about your family's kidnapping," the president replied.

"I warned you all about this," Paternus growled.

"Don't gloat, Robert," chastised the president. He turned back to Doc and said, "We all figured a few nut-jobs would do whatever they could to get vaccinated, but I *never* imagined things would get this out of control. World leaders fear the carnage will escalate with each passing day."

Doc sighed and massaged his throbbing head. "The world clearly isn't ready for an immortality vaccine."

"I agree," the president replied gloomily. "That's why I came to see you. I was hoping you'd attend tomorrow's meeting. I figured you could tell everyone you found a glitch in the vaccine, something that could harm people. We could then say, for safety purposes, that the vaccine is being taken back to the lab for further testing. That should deflate most of the anxiety around the world."

Doc nodded. "That's a brilliant idea. And it's not like we'd be lying. If the vaccine were to fall into the wrong hands…"

"…it could become a Fountain of Death," the president said. "Yes, I remember what you told us."

President Robinson clasped Doc on the shoulder. "Thanks for doing this for me, Doc. Heck, it's not just for me. It's for the entire world."

"Don't mention it, Mr. President. It's the least I can do to prevent a worldwide riot."

"As a token of my gratitude, I took the liberty of securing you a room at the same hotel I'm staying at. That way you and your family can stay in town a few days until your sister and brother-in-law are healthy enough to leave."

Jesse and his siblings hooted and hollered. They rarely got to stay at fancy hotels. Usually they had to stay in rodent-infested motels, or mud huts in third-world countries.

Doc grinned. "This'll be fun. We can hang out, order pizza, and watch some movies."

Goldie spun around in circles, blinking her lights. "Ohhh, I love pizza."

Jesse gave Goldie a funny look. "You can eat?"

"Don't listen to her, she's nuts," Doc said. "She likes to pretend she's a person."

"If ya had put some extra effort in building me, ya could've equipped me with a digestive system," Goldie grumbled.

Mr. and Mrs. Baxter kissed Jesse, Ororo, and Journey goodbye, then Doc led them outside to the helicopter-plane. Once they were all strapped in, Martin blasted off and followed secret service to the hotel.

For the first time since the beginning of their cruise, Jesse and his siblings were getting a chance to chill out and relax.

The interlude of peace wouldn't last long.

Chapter Seventeen: Desperate Times

In the South Pacific...

Aladdin's secret headquarters was located on an artificial island several hundred miles away from the Great Barrier Reef. The island had massive propellers jutting out of the sand, which allowed the enormous man-made structure to float into the sky.

The southern part of the island contained a jungle stocked with exotic animals. The northern part had a giant waterfall and freshwater lake. And the center of the island was dominated by a heavily fortified citadel fortress, with turrets spiraling high into the sky.

Inside one of the spiraling turrets sat Aladdin Salazar, looking over his bed-ridden son. The doctor had just finished checking all of Mikhail's vital signs. He was now in the process of telling the Merchant of Death his son's dire prognosis.

Adjusting his glasses, the doctor said, "I'm sorry, Mr. Salazar. I've done all I can do, but the end is near. I'm afraid your son won't last the end of the week."

Aladdin grabbed the doctor by his throat. "There has to be something we can do, Doctor Jamison!"

Doctor Jamison gagged. "Mr. Salazar, I've given your son every cancer-fighting medication known to man. He's lived several months longer than I thought he would. All we can do now is make him comfortable."

Aladdin growled and tightened his grip. "You and I agree on something. My son's death will be much more comfortable than yours."

Doctor Jamison's already-bulging eyes widened further. "What?!"

Aladdin hurled Doctor Jamison out the window, shattering the glass into thousands of pieces.

Aladdin stormed back over to his son, who was shivering under his blankets.

Annabeth emerged from the shadows. "What should we do, sir? Raid another cancer treatment facility?"

Aladdin shook his head. "No. We've already stolen the best medicine money can buy. The only thing that can save my son is Doctor Xander's immortality vaccine."

Another mercenary, a short-haired teenage boy from Japan, said "Yeah, that plan really fell through."

Aladdin gritted his teeth in an attempt to quell his bubbling rage. He didn't want to start killing *all* of his mercenaries. "Thank you for that blatantly obvious observation, you mindless idiot."

Annabeth leaned toward the Japanese kid and whispered, "Shut up, Raiden. You're going to end up like Doctor Jamison."

She then turned toward Aladdin. "Do you want to try again, sir?"

Aladdin sighed and put his head in his hands. He did not speak for several tense minutes.

He finally lifted his head. "Do we still have a signal on the girl, the one who's name means Beauty?"

Raiden turned on a flat-screen TV hanging from the wall. A 3-D image of the world popped up. A blinking red dot flashed over the New York Metropolitan area.

"Yes sir. It appears she's in Manhattan."

Aladdin turned toward Annabeth. "It was your plan to place a microscopic GPS chip inside her robotic arm, correct?"

Annabeth nodded.

Aladdin smiled. "Consider yourself promoted… *again*. If you keep this up, you may end up with my job."

Annabeth grinned. "Thank you, sir."

Aladdin turned toward Raiden and frowned. "Consider yourself demoted."

"Aw man, not again," Raiden griped.

Aladdin stood up and said, "Gather twenty of my finest mercenaries."

Thundering footsteps echoed throughout the room. Aladdin turned to find one of his ten-foot tall archangels towering in the doorway.

"Perhaps we can be of assistance, Mr. Salazar," the archangel thundered in an eerie, robotic voice.

Aladdin's malicious grin widened. "Yes, perhaps you can. Gather several of your comrades and wait for us in the courtyard."

Aladdin walked over to the shattered window and looked out over the clear, blue sea.

"Everyone get ready. We're about to invade Manhattan."

Chapter Eighteen: The Orphan & The War Vet

Ororo had only been asleep for an hour when she jumped up in a cold sweat. The Janjaweed had just torched her village. Thankfully she woke up before being forced to relive her parents' deaths.

Ororo slid out of bed, making sure not to disturb Journey, who was sleeping next to her. Jesse was sprawled out on the other bed. Several empty pizza boxes were scattered around the room. The TV was on, showing the main menu of the DVD they had watched hours before. She walked past her snoring siblings and made her way into the kitchen.

Ororo filled a plastic cup with tap water and downed the entire thing in one gulp. She then plopped down in a chair in the living room. Doc and Martin were sprawled out on the sofas, snoring almost as loudly as her siblings. Goldie sat off to the side, with all of her lights off. She was plugged into an electrical socket to recharge her batteries. The goldfish in her bowl was asleep as well.

Ororo glanced at the clock. It was shortly after midnight, and yet she was wide awake. Her mind was racing, which she always hated. The only thing capable of calming her nerves was a nice walk. She threw on a jacket, grabbed one of the hotel key cards, and quietly exited the room.

Ororo took the elevator to the deserted lobby and walked past the front desk. Some young guy had his feet on the table, texting away on his cell phone. He didn't even notice Ororo walk by, which suited her just fine. If he had seen her, he probably would have asked where she was going by herself at such a late hour.

As soon as Ororo stepped outside, she started shivering. There was a nip in the air. Just hours before it had been unusually warm out. Now a cold front had moved in, and a storm was brewing.

Ororo pulled up on her collar and walked against the wind. She wove through crowds of young college kids, artists, Wall Street executives, and drunks going to and from bars. A lot of the pedestrians were holding bags and wrapped presents. They were obviously doing last-minute Christmas shopping. Ororo also passed several homeless people slouched against buildings. Her heart went out to them, but she had no money to give.

Ororo turned the corner and passed another shaggy-looking homeless man. He sat outside a busy bar clutching an empty plastic cup. People hurried past him, oblivious to his presence. He might as well have been a fire hydrant. Ororo was about to scurry pass him as well when she noticed the man's artificial leg stretched out on the sidewalk. She then looked at his face. A patch covered his right eye.

The man had his head against the bar window, and his left eye was closed. He wore a tattered, filthy coat. It had just started drizzling, and the rain left dirty streaks along his cheeks.

Ororo plopped down next to the homeless man. "Hello, how are you?"

The man glanced at Ororo and cocked his bushy, unkempt eyebrows. He opened his mouth to speak, but nothing came out. The man cleared his throat and gruffly said, "Sorry, kid. I… I'm not used ta talkin' ta people."

A woman walked by and flipped a quarter into the homeless guy's cup.

The homeless guy stared at his cup in awe. "That's the first change I got all night," he mumbled.

Ororo cocked her head to the side. "Why aren't you used to talking to people?"

The man cleared his throat again. "Well, I usually don't have anyone ta talk to."

Another lady walked by and dropped a dollar. It fluttered onto the homeless man's lap. His hazel eyes grew even wider.

Ororo gestured to all the people walking by. "What are you talking about, dude? The city is full of people!"

The man scoffed. "Yeah, but most of them don't have a heart. I've been on the streets going on seven years, and I can count on one hand the number of times people have talked ta me. They act like I don't exist."

"Oh."

Ororo and the homeless guy sat in silence for a moment. Several more dollar bills fluttered into the man's cup.

The man smirked at Ororo. "You're quite the moneymaker. I've gotten more change in the past two minutes than I have all day."

Ororo shrugged. "I'm a cute kid, what can I say?"

The man burst out laughing and slapped his artificial leg. "Golly, I haven't laughed like that in years."

The man extended his grimy hand. "I'm Jerry, by the way."

"I'm Ororo." She shook Jerry's hand with her robotic one.

"Pretty name. It means 'Beauty', right?"

Ororo nodded. "Wow, I'm impressed. How do you know that?"

Jerry patted his chest. "I'm not an idiot, kid. I consider myself a well-rounded, cultured man."

Now Ororo burst out laughing. "Oh really?"

"Yes, really. I used ta be in the military. I was stationed in Africa a bit, did some peacekeeping in places like Congo, Rwanda, and Darfur."

Ororo lowered her head. "Oh. I'm from Darfur."

Jerry glanced at Ororo's eye patch and robotic arm. He pointed at his eye and said, "Is that how you... uh..."

Ororo nodded, blinking away tears.

"I… uh… lost my leg and eye in Iraq."

Ororo looked up. "I'm sorry to hear that."

Ororo and Jerry continued talking for the next twenty minutes. Jerry asked Ororo where her family was. Without going into detail, Ororo explained her parents were in the hospital, and she was staying with her uncle in a hotel up the street. When Jerry asked why she was out by herself in the middle of the night, she simply replied she needed some air. Jerry then talked about his years in the military, and how he suffered from a severe case of post-traumatic stress syndrome. That was the main reason he was out on the streets. He just couldn't seem to keep a job.

Pretty soon Jerry's cup was overflowing with dollar bills and quarters. He quickly counted the money and gasped.

"Holy mackerel, there's 90 bucks in here!"

A woman in a fur coat walked by and handed Ororo a $10 bill.

"Make that 100," Ororo said, handing Jerry the money.

Jerry giggled like a kid opening a birthday card full of money. "You're amazing, darlin'."

Ororo stood up and stretched. The rain was now coming down in sheets. "It's been fun talking to you, Jerry, but I think I'm going to go visit my folks at the hospital. I miss them a lot."

Recounting the money, Jerry asked, "Aren't visiting hours over?"

Ororo shrugged. "I'll sneak in if I have to."

"Well here, take this." Jerry handed Ororo a fistful of singles. "Use it ta take the subway. That way you can get out of the rain."

"Thanks," Ororo said, grabbing the money. "It was nice meeting you."

Jerry shook his unkempt hair, spraying water everywhere. "You too, kid. Now get outta here before ya catch a cold. Don't worry about me, I'll make this money last all month."

Ororo waved goodbye and started to leave. She stopped when a massive bolt of lightning split the sky in half. Seconds later, a thunderous BOOM rattled windows all throughout the city. The rain started coming down even harder, threatening to drown anyone who opened their mouths.

Ororo pulled her jacket over her head and glanced back at Jerry. He just sat there in the downpour, looking miserable.

"Hey Jerry!" she shouted over the thunder. "You wanna join me? I could use some company. Plus, it'll give you an excuse to dry off."

Jerry grinned, revealing crooked yellow teeth. "Don't mind if I do, darling. Besides, the subway can be dangerous. You need someone to watch your back."

Ororo decided not to mention that her mother had taught her how to incapacitate a man with a single punch to the throat.

Jerry hobbled to his feet. He walked with a limp, but moved pretty fast for a one-legged man with a cheap prosthetic.

Ororo and Jerry rushed into the subway, anxious to escape the relentless downpour. They didn't realize how wet they were until they went underground. Water dripped from their hair and clothes as if they had just jumped into a pool.

Jerry took off his jacket and wrung it out. A puddle of water accumulated under his feet.

"This is the cleanest I've been in years," he said with a smirk.

Ororo scrunched up her nose. Jerry still smelled pretty bad to her.

Ororo and Jerry made their way to the edge of the platform and waited for the train. There weren't too many people waiting with them, just a few drunks and a couple people working the late shift.

A few minutes later, a bright light appeared at the end of the tunnel. The train sped closer and closer, the high-voltage tracks screeching under the immense weight. The train barreled past Ororo and Jerry, creating a gust of wind that rustled their dripping-wet hair. The train finally screeched to a halt and the doors flew open. Ororo and Jerry made their way to the last car and climbed inside just before the door slid shut.

The train quickly jerked forward, nearly knocking Ororo off her feet. She followed Jerry to the rear of the empty car.

Jerry plopped down in a chair and grinned. "Wow, this is fun. I haven't been down here in years. These cars are so nice."

Ororo continued scrunching up her nose in disgust. The subway car was filthy and smelled like urine. But she guessed when you lived out on the streets, even a dirty subway car seemed nice.

Ororo leaned her head against the rattling window and closed her good eye. Seconds later, an explosive blast ripped through the rear of the car. Ororo and Jerry flew all the way to the front of the car and slammed against the wall.

Ororo pushed herself off the ground and looked up. Black smoke filled the car, making it hard to see and even harder to breathe. She pulled her jacket over her mouth and peered into the back. Even through the thick smoke she could see a gaping hole where the rear emergency door used to be.

In between hacking coughs, Jerry grumbled, "That reminded me of when insurgents used to fire on our convoys outside Baghdad."

The smoke quickly billowed out the back of the train, which continued barreling along the track. Ororo and her new pal trudged over to the hole and peeked out. All they could see was the track speeding away from them.

They had just started to turn around when one of Aladdin's armored mercenaries dropped from the top of the car and swung inside, kicking Jerry in the face. Two more mercenaries appeared on hovercrafts and flew inside the car, their heads almost touching the ceiling.

"Not you guys again!" Ororo cried. She ran up and punched the mercenary who decked Jerry, cracking his helmet. He staggered backwards, blinded by his cracked visor.

"I'll take care of him, sweetheart," Jerry said, wiping his busted lip. He hobbled over to the dazed mercenary, grabbed him around his waist, and tossed him out of the car like a ragdoll.

Jerry turned around and cracked a smile. "Who's next?"

The other mercenaries responded by firing energy bolts. Ororo and Jerry rolled around on the ground, narrowly avoiding the blasts. Jerry hopped on a chair and tackled one of the mercenaries off his hovercraft, driving him into the ground. The mercenary's blaster clattered to the front of the car, which Ororo quickly grabbed. Jerry tore off the mercenary's helmet and repeatedly punched him in the face.

Ororo ran up and zapped the other mercenary in the chest. The mercenary flew out of the car like his buddy.

Ororo turned to find Jerry still pounding the living daylights out of the remaining mercenary. She grabbed his shoulder and said, "Uh, Jerry?"

Jerry twirled around and raised his fists. Ororo stepped back and raised her blaster.

"Oh, sorry kid," grumbled Jerry, lowering his hands. "My military instincts kicked in."

"Sorry I startled you." Ororo pointed to the unconscious mercenary, whose face was covered in bruises. "I think he's out."

Jerry nodded. "I think you're right."

Ororo hopped onto a hovercraft and floated into the air, nearly hitting her head against the ceiling. "We need to get out of here. These guys are like cockroaches. If you see one, 100 more are just around the corner."

Jerry nodded again. "So...uh...how do these flying pizza pan things work?"

"Just hop on and lean toward whichever direction you want to go."

Jerry stepped on the other hovercraft and shot upwards, slamming his head against the ceiling. "Ouch! That freakin' hurt!"

The subway car pulled up to the next platform and screeched to a halt.

"Perfect timing," Ororo said.

Ororo and Jerry flew out of the car, startling the few passengers trying to get on. They zoomed up the stairs to the top of the subway station and made their way outside to the bustling streets. Rain continued pouring from the dreary sky. Dozens of people stared at Ororo and Jerry in shock. A few dropped their umbrellas.

"Man, I forgot about the rain." Ororo wiped her good eye. It felt like she was flying through a wall of water. The wind was so fierce that she nearly toppled off her hovercraft.

Jerry raised his hands in the air and shouted, "WOO-OOOO!!! I haven't felt this alive in years!!"

Ororo grinned at the sight of Jerry zooming though the sky, rain pelting his face, his shaggy hair blowing in the breeze.

"Glad you're enjoying yourself!"

Jerry pointed up. "We've got company, kid."

Ororo looked up and groaned. Dozens of armored mercenaries zoomed toward them. Ororo banked sharply to the right and flew through a dark alley. Jerry followed her.

Ororo landed with a thud and jumped off the hovercraft, still clutching her blaster.

"What are you doing, kid?" Jerry asked, landing beside her.

"We can't take all these bozos by ourselves."

Jerry shrugged. "It'll be challenging, but I think we can do it."

Ororo rolled her eye and grabbed Jerry's arm, pulling him toward the street. The unlikely duo scurried to the edge of the sidewalk and jumped up and down in the rain. A taxi sped by and slammed on the brakes, skidding on the slick street. Ororo ran over and threw open the door.

The driver said, "Where would you like to go, kid?" He then glanced at her blaster and put his hands in the air. "Wait, is this a stick up?"

Ororo looked at her gun in embarrassment. "No, we just really need a ride."

She snatched Jerry's money out of his coat pocket and thrust it into the taxi driver's grubby hands.

"Drive us as far as this will take us."

The driver flipped through the money and grinned. "Alright, looks like the cable bill's getting paid this month!"

Ororo and Jerry hopped into the back of the taxi and shut the door. The taxi driver pulled out into traffic and sped off.

Chapter Nineteen: Ororo Blows Up Manhattan

Ororo glanced out the taxi's grimy rear window. She could see mercenaries flying around in the sky, but they weren't following them. Ororo turned back around and breathed a sigh of relief.

"Looks like we lost 'em."

"Great," Jerry said. "So would you mind telling me what that was all about? I mean, it's not every day I find a one-eyed, one-armed African girl being chased by flying assassins."

The taxi driver turned his head ever-so-slightly. Ororo knew he probably thought they were nuts.

"Let's just say my uncle has lots of enemies, and they like to come after his family."

"Hmm. Well, all I know is one day I plan on buying one of those hovercraft thingamajigs. They're freakin' awesome."

Ororo thought Jerry should probably focus on finding a place to live first, but she decided to keep quiet and let him have his fun. After all, he did help her escape.

The back window suddenly shattered and the taxi filled up with a blinding blue light. Ororo and Jerry dropped to the floor while the cab driver swerved into oncoming traffic before veering back into his lane.

The cabbie stopped in the middle of the street and shouted, "What the hell was that?"

Ororo glanced out the back windshield. Five mercenaries zoomed toward them, firing streams of electricity. Another blast flew through the taxi and bounced around before flying out the front. The cabbie's hair stood up on end from all the static electricity.

"Don't stop, dude!" Ororo screamed. "Go, go, go!"

The cabbie cursed and stomped his foot on the gas pedal. The cab took off, leaving a trail of smoke.

Two mercenaries flew next to the cab and aimed their energy blasters at Ororo's window. Ororo screamed and ducked to the floor. The window shattered, spraying even more glass on top of her.

Ororo looked up at Jerry, her left eye wide with fear. Much to her astonishment, Jerry didn't seem frightened at all. In fact, he was grinning.

"I swear, darling, you lead such an exciting life."

"I'm glad you're enjoying yourself," Ororo said, struggling to stay calm.

"Oh my God, we're going to die!" the cabbie screamed, weaving in and out of traffic. Rain poured through the shattered windows, getting everyone soaked. By now there were mercenaries on both sides of the cab.

"Just keep driving!" Ororo shouted, grabbing her blaster. She twirled around and fired several energy bolts out the window. The mercenaries on the left side of the cab backed away. The mercenaries on the right side continued firing into the cab. Energy bolts bounced all over the place. One of the blasts grazed Ororo's robotic arm, sending sparks into the air.

Jerry growled. "No one shoots at my friends and lives to tell the tale."

Jerry grabbed Ororo's blaster and zapped a mercenary in the chest, sending him crashing through the glass door of a convenience store. His hovercraft flew into a parked car, causing the alarm to go off.

Ororo sat up to regain her bearings. The cabbie swerved all over the place, driving up on sidewalks, cutting off cars, and running red lights. He was doing everything possible to keep them alive.

Jerry glanced out the back of the cab. "I think we lost em."

"I doubt it," Ororo grumbled. "Like I said

before, they're like cockroaches. Persistent, super-powered cockroaches."

Jerry made a face. "Those are the worst kind. I hear you can find them on the subway."

Ororo had no doubt. She stuck her head out the shattered window and looked up. Thankfully she didn't see any mercenaries hovering over them. All she saw were lots of clouds, lots of rain, lots of lightning, and lots of giant robots with metallic wings sticking out of their backs.

"Oh no!"

"What is it, darling?" Jerry thrust his head out the window and looked up. He gasped at the sight of six giant winged robots flying directly overhead "Cripes! What are those things?!"

"Robotic assassins," Ororo whispered, her voice quivering in fear.

A mercenary on a hi-tech motorcycle pulled up alongside the cab. He aimed his blaster inside the window and zapped Jerry in the chest, illuminating his tortured face in brilliant blue light. Jerry flew into Ororo, slamming her against the door.

The cabbie glanced back and shouted, "This is *sooo* not worth a big tip!"

When the cabbie turned back around, he screamed bloody murder. One of Aladdin's 'robotic assassins' had just landed in the middle of the street.

The archangel raised his giant, silver hand and bellowed, "Halt, human!"

The cabbie swerved up on the sidewalk to avoid hitting the robot. He slammed into a fire hydrant, sending a massive column of water into the air.

The cabbie's airbag shot out of the steering wheel, snapping his neck back. Ororo and Jerry tumbled into the back of their seats and crumpled to the floor.

The mercenary on the motorbike pulled up next to the demolished cab and hopped off. Several other mercenaries flew over on their hovercrafts. The archangel stormed over, his thunderous footsteps rattling windows up and down the street. Passerbys stared at the bizarre scene in stunned silence. The smart ones ran off.

One of the mercenaries swung open the cab door and reached in to grab Ororo. Jerry clutched the mercenary by his throat and flung him out the back windshield. He then grabbed Ororo's blaster, staggered out of the cab, and spun around in a circle, firing a stream of electricity. The falling rain sizzled as it hit the electrical beam. All the mercenaries ducked for cover.

The archangel stormed over to Jerry and deflected the electrical blasts with his metal hands. The shots ricocheted back toward Jerry, slamming into his chest. Jerry cried out in agony and crashed into the side of the cab.

Ororo rolled out of the car and shouted, "No, leave him alone!"

The archangel turned toward Ororo and thundered, "Come along peacefully, child, and no one else will die."

"Okay, I'll come, just don't hurt him," Ororo said, struggling to keep her voice from shaking. She glanced around and realized they were in the center of Times Square. The iconic One Times Square building towered over them. Its famous LCD billboard broadcasted breaking news footage of the global explosion in kidnappings and terrorist attacks. Aladdin opened a can of worms by kidnapping Ororo and her family, and those worms were now wriggling all over the planet.

Ororo had just put her hands in the air when several flashing police cruisers whipped around One Times Square and barreled toward the archangel. The archangel turned toward the cop cars and raised his hand.

"Halt, humans."

The cruisers skidded to a stop on the slick roads. The police officers hopped out and aimed their guns at the archangels.

One of the cops said, "Freeze. You're under

arrest."

Another cop nervously stammered, "I don't think we have handcuffs big enough for that thing."

Two more archangels dropped from the sky and landed on the cruisers, crushing them beneath their immense weight. The cops pointed their guns at the new archangels and fired off a volley of bullets. The bullets bounced harmlessly off the archangels' chest. Tentacles popped out of the archangels' bluish orbs and wrapped around the police officers' bodies.

A helicopter flew out from behind One Times Square and blasted the archangels with a spotlight.

"This is the New York City Police Department!" one of the cops shouted from a bullhorn. "Put your hands in the air!"

The archangel in front of Ororo raised his massive, metallic hand and fired a blinding laser beam. The laser smashed into the helicopter and sent it spiraling into One Times Square. It exploded on impact, shattering the LCD billboard and engulfing the skyscraper in flames. Glass and flaming wreckage rained down all over the city street. People jumped out of their cars and ran away screaming.

Ororo watched what was going in a stunned daze.

The archangel turned his attention back to Ororo. "Resistance is an unrealistic option, child. Surrender or die."

"Why don't you die, dirtbag?"

Ororo gawked as Jerry hobbled toward the archangel, clutching an energy blaster. He aimed the blaster at the archangel and fired several energy bolts. The bolts bounced off the archangel's head, causing him to stagger backwards.

"Come on, darlin', let's get outta here," Jerry grunted, hoisting Ororo up over his shoulder. Jerry straddled the hi-tech motorbike that belonged to the mercenary he threw out the back of the cab window and set Ororo in front of him.

The other two archangels dropped the police officers they snatched with their metal tentacles and marched toward Jerry.

Jerry pressed down on the gas pedal and tore off down the street. Ororo grabbed the blaster and glanced over her shoulder. The archangels launched into the air and barreled after them, their metallic wings glistening from all the rain and lightning

"This isn't going to work, Jerry! We're sitting ducks!"

"I know, kid. I'm working on a plan."

"Well work on it faster!"

A mercenary on a hovercraft zoomed up to Ororo and Jerry and fired off several energy bolts. Jerry swerved down a one-way street and started driving in the opposite direction, directly in front of oncoming traffic. Ororo screamed and covered her left eye, but she peeked through her fingers. Jerry weaved the motorbike down the center line as cars zoomed by, narrowly avoiding them. The cars honked their horns and drove off the side of the road.

"This is your plan?" Ororo cried.

"Yeah," Jerry grunted. "It's one of those things that seemed like a better idea on paper."

Jerry eventually drove up on the sidewalk, forcing pedestrians to jump out of the way. An archangel landed in front of them, forcing Jerry to turn around and speed off in the opposite direction.

Jerry drove into the parking lot of a gas station and jumped off his bike. Two archangels landed next to him.

"Resistance will result in your immediate incineration," boomed one of the archangels.

"Don't you idiots have any other lines?" Jerry growled. He grabbed the blaster out of Ororo's hands and aimed it at an oil tanker directly behind the robots. The driver of the oil tanker waved his hands and shouted, "Wait, what are you doing?!"

Jerry fired several shots at the tanker. The driver

dashed to the opposite end of the street. The archangels had just turned their heads when the oil tanker erupted in a blinding, scorching fireball. The explosion engulfed the archangels and blew Ororo and Jerry high into the air. They landed with a thud on the far end of the parking lot. Flaming pieces of wreckage rained down all around them.

Ororo coughed and pushed herself off the ground. She could hardly see from all the thick, black smoke billowing into the sky. The rain continued to pour like a monsoon, but it did nothing to extinguish the flaming tanker.

Jerry clambered to his feet and cackled. "I told you I had a plan."

Ororo wiped soot from her torn and tattered clothes. "You're insane. But that's probably why we're still alive."

Two mercenaries hovered in front of Ororo and Jerry and fired their energy blasters. Jerry spun around and blasted one of the mercenaries off his hovercraft, sending him flying through the gas station's plate glass window. His hovercraft crashed in front of Ororo, spinning like a top.

Ororo grabbed the mercenary's fallen blaster and hopped onto the hovercraft. "Let's go, Jerry!"

Jerry zapped the other mercenary and hijacked his hovercraft.

Ororo and her new friend flew away from the brightly-lit New York skyline. Rain continued pouring and lightning continued zig-zagging across the dreary sky. Ororo glanced around and was shocked to see there were no archangels or mercenaries flying after them. She should have been relieved, but something didn't feel right. Ororo immediately took off toward New York Harbor.

"Where are you going, darling?" Jerry asked, struggling to keep pace.

"We need to get away from the city," Ororo replied. "Innocent people are getting hurt because of us."

Jerry pointed toward the horizon. The Statue of Liberty could be seen clutching her illuminated torch.

"We can hide out on Liberty Island. There aren't any tourists at this hour."

Ororo and Jerry leaned as far forward as they could, whizzing through the torrential downpour. They eventually pulled up next to the Statue of Liberty's faded face. They circled her head, looking for a place to hide.

Jerry aimed his blaster at one of the windows on the crown. Before he could fire, a massive, floating aircraft carrier materialized next to the statue's head. Ororo nearly tumbled off her hovercraft in shock.

"What in the world is that?" Jerry muttered.

Ororo noticed for the first time all night Jerry sounded frightened. And for good reason; they were doomed.

Chapter Twenty: The Decapitation of Liberty

Several mercenaries floated off the deck of the aircraft carrier and fired streams of electricity. One of the blasts slammed into Ororo's hovercraft, short-circuiting it. Ororo jumped off the hovercraft and landed on the edge of the Statue of Liberty's crown.

Jerry tried to grab Ororo and was almost immediately shot in the back. He tumbled off his hovercraft and landed on top of the crown as well. He nearly slid off, but Ororo grabbed his legs.

By now all the mercenaries and archangels that had been chasing Ororo were circling the Statue of Liberty's head. They were soon joined by Aladdin, who levitated off the deck of the aircraft carrier on his own hovercraft. His glowing, electrical vipers crackled beneath all the rain.

"Hello Beauty. You put up a valiant fight. I'm most impressed."

"How did you find me?" Ororo asked, her voice quivering in fear.

"One of my mercenaries was smart enough to attach a microscopic GPS chip to your robotic limb, in the off chance you escaped my airship."

Aladdin narrowed his icy blue eyes.

"You should play the lottery. The odds are apparently in your favor."

"Speaking of your stupid airship, I thought we destroyed it," Ororo said, aiming her blaster at Aladdin's head.

"I have an entire fleet of airships at my disposal, child," Aladdin replied in a condescending tone. "Surely you realize by now I'm a firm believer in power by numbers. I have a massive army of mercenaries, a massive army of archangels, and a massive fleet of airships. Now enough with the small talk. When we followed your GPS signal to New York, we expected to find you, Doctor Xander, and your meddlesome siblings. I never thought you'd be wandering the streets with… filth."

Aladdin glared at Jerry. Jerry cocked his blaster and growled, "Who you calling filth, pretty boy?"

Aladdin chuckled. "From the way you fought off my mercenaries, I assume you used to be in the military?"

Jerry puffed out his chest. "Yep. I served my country for nearly a decade."

"How heroic. Unfortunately for you, I despise the United States military."

One of Aladdin's electric vipers shot forward and wrapped around Jerry's neck. Jerry gagged as he floated into the air, gasping for breath.

"No, let him go!" Ororo screamed. She tried to fire her blaster, but Aladdin snatched it with one of his viper cables and chucked it into the ocean.

Aladdin pulled Jerry's writhing body close to his face.

"It's people like you who have made the world the way it is… idiots who blindly follow their corrupt leaders in Washington. Consider this your trial. I find you guilty of crimes against humanity. Your punishment… is *death*."

"NOOOOO!" Ororo screamed.

Aladdin sent electricity coursing through Jerry's body. Jerry writhed around and screamed as his body sizzled. Aladdin then flung Jerry's smoking corpse out to sea.

"You monster!" Ororo cried, her left eye spilling tears.

Aladdin snapped his head around and scowled.

He zoomed toward Ororo and grabbed her by the throat. Ororo gagged and clawed at Aladdin's armored hand.

"I'm only going to ask you once, Beauty. Where is Doctor Xander?"

"I'll…never…tell…you…" Ororo gasped. Her left eye looked like it was about to pop out of her socket. "You'll…have…to…kill…me…."

Aladdin snarled and tightened his grip.

"I may decide to do just that. But for now you're much more useful alive."

Aladdin continued choking Ororo until her world went black.

*

Aladdin dropped Ororo's unconscious body onto the Statue of Liberty's crown.

"Take her aboard the airship," Aladdin commanded with a dismissive wave of his armored hand.

A mercenary flew down and draped Ororo's limp body over his shoulder.

Aladdin flew back about 100 feet and scowled at the Statue of Liberty.

"Decapitate this statue."

All of Aladdin's mercenaries gasped.

One of them finally mustered the courage to mutter, "I beg your pardon?"

"You heard me," Aladdin said, his cheeks flushing red. "Cut her blasted head off."

"But why, sir?" the mercenary sputtered.

"Because I said so, you idiot."

Still staring at the Statue of Liberty's face, and ignoring his stunned army, Aladdin said, "This statue is a symbol of the western world's greed and gluttony. I want it destroyed."

"We shall annihilate it, sir," thundered one of the archangels.

The four remaining archangels surrounded the Statue of Liberty's head and fired fiery red lasers. Giant pieces of her face crumbled off and plummeted toward the base of Liberty Island.

Aladdin grinned. "The Statue of Liberty used to be a welcoming beacon for immigrants. Now it will be a symbol of something else entirely: don't mess with Aladdin Salazar."

Aladdin spun around in mid-air and floated toward his airship. His mercenaries reluctantly followed.

The archangels continued blasting away until all that remained was a headless, smoldering statue clutching a torch. Then they, too, boarded the airship. Seconds later the airship vanished, just as a dozen police helicopters popped up over the horizon.

Chapter Twenty-One: When Dreams Become
Nightmares

On a Bahaman beach, just before twilight…

Jesse and Alex Rodriguez snuggled together as they watched the beautiful Bahaman sunset. The fiery red sun had just plunged beneath a curtain of indigo clouds. Pink and red lines streaked across the rapidly darkening sky. The phosphorescent water sparkled like it was filled with aquatic fireflies. A cool breeze sent Alex's hair fluttering into the air, tickling Jesse's nostrils.

Jesse leaned back and sighed. "Ahhh. This is paradise."

"It sure is," Alex said as she adjusted her teeny, weeny bikini. "You're the love of my life, Jesse Baxter. I can't think of another guy I'd rather spend the rest of eternity with."

Alex was just about to plant a kiss on Jesse's lips when an airship materialized right over their heads. Aladdin floated down on a hovercraft, his viper cables crackling with electricity.

"Give me the immortality vaccine, Jesse Baxter! I know you have it!"

Jesse stood up and shouted, "NEVER!"

Aladdin snarled. "Then *DIE.*"

Over 100 mercenaries zoomed off the airship and surrounded Jesse and his scantily-clad girlfriend.

"Alex, go hide!" Jesse shouted, crouching into a karate stance.

Alex scrambled over to a bunch of palm trees

and hid behind one of the thick trunks.

Jesse turned back to the massive army of mercenaries and waved his right hand. "Ready for me to lay the smackdown on you idiots?"

One of the mercenaries zoomed down and fired a barrage of energy blasts. Jesse did several back flips, narrowly avoiding the bombardment of electricity. The mercenary reached down to grab Jesse. Jesse drop-kicked the mercenary off his hovercraft, sending him flying into a palm tree. Jesse promptly grabbed the mercenary's blaster and twirled around in circles, firing a steady stream of electricity. Within a matter of seconds, all 100-plus mercenaries plummeted off their hovercrafts and crashed onto the island, writhing in agony.

Aladdin cursed. "Blast it! I've forgotten how formidable an opponent you are."

Jesse blew the end of his smoking blaster. "And I've forgotten just how big a douche you are."

"Destroy him!" Aladdin bellowed.

Ten of Aladdin's archangels blasted off the aircraft carrier and fired lasers at Jesse, sending him scrambling.

"Jesse!" Alex cried, peeking out from behind the tree.

"Don't worry about me," Jesse grunted, weaving through laser fire like an Olympic gymnast. "If anything, you should worry about the robots."

Jesse aimed his blaster into the sky and began firing off shots. One by one his streams of electricity sliced off robot heads, sending their decapitated bodies crashing into the sand. Within seconds, all of Aladdin's robots were incapacitated.

Jesse finally stopped jumping and aimed his blaster at Aladdin's head. "You have two options, dirtbag: surrender or fight. Personally I hope you pick the latter."

Aladdin chuckled and clapped his armored hands. "Bravo, young Jesse Baxter. I am most impressed with your fighting abilities. Why don't you join me? Together we can rule the planet!"

Jesse lowered his blaster. "You want me to join you? For real?"

Aladdin lowered toward the ground and hopped off his hovercraft. His heavy armored suit weighed him down so much that his feet sunk into the sand.

"Yes, I am 'for real'. Think of all the things we can accomplish. We can overthrow brutal dictatorships, take out the corrupt American empire, reform the United Nations. We can solve climate change, clamp down on overpopulation, stop biodiversity loss, and finally make Earth into the paradise it once was. Of course, we may have to do some unsavory things in order to achieve those lofty goals, but the 'end' will certainly justify the means."

"Hmmm, sounds tempting," Jesse said.

Alex jumped out from behind her tree. "Jesse, you can't join Aladdin! He's insane!"

Aladdin snarled. "Stay out of this, girl!"

Jesse extended his hand. "You make a convincing case, Aladdin. Let's take over the world. I call Vice Dictator."

Aladdin burst out in laughter and reached for Jesse's hand. "I'm glad we could put aside our minor differences and... what the devil?"

Jesse planted his energy blaster squarely against Aladdin's armored chest. "I was just joshing with you. Since you seem to enjoy the Bahamas so much, why don't I send you somewhere even hotter?"

Before Aladdin could react, Jesse zapped him with electricity. Aladdin shot out to the edge of the beach. A huge wave crashed over him, soaking his entire body.

Alex run over to Jesse and threw her arms around his neck. "My hero! You were so brave!"

Jesse shrugged. "It's all in a day's work."

Alex was just about to kiss Jesse on the lips when a mechanical viper wrapped around his neck and lifted him into the air. Another viper cable slammed into Alex's mid-section, sending her hurling into the trunk of a tree.

Jesse glanced down to see Aladdin marching toward him, his hair dripping wet.

"Foolish child. You actually think you have the capacity to defeat me in combat?"

Jesse gagged and clawed at the viper cable tightening around his throat. His vision began to blur.

Aladdin left Jesse dangling in the air, literally hanging him.

"Please, let him down!" Alex cried, staggering to her feet. "He's dying!"

Aladdin flashed a demonic grin. "Don't worry, my dear. You will be joining young Jesse Baxter very shortly in the ever-after."

Aladdin looked up just as Jesse began to loosen the viper cable around his neck with his bare hands.

"What the devil??" Aladdin snarled.

Jesse used his incredible strength to unravel the viper cable. His head finally slipped through the noose. But he didn't let go; he continued hanging on to the viper cable as he dropped to the beach.

Aladdin's face turned ghostly pale. "What are you----AHHHHH!!!"

Jesse yanked on Aladdin's viper cable and flipped him high into the sky. Aladdin crashed back down on the beach, landing mere feet from Alex.

Jesse collapsed to the ground and gasped for air.

"Jesse!"

Alex had just started running toward Jesse when one of Aladdin's mechanical vipers wrapped around her ankles. Alex crashed face-first into the sand.

Aladdin pulled Alex toward him and wrapped his arm around her throat. "Do you love this woman, Jesse Baxter?"

Jesse clambered to his feet and gasped, "Yes! Please... let...her...go..."

Aladdin tightened his grasp around Alex's neck.

"You can have the wretched girl, under one condition. Give me the Fountain of Youth."

"Don't give in, Jesse!" Alex shouted, squirming in Aladdin's arms. "I'm not worth it!"

"Yes you are, babe," Jesse said. "Yes you are."

Alex smiled. "I love it when you call me babe."

Jesse grabbed a coconut that just happened to be lying by his feet and hurled it at Aladdin, clonking him on the forehead. Aladdin collapsed into an unmoving heap, allowing Alex to dash toward Jesse and jump into his arms.

Jesse grinned. "Hey babe."

Alex grinned back. "Hey yourself."

They were just about to kiss a third time when Journey popped up out of nowhere and smacked Jesse in the face with a pillow. That's when Jesse fell out of bed and crashed onto the floor.

Jesse looked up to find Journey hovering over him, laughing her head off. Jesse glanced around and realized he was back at the hotel. He groaned and rubbed his eyes. It had all been a dream… a glorious, wonderful dream. And now thanks to his rotten sister it was over.

"You were so funny!" Journey cackled, wiping away tears. "You kept kicking your feet and punching the air. And you mumbled something about Alex Rodriguez and puckered your lips. Did you enjoy your exciting dream?"

"Yes, as a matter of fact I did," Jesse grumbled. He got up off the ground and straightened his shirt. "Why did you have to interrupt me?"

"Because you woke me up with all your moaning and groaning," Journey replied. "If you're going to keep me awake, then I'm doing the same to you."

Jesse rubbed his eyes again and looked over at the flashing alarm clock. "Great, it's 2:00 am and I probably won't be able to fall back asleep. I'm going to be tired all day."

"Then let's watch cartoons," Journey said. She

grabbed the remote and turned on Cartoon Network.

Jesse yanked the remote out of her hands and changed it to Nick at Nite. "You're not allowed to watch the Cartoon Network after 8:00pm. That's when all the 'bad' cartoons come on."

Journey crossed her arms. "Are you freaking kidding me? I almost died like 50 times over the past two days. I think I deserve to watch a little obscene television."

Jesse sighed and threw the remote on her bed. "You make a good point. Go ahead and corrupt your mind."

Journey flipped the channel back to the 'bad' cartoons.

Goldie wheeled into the room, blinking her lights. "Ohhh, I love this channel. Is *Rick & Morty* on? That show cracks me up."

Jesse rolled his eyes and glanced around the hotel room. It suddenly dawned on him that his other sister was missing.

"Where's Ororo?"

"She probably went on one of her late night walks," Journey said without looking up from the TV. "You know she has sleeping problems."

Jesse was starting to get worried. "She shouldn't be out wandering the streets of New York by herself."

"No one's going to mess with Ororo," Journey said, snacking on some complimentary hotel mints. "If they do, she'll punch them in the throat with her cyborg arm."

Goldie cackled. "Man, I'm really starting to love you kids. You're so violent! You're like Tom and Jerry, but with more blood and more explosions."

"No one should be going out on their own, especially after what's happened the last couple days," Jesse said, ignoring Goldie's nonsensical ramblings.

"Chill out, bro," Journey said. "It's not like Aladdin and his goons are going to attack us in New York."

"And even if they did, we kicked their butts," Goldie said. "We could totally do it again."

"Yeah, they don't want none of this." Journey patted her chest like she was a professional wrestler.

Journey barely finished her sentence when a thunderous knock rattled the door.

"This is secret service. Open up immediately."

Jesse rushed into the living room. He walked past Doc and Martin, who were still sprawled out on the sofas, snoring obnoxiously, and opened the door. Four secret service agents hurried in, scanning the room with their guns drawn.

Goldie wheeled toward the agents, four laser guns protruding from her robotic belly. "Is there a problem, fellas?"

"Just a safety precaution…uh…ma'am," replied one of the agents as he peeked behind the sofa.

President Robinson walked into the room a few seconds later, flanked by two more secret service agents. His jacket was unbuttoned, like he had just thrown it on, and he wasn't wearing a tie. He looked like he just rolled out of bed.

"Hello, Mr. President," Jesse said, patting down his bed-hair. He thought he should look at least halfway presentable in front of the leader of the free world.

"Hey, Jesse," the president said, looking a tad confused and flustered. "Where's your sister?"

"I'm right here, Barry," Journey said, raising her hand.

For the briefest of moments, the president smirked. Jesse smiled, too. It was kind of humorous to hear an 11-year old girl refer to the most powerful man on Earth by his first name. But the smile quickly disappeared.

"Not you, hon. Your other sister, the one with the eye patch. Uh… Ororo."

The color drained from Jesse's face. "She's not here, Mr. President. We think she went for a walk."

The president sighed and massaged his head. "I

think she may have done more than go for a walk, son."

By now Doc and Martin were wide awake.

Rubbing the sleep from his eyes, Doc grumbled, "What's going on? Is it morning already?"

"No, but it looks like our day is going to start a tad prematurely," the president said gravely. He grabbed the remote off the table and turned on the TV. He then changed the channel to CNN.

The news anchor was rattling on about some wild shoot-out in Manhattan. Everyone in the room shut up and listened as the reporter detailed how a one-armed, one-eyed girl and a one-armed, one-eyed middle-aged man waged guerilla warfare with a massive army of robots, 'flying bikers', and the 'Merchant of Death'.

Jesse and everyone in the room watched in stunned horror as CNN broadcasted amateur and security footage of Ororo and her shaggy-haired friend zooming through the streets of Manhattan, evading a barrage of energy blasts. They showed the destruction of Times Square, the inflamed gas station, and the freshly-decapitated Statue of Liberty.

"Holy moley!" Goldie shouted, blinking her lights. "Ororo blew up Manhattan! That kid is so freakin' awesome!"

"Jumping Jupiter," Doc whispered. He looked up at the president and asked, "When did all this occur?"

"Approximately 30 minutes ago," the president replied, still staring at the eerie footage of the headless Statue of Liberty clutching her torch on Liberty Island.

"Why would Aladdin single out Ororo?" Martin asked in between yawns. "Why wouldn't he come after us?"

"More importantly, how did he find her?" Doc said, more to himself than anyone else.

Before anyone could articulate a theory, CNN cut away from the headless Statue of Liberty and showed the anchor shuffling some papers.

"My producer has just informed me that the man presumed to be behind these devastating terrorist attacks,

Aladdin Salazar, also known as the 'Merchant of Death', has downloaded *another* video on the internet. Many of you may recall that Mr. Salazar downloaded a similar video several days ago. I'm being told we're now showing the video in its entirety."

CNN cut away from the anchor and broadcasted the video. An image of Ororo tied to a chair appeared on screen. Two armored mercenaries stood beside her, clutching energy guns. Jesse clenched his fists and gritted his teeth.

Aladdin Salazar's scarred, humorless face suddenly popped up on screen. "Hello, Dr. Xander. It was nice seeing you again after all these years. I don't appreciate the way you trashed my airship, but I'm willing to let bygones be bygones."

Aladdin stepped back and gestured toward Ororo, who struggled against her bounds. "As you can plainly see, I have kidnapped your niece. If you ever want to see her again, bring me your immortality vaccine to the following coordinates."

The coordinates flashed on the bottom of the screen.

"That's the middle of the Pacific Ocean," Goldie said. "There aren't even any islands there!"

Aladdin continued talking. "There's nowhere to land, so simply hover above the ocean. One of my airships will meet you there. As long as you hand over the vaccine... the *real* vaccine... and as long as it cures my son, your niece will live. If you do not... if you attempt to trick me again... then she will die. But I will not stop there."

Aladdin's face once again filled the entire screen. His thin lips were curled into an evil scowl. "If you do not save my son, then I will unleash the full wrath of my military might. I will order my massive army of mercenaries and archangels to wage unholy war against every country represented by the United Nations. I will also kindly request that all the dictators, terrorists, and warlords I've weaponized over the years join me, to wage a global uprising against the corrupt powers-that-be. And don't think these warlords and dictators won't come to my aid. Just like the United States is addicted to oil provided by Middle Eastern despots, many dictators and terrorists are addicted to the futuristic weaponry I provide them. They will help me if I request their assistance."

Aladdin pulled the camera even closer. "I am not bluffing, Xander. If I detect any movement by the U.S. military or NATO forces, the war will commence *immediately*. Countless thousands will perish, and their blood will be on your hands. You have 48 hours."

Aladdin stormed off screen, leaving the image of Ororo struggling in her chair.

Chapter Twenty-Two: Doc's Crazy Plan

"I should have killed that psychopath when I had the chance," Doc growled. He kicked over a small table, sending a lamp crashing to the floor. "Mikhail's terminal illness has caused my former student to quite literally lose his mind."

Martin tapped his fingers together and quietly said, "Say what you want about Aladdin, but there is something morbidly admirable about a man willing to kill untold thousands in order to save his only child."

Goldie wheeled around in circles, flashing her lights. The goldfish in her fishbowl burrowed into the sand. "There ain't nuthin' admirable about Aladdin. He's a nutjob who needs ta be taken out!"

The president sighed and plopped down on the sofa next to Martin. "I want to rescue your niece just as badly as you do, Xander. But we simply cannot give in. All the psychopaths causing chaos around the globe will become even more emboldened if we cave to Aladdin's demands. They'll know that if they kidnap enough people, cause enough damage, we will give them your vaccine. We simply cannot afford to put ourselves in that position."

Jesse expected his uncle to go off on the president. He certainly did not expect him to nod and mumble, "I know, Mr. President. I know."

"What do you mean you know?!" Jesse shouted. "Nothing is more important than Ororo's safety!"

"Jesse, stay out of this!" Doc snapped.

Jesse was so taken aback that he shut up.

The president stood up and clutched Doc's

shoulder. "I will have Paternus gather with our top military brass and come up with a rescue plan. Aladdin is giving us 48 hours, so we have a considerable amount of time to figure this out. Aladdin may be insane, but he wouldn't dare think about harming your niece. She's his only bargaining chip. First, though, we need to go to the U.N. and inform the world we will not bow to terrorist demands. Once you declare your immortality vaccine to be a health hazard, all the attacks and kidnappings should dissipate. We can then focus on rescuing your niece and taking out the 'Merchant of Death' once and for all."

Doc continued to nod. "I agree, Mr. President. We simply can't give Aladdin what he wants, even if it is for his terminally ill son."

"But Uncle Xander!" Jesse sputtered.

"Enough, Jesse!" Doc shouted.

Jesse crossed his arms and scowled. He couldn't believe what he was hearing.

The president continued clutching Doc's shoulder. "Don't worry, Zach. We'll get that son of a gun."

"I appreciate that, Mr. President," Doc said, shaking his hand. "Now if you don't mind, I'd like to get a little more rest before our big meeting later today. I need to be refreshed if I'm going to convince the entire world my vaccine is no longer effective. I'm not exactly the world's greatest liar."

"Of course. Secret service will come get you around 8:00am. Speaking of which, I'd like one of my agents to remain in your room."

Doc twiddled his thumbs. "Er, that's not necessary, sir. We have Goldie."

Goldie wheeled over to the president and popped open her belly, revealing an impressive arsenal of laser blasters, tasers, and cruise missiles.

"I'm better than 20 secret service agents combined," she bragged.

The president frowned. "I'd still like an agent to

stand outside your door."

Doc shrugged. "Suit yourself, Mr. President."

The president shook Doc's hand one more time and turned to Jesse and Journey. "Don't worry, kids. Your sister will be safe and sound before you know it."

Jesse continued scowling.

The president walked out of the room, quickly followed by his secret service agents. Doc shut the door. Jesse could hear an agent whispering to one of his colleagues. The president must have ordered *two* agents to stand guard.

Mere seconds after the president departed, Jesse and Journey started shouting. Doc walked into the bedroom and everyone followed him.

Jesse grew even angrier when Doc shut the bedroom door and turned up the volume on the TV.

"My sister is being held by your psychotic student, and you want to watch TV?!" Jesse shouted, his cheeks flushed from anger.

Doc turned to face Jesse and, in an eerily quiet whisper, said, "That was all an act, you nincompoop. Now shut up and listen to me."

Jesse and Journey exchanged confused glances.

"An act?" Jesse said.

"Yes," Doc said in exasperation. "Ororo will be rescued, but I'm doing it on my own. It's way too risky for the U.S. military to get involved. This needs to be a covert, surgical operation."

"Wait, what?" Jesse sputtered.

Doc kissed Jesse and Journey on their heads, then turned toward Goldie. "Are you ready, you bucket of bolts? I know how much you love suicide missions."

Goldie cackled and spun around in circles. "I was born ready, Doc. Let's go kick some butt!"

"I'd like for you to come along, too, Martin. That is, if you feel you're up to it."

Martin sighed. "You know how much I hate suicide missions, Doc, but I can't let you do this alone. If you're going to throw your life away, then I'll be right beside you."

Doc smiled and turned to Goldie. "Do you still have a signal on Ororo?"

"Of course. By the way, she's not at the coordinates Aladdin gave you. She's several hundred miles away, near the Great Barrier Reef. It must be Aladdin's secret lair."

"Wait a minute, you know where Ororo is?" Jesse asked.

Doc wrung his hands. "Er, yes. Shortly after I busted you guys out of Aladdin's airship, I... uh... tagged you with microscopic GPS devices."

"You did?" Journey asked. "Where'd you put 'em?"

Doc rubbed the back of his head. "It's a tiny flying bug, sort of like my nano-bots, only slightly bigger. I had it fly inside your ear canals."

Jesse and Journey instinctively dug into their ears.

"It's way in there. You're never going to find it. I know you guys are probably mad I tagged you with a tracking device, but I figured it was a necessary evil. You know, in case one of my psychotic enemies managed to kidnap you."

"We forgive you, Doc," Jesse said. "Now how are you planning on saving Ororo?"

"Well, Aladdin has no idea we know where he's keeping her," Doc said, pacing back and forth. "So he'll be caught completely off guard if I invade his secret lair, rescue Ororo, and trash his hideout with an infestation of robotic locusts."

Jesse nodded in understanding. Doc planned on doing to Aladdin's secret lair what he did to his airship.

"Brilliant plan, Doc," Jesse said. "There's just one thing; you're not going without me."

"Me neither," Journey said defiantly.

Doc narrowed his eyes. "Oh yes I am. This is going to be a dangerous mission. You kids are staying right here."

"Oh no we're not," Journey said, crossing her arms. "If you don't take us, we're going to tell the president on you."

Doc threw his hands in the air. "Fine! Your parents are going to kill me if we miraculously survive this, but I guess I don't have much of a choice."

Jesse and Journey cheered.

"Shhh! Keep quiet," Doc whispered, turning up the volume on the TV even higher.

"The first thing we need to do is head back to our lab and load up on weapons," Martin said. "Aladdin's fortress is probably crawling with mercenaries and robots."

"I agree," Doc said. "But before that we need to figure out how to bypass all the president's secret service agents without arousing suspicion."

"I have a plan," Goldie said.

Goldie fired a laser out the bedroom window, shattering it into thousands of shards of glass. Wind and rain swept in, getting everyone wet.

"Are you insane?" Jesse shouted. "We're on the 15th floor! How are we supposed to get down to the parking lot?"

Secret service started banging on the door. "Hey, what's going on in there?"

"Great thinking, Goldie," Jesse grumbled. "Now secret service is onto us---*ahhhh!!!*"

A mechanical cable popped out of Goldie's body and wrapped around Jesse's mid-section. Three more cables snatched up Doc, Martin, and Journey.

"Goldie, what are you---holy moley!"

Jesse shut up as a propeller extended out of Goldie's back and started whipping around. Goldie flew out the shattered window, dragging Jesse and the gang with her. Just as they left the room, secret service barged in and gawked out the window in flabbergasted astonishment.

One of the agents whipped out a phone and

shouted, "Doctor Xander and the Baxter children are trying to escape! Get outside and block their plane!"

But it was too late. Goldie was already zooming toward Doc's plane, which was hoarding several parking spaces near the front of the hotel.

Goldie hovered ten feet above the ground and released her cables. Jesse and the gang fell to the parking lot in crumpled heaps.

Goldie landed next to them and wheeled inside the plane. "Get up, ya wusses. We ain't got all day."

Jesse pushed himself off the ground and muttered, "Jeez, Goldie, you could've at least warned us you were releasing your cables."

"If I have any cracked vertebrae I am *soooo* suing your flying garbage can, Doc," Journey grumbled as she staggered to her feet.

Once Jesse and the gang picked themselves up and hurried aboard the plane, Goldie flipped on the propellers. The plane lifted into the air just as a dozen secret service agents rushed outside, their guns drawn.

"Get down here!" one of the agents shouted, aiming his gun at the plane.

Doc looked out the window and chuckled. "Idiots. Do they really think we'd believe they'd shoot us?"

The agent proved Doc wrong by firing several shots at the propeller. Doc cursed and ducked under his chair.

"Jumpin' Jupiter, they really are shooting at us!"

"Not for long," Goldie said. She flipped on the turbo jet engines and blasted off toward the western seaboard, flying several times faster than the speed of sound.

Chapter Twenty-Three: Eat Your Heart Out, Batman

Even though they took off from Manhattan, Jesse and the gang arrived in LA in no time. Doc's hi-tech plane was so fast that they reached the opposite end of the country in a fraction of the time it would have taken a normal plane. Word must have leaked that they were on the run, however, because dozens of flashing police cruisers surrounded Doctor Xander's estate.

As soon as Doc's helicopter-plane came into view, all the cops hopped out of their cars and pointed their guns into the sky. The laser cannons sticking out of Doc's lawn, the electrified fence surrounding his estate, and the robotic 'death hawks' circling overheard kept the cops at bay. Otherwise they probably would have already raided his mansion.

Doc landed his helicopter-plane right outside the front door of his mansion. One of the cops whipped out a bullhorn and shouted, "Doctor Xander, we'd like to have a word with you. Please make your way outside your fenced-in property."

"It's a trap, Doc," Jesse said as they hurried inside his mansion. "Don't fall for it."

"What would I do without your acute observations, my dear nephew?" Doc said with a smirk.

Once everyone was inside the mansion, the steel door slammed shut. Doc led Jesse, Martin, Journey, and Goldie through his sprawling lobby and inside his sliding bookcase. When Jesse entered Doc's underground lab, his jaw dropped at the sight of all the futuristic planes, vehicles, and weapons scattered all over the place.

"Doc, this place is amazing," Jesse stammered, looking around in awe. He had been to Doc's mansion many times, of course, but he had never been granted access to his secret dungeon.

"Thanks. I'd give you guys a tour, but time is off the essence."

Doc opened a massive, steel-plated door and started pulling out all sorts of hi-tech weapons, vests, and helmets. The first objects Doc passed around were shiny black helmets that bore a striking resemblance to the ones worn by Aladdin's mercenaries.

Jesse put the helmet on his head. It was a tad too big, but he snapped the chin-strap on and it stayed in place. Jesse then fiddled with the visor, which gave everything a reddish tinge. He was shocked when a holographic map of the world popped up in front of him.

"These helmets will protect you from most energy blasts," Doc said as he continued pulling weapons out of the closet. "They're computerized and connected to the internet, allowing you to instantaneously pull up pivotal information. If you need to know how to get somewhere, just state your destination and a holographic map will materialize on the visor. The helmets also have a night-vision function and allow you to see in infra-red as well."

"This is so cool, Doc," Jesse said, flipping through all the maps popping up on his visor.

The next objects Doc passed around were laser-proof vests. Just like with the helmets, the vests were a tad too big for Jesse and Journey. But that just meant they protected even more of their exposed body parts. Doc also handed out flexible, fabric-like plates of armor for their arms and legs. The plates were magnetic so when they overlapped they clung together. Jesse and Journey also received thick, laser-proof gloves.

Doc then handed out heavy belts loaded with all sorts of crazy, hi-tech weapons, including laser blasters, 'dazzler' guns that fired bursts of blinding light and ear-shattering sound beams, taser guns that fired electrified darts, tear gas guns, and grappling hooks. After that he passed out shoulder straps that contained dozens of electromagnetic pulse grenades. According to Doc, the EMP grenades were capable of short-circuiting any robot as long as the robot's inside circuitry was exposed. Jesse, Journey, and Martin placed the grenade straps over their vests.

The last weapons Doc handed out were plasma swords. Jesse pressed the button on his sword handle. A glowing red plasma blade popped out of the end.

"Whoa, awesome!" Jesse exclaimed, swinging the blade in front of his helmeted face.

"The blades are made of plasma, which is the fourth state of matter, right after solids, liquids, and gasses," Doc said, wielding his own plasma sword. "It's capable of slicing through almost anything. It should prove most effective against Aladdin's archangels."

Journey posed in front of a giant mirror.

"Eat your heart out, Batman," she said beneath her gigantic helmet.

While Jesse and Martin admired their arsenal of hi-tech gadgets, Doc loaded Goldie up with extra cruise missiles, electrified taser darts, and tear gas. He then walked over to a refrigerator and withdrew a small vial of a grayish-looking liquid.

"What's that, Doc?" Jesse asked.

Doc grimaced and reluctantly replied, "Er, it's my immortality vaccine."

Jesse cocked an eyebrow. "Why are you taking it with you? Please tell me you're not seriously thinking about giving it to Aladdin."

Doc shook his head. "I don't intend to, but in the incredibly likely event that our rescue mission is a bust, it'd be wise to have a bargaining chip."

Jesse gulped at Doc's lack of faith in their chances.

Doc slipped the immortality vaccine inside his utility belt and asked, "Is everyone loaded up on weapons?"

"Yep," Jesse said, patting his sagging belt. "Let's go kick some butt, Doc."

Doc led Jesse and the gang aboard another one of his helicopter-planes. The launching pad elevated to the ceiling, which opened up to the still-dark sky.

The plane's propellers began whipping around, lifting it into the sky. Doc's mansion was still surrounded by cops, but now they were joined by a SWAT team.

"Doctor Xander, this is the LAPD!" one of the cops shouted in a bullhorn. "You are ordered to land your plane and surrender yourself. If you do not, we will have no choice but to invade your property."

Doc responded through his plane's speaker. "That would be an extraordinarily stupid move. My mansion has an impenetrable security system."

Several cops tried to scale the fence. They were immediately zapped with electricity and fell to the ground in smoldering heaps. The electricity wasn't potent enough to kill them, but it did succeed in rendering the police officers unconscious.

A SWAT helicopter flew over the fence and zoomed toward Doc's plane. Giant laser guns popped up out of the lawn and fired several warning shots at the approaching helicopter. Doc's 'death hawks' swooped down and fired shots as well. The helicopter immediately turned around.

Having made his point, Doc blasted off toward the Pacific. Jesse glanced out the rear window and watched in muted amusement as the small army of cops and SWAT members gawked at each other in stunned silence. He imagined the president wouldn't be too thrilled they allowed Doctor Xander and his rag-tag army of teenagers and a flying cyborg goldfish to slip through their fingers.

Chapter Twenty-Four: The Birth Of The Merchant Of
Death

Jesse and the gang were out over the Pacific in
no time. Martin piloted the helicopter-plane while Jesse
and Journey rested in the cabin. Goldie read a lusty
romance novel while Doc tinkered with one of his laser
blasters, trying to make it even more powerful.

Jesse yawned and stretched his arms. "Are we
there yet?"

"We've only been in the air for 20 minutes,"
Doc said. "Of course we're not there yet."

Jesse looked out the window for a few minutes.
The sky was still dark, but he could see a soft gray light
off on the horizon. They were rapidly flying toward the
setting sun. Pretty soon they would cross the
International Date Line, which would technically thrust
them one day into the future. It really didn't mean much,
but Jesse still enjoyed telling people he skipped a day.

Jesse glanced over at Doc, who was now
tinkering with Goldie's body.

"Hey Doc, you never did tell us why Aladdin
turned bad."

Doc dropped his screwdriver. "Oh. Uh... I
didn't?"

"Nope. What happened to him? What made him
go nuts?"

Doc sighed and rubbed the back of his head. "To
be honest, I'm not entirely sure. His father used to work
for a Russian intelligence agency before moving into the
seedy, dangerous world of illegal arms trafficking. But
his mother brought Aladdin to the U.S. when he was

young to escape that lifestyle, so you can't really blame his father for influencing him. His father was a fugitive on the run from every nation on Earth... much like Aladdin is now, ironically.

"Aladdin was a normal, albeit exceptionally intelligent, student at Harvard," Doc rattled on. "He was so bright, in fact, that I had him accompany me on some of my top-secret, government-sanctioned humanitarian endeavors. I had your parents join me as well. Even though I was their professor, we all become very close during our travels. Our trips around the world helped us forge a bond... a bond I once thought was unbreakable. Boy was I wrong."

"Sometimes I get angry when I go to poor countries and see people living in horrible conditions," Jesse said. "Maybe that messed him up."

"You may be on to something," Doc said quietly. "On weekends we would visit impoverished villages in Africa, South America, and Southeast Asia. We'd feed the poor and downtrodden, combat slave trafficking, and help endangered wildlife. And during the week we'd remain in the states, so I could teach and they could study."

Doc paused a moment, deep in thought.

"I truly think it was this stark contrast that corrupted his mind," Doc finally said. "There were many weekends when Aladdin would literally watch a malnourished child die in his arms. Then he'd come back to the states and see kids driving fancy cars and gorging on food. He always felt there was a plethora of injustice and hypocrisy in the world. I always got the feeling he felt it was necessary to stop the western world from influencing other nations."

"What do you mean?" Jesse asked.

"Well, Aladdin always hated how the U.S. and other first-world countries gobbled up so many natural resources. He was disgusted by the fact that the wealthy few destroyed the planet while the impoverished majority suffered. That's why he provides weapons to terrorists, dictators, and warlords. He wants to create a buffer against western influence, so we don't corrupt other nations. And as much as I hate to admit it, he does have a point. If everyone alive today lived like the average American, we would need three Earths just to provide enough food and resources. So his cause is noble. But his methods are deplorable."

"So you're saying Aladdin started out as a good guy, but all the injustices of the world turned him evil?" Jesse asked, seeking clarification.

"Precisely," Doc said. "The Aladdin of today is nothing like the man I once knew and loved like my own brother. If this world is to ever know peace, Aladdin must be stopped."

Jesse felt a chill ripple down his spine. He himself had been sickened by the many injustices he had encountered during his travels around the globe. Could he one day end up like Aladdin? No... he would never allow himself to become so ruthlessly evil. Still, it was something he'd have to pay attention to. He'd have to make sure the evil he fought against *never* found refuge in his soul.

"I still find it hard to believe that's all it took to make Aladdin so evil," Jesse finally said after a moment of silence.

Doc shuffled in his chair and said, "Well, there was one major catalyst that aided in thrusting Aladdin into the dark side. I'm sure you've heard the name *Isaac Kelvin?*"

Another chill rippled down Jesse's spine. He knew Isaac Kelvin all too well. He was one of the most evil men the world had ever known. There were specials about him on the History Channel all the time.

"Of course I do, Doc. Who hasn't?"

"Well, you may not have known that during my time at Harvard I worked with Kelvin. This was years before he became a genocidal lunatic of course. We became good friends... best friends... and traveled around the world together on countless humanitarian missions. Kelvin eventually became my lab assistant. This would become my greatest regret in life, because it was under my tutelage that Kelvin learned how to build and develop futuristic weapons of mass destruction."

Jesse and Journey exchanged alarmed glances.

Munching on popcorn, Martin said, "I can tell this story is about to get good."

"You already know all this, Martin," Doc said with a roll of his eyes. "*ANYWAY*, Kelvin was obsessed with black magic, sorcery, and his Egyptian heritage. He was also a radical environmentalist. He felt humans were like locusts feasting on the Earth. He also felt sympathetic to ancient civilizations and societies wiped out by Europeans, like the Mayans, Native Americans, African tribes, and many others.

"I grew increasingly alarmed over Kelvin's odd, cultish behavior. Our friendship soured when he began to talk about *'taking back the world'* and *'rebuilding the societies of old'*. It was around this time that he joined a freakish cult called the Phoenix Society."

"The Phoenix Society?" Jesse said with a smirk. "What kind of lame name is that?"

"The Phoenix Society was far from lame," Doc said solemnly. "In fact, it was one of the deadliest terrorist organizations the world has ever known. It was a group of insane extremists who wanted to resurrect ancient empires, like the Greeks, Egyptians, Romans, Aztecs, and Babylonians. They claimed these dead empires would *'rise from the ashes of the old world and converge to create a new one'*, like a proverbial phoenix."

Doc made quote marks for dramatic effect.

"That's... weird," Jesse said.

"Kelvin's cult was very weird," Doc agreed. "Most of the cult members thought they were the descendants of famous generals, queens, and kings. Kelvin thought he was the descendant of Ramses, the Pharaoh Moses supposedly tangled with. A few of his henchmen even thought they were the reincarnations of ancient gods and goddesses."

"Okay, now that's *very* weird," Goldie said.

"So Kelvin really dabbled in black magic?" Jesse asked, intrigued.

"He tried to," Doc said. "But as any rational person knows, magic is simply all about illusion. A quick sleight of hand, smoke and mirrors, all that jazz. So Kelvin made machines and gadgets that mimicked the magic he strived to wield. One of his greatest and deadliest inventions was a flying pyramid."

Jesse smirked. "How was that dangerous?"

"It was basically a giant flying tank that rained bombs and bullets down upon hapless armies and cities," Doc said dourly.

Jesse gulped. "Okay, that does sound dangerous."

Doc took a sip of Coke before continuing his tale.

"The Phoenix Society, for all its horrifying flaws, actually had a noble goal... in theory, at least. They wanted to rebuild the world, make it cleaner and more pristine. They wanted to stop rampant deforestation, reverse climate change, and bring endangered wildlife back from the brink of extinction. They also wanted to eradicate gluttony, greed, famine, war, and senseless discrimination."

"That doesn't sound so bad," Journey said.

"Yes, but their methods for achieving their idealistic goals were barbaric at best and innately evil at worst. Kelvin and his diabolical cohorts felt the human race was diseased, that it needed to be wiped out so they could rebuild society in their own grotesque image. They claimed this was the only way to save Earth from environmental catastrophe."

Journey gulped. "Okay, maybe that does sound bad."

"Kelvin and his psychotic followers began launching devastating terrorist attacks," Doc continued. "The U.S. and U.K. were hit particularly hard, as were

Brazil, Indonesia, China, and Russia."

A light bulb went off inside Jesse's head.

"Those are the countries with the most deforestation and pollution, right?"

Doc winked at his insightful nephew. "Bingo."

"Was Kelvin ever arrested?" Jesse asked.

Doc sighed. "No. After wasting many months waging a costly counterinsurgency, the U.N. worked out a deal where Kelvin and the Phoenix Society could set up an empire in the Sahara Desert, just west of Egypt. This fragile peace treaty did not last long. Kelvin and his followers grew increasingly power-hungry. They invaded Egypt in the middle of the night. By the time the sun rose the following morning, the entire country was in ruins.

"Kelvin and his society of deranged lunatics didn't stop there," Doc elaborated as Jesse and Journey listened with rapt attention, captivated by their uncle's riveting tale. "They quickly invaded other African countries: Sudan, Libya, Congo, you name it. Then they marched eastward, through the Sinai Peninsula, Saudi Arabia, Yemen, Syria, all the way to the doorsteps of Iraq and Israel. They did all of this in a matter of weeks. By the time the rest of the world mobilized, the Phoenix Society had dramatically increased the size of their empire.

"But like most conquest-driven dictators throughout history, Kelvin stretched his forces to the limit. This made the Phoenix Society ripe for a coordinated global assault."

By now the Baxter kids were on the edge of their seats, about to fall off the bed. They loved a good war story.

"After an emergency session at the United Nations, it was decided the U.S. would lead an invasion of North Africa. Since I knew Kelvin better than anyone, I helped lead the assault. Your parents joined me, as did Aladdin."

"Really?" Jesse said in astonishment. "Why?"

"Ariel, Hank, and Aladdin were my star pupils at Harvard," Doc explained. "They joined me on many top-secret missions I partook on behalf of the U.S. This was shortly before Aladdin went nuts, mind you.

"So with Aladdin and your parents in tow, not to mention several thousand marines and special-forces, we launched a daring midnight raid against the heart of the Phoenix Society's sprawling empire. Israel attacked from the east while more U.N. forces attacked from the south. Within days the Phoenix Society's empire was in shambles. We eventually launched an attack on Kelvin's pyramid citadel. Kelvin tried to retreat, but his pyramid was bombarded with missiles from stealth fighters, and his flying fortress plunged into the Mediterranean Sea. Everyone inside the pyramid was killed, including Kelvin. That's the good news. The bad news, however, was the fact that Aladdin was actually quite sympathetic to Kelvin's cause. He and I had a falling out shortly afterwards, and it was soon discovered Aladdin decided to take up Kelvin's cause of thwarting climate change by any means necessary. And that, my dears, is how the 'Merchant of Death' was born."

"Dang," Jesse grumbled. "Everything makes sense now."

The rest of the flight was eerily silent, and for good reason: the fate of the planet depended on Jesse and his family defeating one of the deadliest tyrants the world had ever known.

Chapter Twenty-Five: The Unlikeliest Friendship

Inside Aladdin's island fortress...

Ororo was being held in a solid steel prison cell. The bars in the front of the cell were replaced with vertical ruby-red laser beams. Like the prison on Aladdin's airship, it was actually rather nice. It had a cot, a sink, and a toilet. But there was absolutely no privacy. Two heavily armed and armored guards marched in lockstep outside the cell. Several cameras hung from the ceiling, watching Ororo's every move.

Ororo knew escape was impossible, so she didn't even try. Instead she lay on her cot and tried to get some rest. She was just about to doze off when thundering footsteps jolted her upright.

Ororo looked up to find Aladdin towering outside her cell. He still wore his armored exoskeleton, but his electric vipers weren't wagging around over his head. She was glad; the hissing vipers *really* freaked her out.

"I'm sorry to disturb you, Beauty. I just like to check on my guests. Are you comfortable?"

"Shove it, Aladdin," Ororo snapped. "You're not kidding anyone. Let's call it like it is. I'm your prisoner."

"I'm sorry you feel that way. I personally feel like you're doing me a favor."

"I'm *what??*" Ororo hollered, jumping off her cot. "Okay, you seriously must have bumped your head, because I wouldn't do you a favor if my life depended on it!"

"But you are doing me a favor, Beauty. Because of you, your Uncle Xander is on his way to my rendezvous point in the middle of the Pacific. Once he hands over his immortality vaccine, I'll let you go. Then I can cure my son of his horrible illness. Everyone will be happy. What's the problem?"

Ororo sighed and leaned her head against the cold steel wall. "I truly do feel bad for your son, Aladdin. But you're going about this all wrong. There are millions of sick and dying children all over the world. I've met a lot of them. I've watched many of them pass away. Quite a few were good friends of mine. Why should Mikhail get to live while everyone else suffers and dies?"

"I don't care about anyone else," Aladdin replied coldly. "No one on the face of this Earth is more precious or important to me than my son. I will do whatever it takes to save him."

"Even kill a homeless war vet?" Ororo growled.

Aladdin's cold demeanor turned even frostier. "Your friend was a mentally ill man. I did him a favor by putting him out of his misery."

Ororo jumped up and marched over to the laser-bars separating her from Aladdin. "Jerry was not mentally ill! He was… well, okay, maybe he had some mental issues, but he didn't deserve to be electrocuted and tossed into New York Harbor!"

"Don't blame the veterinarian for putting down a rabid dog," Aladdin said callously, augmenting his image as a cold-hearted supervillain.

Ororo quivered in rage. "Don't you *DARE* talk about him like that! Jerry may have had some problems, but he was a good person! He didn't deserve to die!"

"Your friend didn't deserve to die?!" Aladdin exploded, his icy blue eyes wide with rage and malice. "My wife didn't deserve to die! My son is most likely days from death, and he most certainly does not deserve to die! You ask me why I should be allowed to choose who lives and dies? Why don't I ask *you* why you get to decide, Beauty? Why is it *your* decision? What makes *you* so special??"

Ororo had no idea how to respond to Aladdin's sullen outburst. So she simply stared at the Merchant of Death in silence.

Aladdin's hardened face softened. "I didn't mean to go off on a tirade, Beauty. I really am not a bad man. It's just sometimes I'm forced to do bad things. As long as the end justifies the means, I'm willing to do it. And the end result of my son living a full and healthy life is worth all kinds of horrible 'means'."

Ororo plopped back down on her cot and closed her left eye. When she opened it, Aladdin was gone. His two armored mercenaries continued marching in lockstep.

Ororo had suffered a lot of hardships during her short, brutal twelve years on Earth. But she never felt this hopeless... this alone. Not even when her family was wiped out in Darfur. Ororo did everything she could to fight back her tears, but it was a losing battle. The tears poured from her one good eye like a raging river bursting forth from a collapsing dam. She had no idea how long she sat there feeling sorry for herself, but she abruptly stopped crying when a familiar cough echoed off the steel walls.

Ororo wiped her eye and looked up. Mikhail sat outside her cell in a wheelchair, covered in blankets. He looked even sicker than before. His face was as white as freshly fallen snow, and his eyes were puffy and red. Ororo's heart nearly cleaved in two at the sight of him. He almost resembled a living skeleton.

One of the guards hovered over Mikhail and nervously said, "Mr. Salazar, your father would not approve of you communicating with the prisoner. Why don't you go back to your---"

Mikhail raised his frail hand, prompting the guard to shut up. In a surprisingly deep, clear voice, Mikhail said, "I won't be long, Tom. I just want to talk to Beauty for a brief moment... in *private*."

The two guards glanced at each other before walking to the other side of the hallway. They were out of earshot, but kept Mikhail firmly in their sights. Ororo guessed Aladdin must have made it perfectly clear his son was to be protected at all costs.

Ororo hopped off her cot and walked to the front of the cell. The light from the lasers reflected off her robotic arm.

"Hello, Mikhail," Ororo said.

Mikhail coughed and wiped his runny nose with a handkerchief. Speaking so low she could barely hear him, Mikhail said, "I just wanted to apologize for everything my dad's put you through. I feel horrible. If I wasn't so sick, none of this would have happened. I'm so, so sorry."

Mikhail started coughing again.

Ororo's heart was once again on the verge of cracking in half. She lowered her head and quietly replied, "I'm sorry you're so sick. My... brothers and sisters were about your age when they were killed in Darfur."

Mikhail nodded before coughing into his handkerchief. "Like I said, I just wanted to apologize for my dad's craziness. I've been trying to talk him out of attacking your family. But I'm so drugged up on chemo that I can barely think straight. I hope you can forgive me."

"Of course I forgive you," Ororo said, moved by Mikhail's remorse over his father's deplorable actions. "None of this is your fault. But my uncle and siblings are undoubtedly on their way. Can you please convince your father to let us leave here alive?"

Mikhail continued nodding. "I'll talk to him."

Mikhail suddenly started hacking up blood. One of the guards rushed over and pushed him to the infirmary.

Ororo plopped back down on her cot and cried, but not because she felt sorry for herself. She cried for Mikhail... for all the sick children who would die before getting a chance to make their mark on the world.

Doctor Xander's immortality vaccine would never bring back all the loved ones Ororo lost in Darfur. But perhaps it would save kids like Mikhail.

All she could do was hope. If there was one thing the world could never have enough of, it was hope.

Chapter Twenty-Six: Invasion Of Death Island

"Everyone get ready. We're almost there."

Jesse and the gang heeded Doc's orders and made sure they were fully armed. They had flown so far, so quickly that they outraced the setting sun and were now literally flying through the next day. The sun filtered through high cirrus clouds, illuminating the bright blue ocean. Jesse pressed his head against the window, anxious to get a glimpse of Aladdin's secret lair.

"So do you think Aladdin is hiding out on another airship?" he asked.

"I'm not sure," Doc replied, fiddling with his EMP grenade strap. "I thought he might have set up base on a deserted Pacific island, but there aren't any islands at Ororo's coordinates."

"Are you sure about that, Doc?" Martin called from the cockpit.

Jesse, Doc, Goldie, and Journey rushed into the cockpit to see what Martin was talking about.

"Of course I'm sure. I've scanned every map I could find, and I... jumping Jupiter!"

Doc staggered backwards, stepping on Journey's foot.

"Ouch! Watch your freaking step, Doc!" she shouted.

"Sorry, Journey," Doc grumbled. He went back to staring out the front of the plane. Off on the horizon was a massive island. Only it shouldn't have been there.

"What's that sticking out of the sand?" Jesse asked. "Are those propellers?"

As they got even closer, it became apparent Jesse was correct. The island had dozens of massive propellers sticking out all over the place.

"No wonder Aladdin's lair has never been discovered," Doc murmured. "He created a floating island."

"That's actually pretty cool," Goldie said, sounding impressed for a cynical robot.

As they flew over the island, Jesse became even more stunned. In the northern part of the island was a giant waterfall that cascaded into a massive lake. On the southern end was a dense jungle. Exotic birds flew over the high treetops. And in the center of the island was a monstrous citadel fortress with a dozen towering turrets that spiraled high into the air. Beside the citadel were half a dozen airships. Two of them were fully constructed. The other four were in the process of being built. It appeared Aladdin was creating his own air force.

"Um, Doc? How the heck are we supposed to invade that thing?" Jesse asked.

"I honestly have no idea," Doc replied. "We're just going to have to wing it."

Journey crossed her arms. "You know, uncle, sometimes you don't act like a genius."

"We all have our shortcomings," Doc replied sheepishly.

Several massive laser cannons suddenly popped out of the sand and fired at the plane.

"Cripes! We've been spotted!" Martin shouted, weaving the plane through the crossfire.

"Put the plane in auto-pilot, Martin," Doc commanded. "Goldie, take us down to Death Island."

"Can we not call it that?" Jesse asked.

Once Martin did what Doc ordered, Goldie wrapped everyone up in her metallic cables. She then flew out of the plane, carrying her precious cargo with her. The laser cannons continued firing on the plane, allowing Goldie to levitate down to the island relatively unscathed. She lowered into the jungle, out of harm's way.

Once Jesse and the gang were on the ground, Goldie retracted her cables and spun around in the mud. "Hehehe, this is so much fun. I hope I get to zap like 100 bad guys."

"Psycho," Jesse mumbled.

Jesse and the gang huddled under a towering palm tree. Several toucans and macaws flew by, pretty much ignoring them. Howler monkeys could be heard screeching off in the distance. Giant flying insects buzzed around overhead.

"So what's the plan, Doc?" Jesse asked, adjusting his helmet. His vision continued to have a red tinge to it. A transparent map of the island popped up on his visor.

"In a moment we're going to dash toward the front entrance of the citadel," Doc replied in a hushed whisper. "Goldie will blow down the doors and knock out whoever's waiting inside. I released my locusts as soon as we exited the plane, and they are now burrowing their way into the heart of Aladdin's fortress. Soon the locusts will have hacked into Aladdin's surveillance system, giving us Ororo's exact whereabouts. Then we…"

Doc was interrupted by a 'ringing' noise coming from his helmet. He read the information scrolling across his visor and said, "Okay, the locusts are faster than I expected. They've already hacked into the island's computer database. Ororo is being held in the center of the fortress. The plan is to barge in, grab Ororo, and fly out. My locusts will take care of the island. There's no need for us to stick around and watch the show. I'm sure you all remember what happened on Aladdin's airship."

Jesse shivered as he recalled plunging into the icy Arctic. He knew the South Pacific was a lot warmer than the waters off the coast of Greenland, but he still didn't want to be around when millions of self-replicating robotic locusts went on a feeding frenzy.

"Your plan is nuts, Doc, but I guess it's all we've got," Jesse said.

"Thanks for the support, kid," Doc grumbled.

Jesse and the gang began making their way out of the dense and humid jungle. They had only gone about 100 yards when the rustling of leaves and thundering footsteps stopped them in their tracks.

"What the heck is that?" Jesse asked, unable to hide the fear and apprehension in his voice.

Jesse's question was answered seconds later when three massive elephants exploded out of the brush and charged straight toward him. The elephants were covered in gleaming black armor. Three mercenaries rode on their backs.

"Run for your lives! We're going to die!" Martin screamed, jumping behind a palm tree.

"What a wuss," Goldie said, flying into the air. She fired streams of tear gas at the elephants. The gas stopped two of the elephants, but the third one kept stampeding toward Journey.

Jesse ran directly in front of the elephant and fired his dazzler gun. He couldn't hear the blast, but he could see the light. His red-tinged visor saved him from being blinded. The 'dazzler' blast must have been pretty intense, because the elephant skidded to a halt and wildly shook his head. The elephant then staggered off to the side, temporarily blind and deaf. The mercenary toppled off the elephant's back and plummeted into a pile of dung.

Jesse blew the end of his gun. "Piece of cake."

"Don't get cocky yet, kid," Doc said, pointing off into the distance.

Jesse looked up and groaned. More mercenaries were on the way, along with an army of ferocious wildlife. Several mercenaries were riding giant, aggressive ostriches. The others ran toward them with lions, bears, tigers, jaguars, wild boars, and mountain lions. Jesse noticed all the animals wore electric collars. He assumed that was how Aladdin and his mercenaries kept them in check.

"Take out the animals with tear gas, electric darts, and your dazzler guns," Doc commanded.

"What about the mercenaries?" Jesse asked.

"Hit them with everything else," he snarled.

Jesse and the gang formed a line in the jungle and whipped out their various weapons. The mercenaries and animals continued racing toward them.

"On the count of three, fire your weapons," Doc said. "One...two..."

"Just shut up and fire, Doc!" Jesse hollered.

A relentless bombardment of blinding light, deafening sound, crackling electric darts, and suffocating tear gas rained down on the rapidly approaching army. The animals skidded in the mud and ran off in the opposite direction. The mercenaries who stayed behind were met with a relentless onslaught of low-energy laser blasts. Within a matter of seconds, all the mercenaries and animals were either knocked out cold or dashing back toward Aladdin's fortress.

Jesse and the gang 'woo-hooed' and high-fived each other.

"Wait, what's that noise?" Martin asked, spinning around in a frantic circle.

The island began to rumble, like it was under siege from an earthquake.

"I think that was just the first wave," Doc said, his voice shaking in fear. "Everyone get ready to----"

Doc was interrupted by the trumpeting of a massive elephant that had just exploded through the brush. It was the largest elephant Jesse had ever seen, well over twenty feet tall. He was covered in black armor, just like his smaller cousins. Two mercenaries stood on his back, armed with energy blasters.

The elephant skidded to a stop and raised his front legs.

Jesse grabbed Journey, who was frozen in fear, and yanked her out of the way just as the giant elephant brought his massive front feet crashing into the mud. If

Journey had stayed put, she would have been flattened.

Several more elephants barged into the clearing, as did several mercenaries on hovercrafts. Even more mercenaries appeared with another wave of ostriches, lions, bears, tigers, alligators, mountain lions, and wild boars.

Goldie released tear gas and electric darts while Jesse and the gang dodged alligator jaws, bear paws, and energy blasts.

Jesse watched in horror as toucans, macaws, and parakeets began attacking Goldie, pecking at her fishbowl-head.

"Stop it, ya dang birds!" Goldie shouted. "You're gonna crack my bowl!"

Goldie's entire body suddenly crackled with electricity, zapping all the birds. The birds squawked and flew to safety.

"Works every time," Goldie cackled.

A giant grizzly bear barged toward Jesse, who was firing his laser blaster from behind a tree. The bear swatted at Jesse's helmet, nearly knocking his head off. Jesse tumbled to the ground, his gun clattering into the brush.

Jesse moaned and grabbed his throbbing head. The bear pressed his claws into Jesse's vest and towered over him, baring his razor sharp teeth. The bear opened his mouth and growled, nearly suffocating Jesse with his horrible breath.

Jesse closed his eyes and waited for the bear to bite his head off. He hoped it would be quick. He then heard a zapping sound and a yelp. Jesse opened his eyes just in time to see the bear topple off of him. Journey ran over, clutching her taser dart gun.

"Since you saved my life, I thought I'd return the favor," Journey said, helping Jesse to his feet. "Are you okay?"

"I just got rescued by my 11-year old sister," Jesse grumbled. "Of course I'm not okay! That's embarrassing!"

Journey shook her head and pulled Jesse out of the brush. The both fired volley after volley of tear gas and electric darts. By now most of the animals had realized Jesse, Journey, Doctor Xander, Martin, and Goldie were not worth the effort of a tasty meal and scurried into hiding. Most of the mercenaries were knocked unconscious. But the giant elephant was still running around in circles, trying to crush Jesse beneath his massive feet.

Jesse grabbed a hanging vine and swung through the air, kicking a mercenary off his hovercraft. Jesse dropped from the vine onto the hovercraft just as the elephant barged past. He flew over the elephant's back and blasted the two mercenaries riding him with his dazzler gun. The mercenaries tumbled off. He then jumped on top of the elephant and fired the dazzler gun at his floppy ears. The elephant shook his head, his trunk and ears flying all over the place.

"Let's invade the fortress!" Jesse shouted, continuing to fire his dazzler gun at the elephant. The elephant charged out of the jungle, trying to escape the deafening noise bombarding his eardrums.

Doc, Martin, and Journey hopped onto hovercrafts and flew after Jesse. Several mercenaries brought up the rear, firing energy bolts at their backsides.

Jesse and the stampeding elephant were the first ones to burst forth from the jungle. As he barged through 'no-man's land', sirens blared and the massive propellers jutting out of the island began whipping around in circles, lifting the island into the sky. The propellers blew sand everywhere, creating a massive sandstorm.

"Great, Aladdin is making our escape even more impossible," Jesse grumbled. Thankfully his helmet protected his eyes from the blowing sand.

Dozens of mercenaries fired at Jesse and his family and friends from the citadel's spiraling turrets. Jesse and the gang returned fire. Several mercenaries were zapped out of their windows. A few shots bounced off Jesse's elephant, but did nothing to slow him down.

Goldie flew out in front and fired off several miniature cruise missiles. The missiles slammed into the citadel's massive steel door, blowing the front entrance into thousands of pieces. Before the smoke had even settled, Jesse and the gang barged inside.

Jesse hopped off his elephant, who continued stampeding through the citadel lobby. A few startled mercenaries dropped their blasters and dashed in the opposite direction. The elephant turned a corner and disappeared. Jesse could only imagine how much damage he was causing.

Dozens of mercenaries immediately began firing at them from the second-floor balcony hanging over the lobby. Jesse weaved through the relentless crossfire.

Jesse gasped as one of the blasts hit Journey squarely in the chest. She tumbled off her hovercraft and crashed to the floor.

Jesse kneeled in front of his little sister and unloaded his laser blaster, doing his best to protect her. Several shots slammed into his chest and sent him flying into the wall. He crumpled to the ground and clutched his throbbing stomach. His laser-proof vest and helmet were doing a decent job of protecting him, but the shots were still bruising and battering his body.

Goldie flew high into the air and released another volley of cruise missiles. The missiles detonated the entire balcony. The balcony collapsed into a pile of rubble, burying most of the mercenaries.

Jesse helped Journey to her feet. "You okay, sis?"

Journey coughed and muttered, "Yeah, I just had the wind knocked out of me. Let's go rescue Ororo. I miss her."

Jesse and Journey both hopped onto her hovercraft and zoomed down the hallway with Doc, Martin, and Goldie. They were now in the belly of the beast, and it would take every iota of courage and cunning they possessed to leave 'Death Island' alive.

Chapter Twenty-Seven: The Archangel Assembly Line

Ororo had just drifted off to sleep when the sirens went off. She bolted out of bed and glanced out her laser-encased cell door. The guards had stopped marching and were whispering to one another.

Ororo walked toward the laser-bars in a not-so-subtle attempt to eavesdrop. The guards turned their heads and whipped up their energy blasters.

"Get back on your cot, Beauty."

Ororo rolled her eye and went back to her corner. She hated how everyone kept calling her 'Beauty'. She wondered how an American girl named 'Joy' would appreciate being referred to as Ayo, an African version of the word.

Ororo plopped back down on her cot. She had a vague idea of why the sirens were going off, but she wasn't about to get excited until she knew for sure.

Aladdin's voice suddenly blared from all the island speakers. "The citadel is under attack! All available forces need to report to the front of the fortress to repel the invasion! I repeat, we are under attack!"

The guard on the left said, "You wait here, someone should keep an eye on the girl."

"Okay," replied the guard on the right as his friend dashed off. The guard turned toward Ororo and barked, "Stay in your corner!"

Ororo did her best to keep her emotions in check, but even she couldn't hide her happiness. She grinned like a 5-year old on Christmas morning.

"Wipe that stupid smile off your face," the guard snapped. "It'll be a cold day in Hades before your crazy uncle makes it down here. In fact, I..."

The guard was interrupted by a laser beam slamming into the side of his head. He collapsed into an unmoving heap.

Ororo jumped off her cot and ran back over to the laser-bars. Goldie flew by and hovered in mid-air.

"Goldie!" Ororo squealed, jumping up and down in excitement.

"Hey kiddo. Didja miss me?"

"Yes!" she shrieked, still hopping around in circles. "Get me the heck out of here!"

Doc and Martin flew over on their hovercrafts and hopped off. Jesse and Journey arrived a few seconds later.

"Jesse! Journey!" Ororo was so excited she nearly leaped into the laser-bars.

"Ororo, thank goodness you're okay!" Journey exclaimed.

Jesse knelt in front of the laser-bars and frowned. "How are we going to get her out of here, Doc?"

Doc lifted his helmet. "Jumping Jupiter, what an ingenious use of lasers!"

"Don't mess your pants, Doc," Goldie said. "I know ya get excited over hi-tech gadgets, but we need ta get a move on!"

"Right," Doc replied sheepishly. He pulled out an EMP grenade and placed it up against the cell wall, right next to the first vertical laser beam. Ororo watched as he fiddled with the detonator so that it wouldn't explode.

"Ororo, lean against the back wall and cover your arm," Doc ordered. "I programmed the grenade to unleash a burst of electromagnetic energy. The blast will short-circuit any exposed piece of machinery."

Ororo did as Doc ordered and leaned against her prosthetic.

Doc pointed at Jesse and the gang. "Follow me to the back of the hall. This blast will knock out our electronics as well."

Goldie blinked her lights and immediately took off. Jesse and Journey hopped on their hovercraft and zoomed after her, followed by Doc and Martin. Seconds later, the EMP grenade released a brilliant, green flash. The laser-bars instantly dissipated. Ororo dashed out of the cell and stampeded toward her brother and sister.

"I missed you guys so much!" she shrieked ecstatically, giving Jesse and Journey suffocating bearhugs.

"We missed you too, sis," Jesse said, returning the asphyxiating embrace.

Ororo let go of her siblings and hugged Doc and Martin.

"I'm glad you're okay, kiddo," Doc beamed.

Goldie blinked her lights and said, "All right, enough with the mushy stuff. Let's get moving!"

Doc handed Ororo a laser blaster and pulled her onto his hovercraft. There wasn't much room, but they made it work.

"Goldie, get us out of here," Doc commanded.

Goldie had just started to lead Ororo and the gang down the hall when half a dozen mercenaries rounded the corner and fired streams of electricity.

Goldie spun around and took off in the opposite direction, nearly colliding into Ororo.

"We're takin' a detour, guys!" Goldie shouted behind her.

Ororo and Doc fired laser blasters at the rapidly approaching mercenaries while they zoomed after Goldie. Jesse, Journey, and Martin brought up the rear.

Goldie led everyone down several narrow hallways. The flashing red lights and blaring sirens gave Ororo a throbbing headache. It also didn't help that energy bolts kept whizzing past her head.

Ororo and the gang finally flew inside what appeared to be a monstrous factory. There were assembly lines all over the place. Except these assembly lines weren't building cars or TVs. They were constructing archangels... dozens of them. Several half-constructed robots were on each conveyor belt, being put together by robotic arms.

Even more frightening than the sight of dozens of half-built killer robots was the horrifying sight of 50 completely finished archangels lined up against the back wall. Ororo was relieved to see that they weren't activated.

"Why did you bring us in here, Goldie?" Doc shouted, narrowly avoiding energy bolts from the mercenaries chasing them. Ororo nearly toppled off the jerking hovercraft.

"Sorry, Doc," Goldie said. "I thought this was a short-cut. But while we're in here we might as well destroy some robots."

Goldie fired cruise missiles at the nearest conveyor belt. Several partially-constructed archangels erupted in flames, sending a scorching fireball high into the air.

Ororo and the gang followed Goldie's lead and fired at other assembly lines. They also fired at several of the fully completed archangels leaning against the back wall. Ten of the archangels were totally blown apart, while others suffered minor damage. Within seconds, the massive room was filled with thick, black smoke.

By now over a dozen mercenaries had entered the factory. Ororo, Jesse, and the gang were quickly becoming overwhelmed by Aladdin's vast army.

"We need to get out of here," Ororo said, dodging a stray energy blast. She once again nearly toppled off the hovercraft, but Doc grabbed her.

Ororo had no more than uttered those words when the lights flickered on and off and the fully constructed archangels started moving. 40 pairs of eyes glowed bright red.

"Oh no..." Ororo muttered.

All 40 remaining archangels turned their heads and stared directly at Ororo and the gang.

"Intruder alert," the archangels said simultaneously in their eerie, robotic voices. "Targets have been identified: Doctor Zachary Xander, Martin Carter, Jesse Baxter, Ororo Baxter, Journey Baxter, and a nameless robotic flying garbage can."

"My name's Goldie, ya boneheads!" snapped the 'nameless flying garbage can'.

"Targets must be destroyed," the archangels thundered, their loud, mechanized voices rattling the factory walls.

"No, 'targets' must be allowed to escape!" Ororo shouted.

All 40 archangels stepped forward and raised their giant hands.

"Die, intruders!"

80 lasers ejected from the archangels' hands. Ororo and Doc swooped down at the last possible second, narrowly avoiding the fiery red beams. The lasers slammed into the walls and ceiling, sending chunks of steel and concrete crashing to the floor. Some of the debris crushed a couple conveyor belts.

"Hang on, kids," Doc shouted, clutching Ororo's shirt so she wouldn't fall off the rattling hovercraft. "We're about to make a dramatic exit!"

Ororo braced herself as Doc leaned as far forward as he could. She glanced back and was relieved to see Jesse and Journey right behind them, followed by Martin and Goldie. All six of them whizzed toward the open doorway. They were less than 100 feet away when a massive steel door slid in front of the exit. Doc barely pulled up in time, once again nearly knocking Ororo off the hovercraft.

The massive army of archangels extended their wings and flew into the air.

"Escape is impossible, humans. Prepare for immediate incineration."

"What do we do, Doc?" Ororo asked, her voice quivering in fear.

"We fight to the bitter end," Doc said gravely,

unloading his laser blaster at a nearby archangel. "If we're going down, we're taking all these buckets of bolts down with us."

"Don't worry, kids," Goldie said, spinning around in circles and unloading lasers and cruise missiles. "There's six of us and dozens of them. The odds aren't great, but they could be a heckuva lot worse."

A laser suddenly slammed into Goldie's backside. Ororo gasped as Goldie flew all the way across the room and crashed into the wall. Her fishbowl head shattered and her goldfish plummeted to the ground. Goldie slid to the floor in an unmoving heap, beside her flopping, dying goldfish.

Doc landed his hovercraft with a thud. Ororo and Doc both hopped off and dashed over to Goldie's smoldering body. Doc knelt beside Goldie and popped open a concealed control panel on her side.

Frantically pushing buttons, he murmured, "Come on, Goldie, stay with me."

Sparks flew out of the top of Goldie's shattered head, causing Doc to jump back in alarm.

Ororo glanced down at Goldie's goldfish. The poor fellow had finally stopped flopping around. She then looked up to see Jesse and Journey weaving through dozens of laser beams and energy blasts. Martin was on the far side of the factory, waging his own laser battle.

Five archangels hovered over Ororo and Doc. Tentacles wriggled out of their glowing chests.

"Escape is impossible," boomed the center archangel. "Surrender and our creator, Lord Salazar, may grant you mercy. Resist and face imminent incineration."

Ororo responded by blasting the archangel in the face. The archangel's head snapped back as sparks flew out of his damaged left eye.

Doc unsheathed his plasma sword and swung it at the damaged archangel's right leg, slicing it in half.

Ororo ran behind the archangel and blasted him in the back. The archangel toppled to the floor.

Another archangel flew toward Ororo and wrapped her up with tentacles. The same archangel ensnarled Doc with tentacles and dangled him in the air. Doc's plasma sword slipped from his grasp and clattered to the floor. The archangel's tentacles immediately tightened around Ororo's chest, cutting off her air supply.

Ororo tried gasping for air, but every time she inhaled, the tentacles constricted her like anacondas squeezing a mouse. Her world slowly began fading to black.

Chapter Twenty-Eight: Attack Of The Robots

"Ororo!" Jesse cried from the far side of the factory.

He tried flying toward her, but a mercenary blasted the bottom of his hovercraft, flipping it over. Jesse and Journey crashed onto scaffolding hanging above an archangel assembly line. Jesse's left ankle slammed onto the metal flooring of the scaffold, nearly shattering. Journey landed next to him. Her helmet popped off and tumbled over the side.

Five mercenaries flew over Jesse and his stunned sister, as did six archangels. They all fired at once, bombarding Jesse and Journey with energy blasts and lasers. One of the blasts slammed into Jesse's laser-proof vest, sending him flying into the railing. Another blast sent Journey collapsing to the floor of the scaffold.

Jesse grabbed Journey and pulled her close. The scaffold began to creak from all the blasts. An archangel landed in front of Jesse, causing the creaking to intensify.

"Escape is impossible," the robot thundered. "Surrender or…"

"Yeah, yeah, we know," Journey snapped. "You're going to 'liquidate us', blah blah blah…. You morons keep saying the same freaking thing!"

Journey ran toward the archangel and chopped his leg off with a plasma sword. Jesse hobbled over and blasted the archangel in the chest with a laser gun. The archangel toppled over the railing and landed on the conveyor belt down below.

The archangels and mercenaries continued their

aerial bombardment, causing the scaffold to suddenly collapse. Jesse and Journey landed on top of the pile, but the force of the impact left cuts and bruises on their faces.

Journey wiped blood from the top of her forehead.

"I should be in bed watching *Spongebob Squarepants* like a normal kid, not fighting giant killer robots," she grumbled.

"I thought you hated Spongebob," Jesse said, clutching his stomach.

"I do," Journey said, staggering to her feet. "That should tell you how much I hate these douche bags."

She pointed to the mercenaries and archangels circling overheard.

"Give it up, kids," a mercenary snapped. "Don't make us hurt you."

Jesse sighed and raised his arms in the air. "Okay, okay, we surrender."

"Oh no we don't!" Journey shouted, tossing an EMP grenade into the air. She tackled Jesse off the conveyor belt, then pulled him beneath the assembly line.

"You blasted kids!" the mercenary shouted.

A split-second later the grenade detonated, blowing all the mercenaries off their hovercrafts. The green light from the EMP blast bathed over the archangels, causing several of them to short-circuit and plummet to the floor. A headless archangel slammed onto the ground right next to Jesse and Journey. Sparks sprayed out of his severed neck.

Jesse stared at Journey in shock.

"You are one crazy little girl."

"Crazy like a fox," Journey said as she rolled out from beneath the conveyor belt. Jesse followed after her, in complete awe of his spunky, bat-poop crazy little sister.

Jesse and his injured but resilient Brazilian sister

hobbled toward Ororo and Doc, who were still being strangled by an archangel.

"Let them go, scumbag!" Jesse shouted. He unsheathed his plasma sword and chopped of the archangel's left leg. The archangel tumbled forward and fell on his hands and knees. Ororo and Doc fell to the floor, but they were still entangled in tentacles.

Journey fired lasers at the archangel's head, blowing out his left eyeball. Jesse ran behind the archangel and slashed a gaping hole in his back with a plasma sword. The archangel finally stopped moving.

Ororo and Doc ripped the tentacles from their neck and gasped for air.

Jesse helped Ororo to her feet while Journey checked on Doc.

Martin landed next to Jesse and fired lasers at the massive army of archangels and mercenaries flying toward them.

Jesse, Ororo, Journey, Martin, and Doc stood back-to-back, unloading their hi-tech arsenal at the killer robots and mercenaries circling overhead. Several of the mercenaries were blasted off their hovercrafts. The hovercrafts clattered to the ground, but they were well out of anyone's reach.

The archangels and mercenaries backed off, but Jesse knew they were simply buying time. Soon Jesse and his family would be out of ammunition. When that happened, they'd have no choice but to surrender.

"It's been nice knowing you all," Journey said, her face glowing crimson from her laser blaster. "And to think I've never kissed a boy."

"You're not missing much," Ororo grunted as she blasted off the head of a nearby archangel. "It's a lot of bad breath and slobber."

"I don't like the fact you know *anything* about kissing a boy," Doc grumbled, feeling a tad over-protective of his favorite one-armed niece. His shaggy hair started standing up-on-end from all the electrical blasts whizzing past his head.

Two archangels suddenly erupted in flames and fell to the ground. Goldie flew up behind them, blinking her lights and firing a barrage of lasers. Her fishbowl head was gone, but her feisty, never-say-die attitude appeared to still be intact.

"Sorry for the delay, guys. My self-repair mechanism took a while ta kick in."

Goldie continued to unload her arsenal. Laser beams, tear gas, and miniature cruise missiles flew all over the place. A couple of the cruise missiles blew apart one of the factory's massive control panels, plunging the factory into darkness. Lasers and energy blasts illuminated the pitch-black room in eerie blue and red light. Flaming pieces of wreckage added additional light, as did the countless number of explosions. The archangels' glowing eyes gave away their locations, making them easy targets.

Jesse and the gang hopped on fallen hovercrafts and started zooming around. Jesse, Journey, Martin, and Doc hacked off archangel heads with their plasma swords while Ororo blasted them with her laser blaster. And of course Goldie continued her ruthless aerial bombardment. Within a matter of minutes, half the archangel army was obliterated, littering the factory floor with flaming pieces of metal and sparking wires.

The lights eventually flickered back on, allowing the mercenaries and archangels to see their targets.

"Stupid back-up generators," Jesse grumbled weaving through criss-crossing electrical blasts.

Jesse overheard one mercenary shout, "Unleash a Motherboard Archangel!"

Another mercenary shouted back, "Won't Aladdin be mad? Those are meant for our clients!"

"Just do it," the other mercenary demanded. "This is an emergency!"

Jesse quietly wondered what the heck a Motherboard Archangel was. His question was answered seconds later when a giant hole opened up in the center of the factory. Out of the hole emerged a 100-foot tall archangel with monstrous, gleaming wings and massive, black cables protruding from its head. The cables went all the way down the robot's back, giving it a feminine appearance.

"Oh jeez," Jesse grumbled as he struggled not to mess his pants.

The Motherboard Archangel towered over everyone in the factory. She was so tall that her head nearly touched the ceiling.

The Motherboard Archangel's eyes glowed fiery red. In a robotic, feminine voice, she thundered, "Prepare to be annihilated, humans."

"At least she has a larger vocabulary than the smaller archangels," Journey observed. "She said *'annihilated'*."

The Motherboard Archangel took her first step, shaking the entire factory. Her chest opened up, revealing a normal-sized 10-foot tall archangel. The archangel jumped out of the chest cavity, spread his wings, and took to the air, firing lasers. Another archangel appeared, jumped out of the chest cavity, and took to the air. Then another one appeared.

"Jumping Jupiter! Aladdin's created a mobile robot factory!" Doc cried.

"There's plenty more where that came from," cackled a nearby mercenary, firing a stream of electricity at Doc's head. "Mr. Salazar is creating a whole army of Motherboard Archangels. Once they're completed, no country on Earth will be able to stop us, not even the stupid United States."

"What do we do, Doc? We're running out of weapons!" Jesse cried, tossing EMP grenades at the horde of archangels zooming toward him.

"Attack the Motherboard," Doc commanded, barely dodging an energy bolt whizzing past his head. "If we don't take her down, she's going to keep popping out archangels."

Jesse, Ororo, and the gang focused their firepower on the skyscraper-sized Motherboard

Archangel. Their laser beams and EMP grenades seemed to do nothing against her gleaming armor. Motherboard cocked her massive head to the side, almost as if she were observing Jesse and his family like curious specimens in a lab.

"Resistance is futile, humans. Prepare to…"

"Oh my Gosh, shut up already!" Journey screamed. She tossed an EMP grenade inside Motherboard's chest cavity, just as another archangel was preparing to leap out. The EMP blast shirt-circuited the archangel. More importantly, it seemed to affect Motherboard. She staggered backwards, stepping on a conveyor belt stacked with partially-constructed archangels.

"Great thinking, Journey!" Jesse exclaimed, decapitating a normal-sized archangel with his plasma sword. "Everyone fire at Motherboard's chest!"

Unfortunately they didn't get the chance. Motherboard's chest cavity instantly closed up, just as Jesse lobbed another EMP grenade. The grenade detonated harmlessly against her impenetrable armor.

"At least we got her to stop reproducing," Jesse observed gloomily.

Motherboard swatted at Jesse like he was a fly. One of her giant fingers grazed his hovercraft, sending him plummeting toward the floor. Goldie swopped down and grabbed him with one of her metallic cables.

"I swear, I'm gonna start charging ya kids every time I have ta save your lives! I should have Doc install an Uber app inside me."

"I hope you take rain checks, because I'm broke as joke," Jesse cracked, dangling beneath Goldie's hovering body.

A damaged archangel with a missing right eye flew in front of Goldie and aimed his hand at her body.

"Prepare to die, robot traitor."

"Prepare ta become a traitor yourself," Goldie shot back.

Goldie fired a dart into the archangel's damaged

eye. The archangel started quivering in mid-air like he was being electrocuted. His left eye flickered on and off for a few seconds before finally stabilizing. The archangel then turned around and fired a laser at another archangel. The archangel's head detonated in a fiery explosion.

"What did you do to him?" Jesse asked, staring at the 'Benedict Arnold' archangel in awe.

"I infected his computer brain with a virus," Goldie explained as she zoomed around the room, ejecting the last of her cruise missiles. "Now instead of attacking us he's gonna blast his friends."

"Why don't you infect all of them, then?" Jesse asked. "Wouldn't that make our lives a heck of a lot easier?!"

"Why don't ya ask your nutty uncle?" Goldie snapped. "He's the one who equipped me with only one virus dart!"

Doc flew by and shouted, "How was I supposed to know we'd be fighting 50 zillion robots?"

Goldie's infected archangel started going after the other archangels. He fired rockets and lasers at them when they weren't paying attention, blowing their heads off.

Motherboard pointed her massive index finger at the infected Archangel.

"Archangel 087B has been compromised. Terminate him immediately."

The rest of the archangels momentarily forgot about Jesse and his pals and bombarded poor Archangel 087B with lasers. The relentless assault took off all his arms and legs. Eventually even his head flew off. Archangel 087B crashed to the ground in a smoking pile of charred steel and wires.

"Well that backfired," Goldie grumbled.

"Hey Goldie, I have an idea," Jesse said, still dangling from a cable.

"That's a first," Goldie chortled. "Man, I crack myself up. I should do robot stand-up."

"No, seriously, take me up to Motherboard's face."

Goldie blinked her lights like an out of control fire truck. "Are you nuts, kid?"

"Yes I am! Now do it!"

Goldie sighed and flew toward Motherboard's titanic face, with Jesse still dangling from her body. Jesse gulped when he flew in front of Motherboard's monstrous, flickering red eyes. They were almost as big as his entire body.

Goldie flew under Motherboard's armpit, back up over her shoulder, and right next to the side of her gargantuan head.

"This is your stop, kid."

Goldie released her cable, sending Jesse tumbling onto Motherboard's right shoulder. Jesse scrambled to his feet and nearly slipped off of Motherboard's glistening metallic armor. He swung his arms in circles, then whipped out his plasma sword and plunged it into Motherboard's neck.

Sparks flew out of the incision. The Motherboard Archangel squawked, almost like Jesse was causing her pain. Jesse withdrew the sword and started slashing away at her neck, exposing a bunch of circuitry.

Goldie flew back around and shouted, "Good thinking, kid! Now toss a grenade in there and hop off!"

Jesse unlatched an EMP grenade, planted it inside Motherboard Archangel's exposed neck, and jumped off her shoulder. He had only fallen about twenty feet before Goldie caught him with one of her metallic cables. Goldie carried Jesse away from the giant robot just as the grenade detonated in a brilliant green flash. Half of the Motherboard Archangel's face blew off. Motherboard staggered backwards, but managed to stay upright.

"Jeez, what does it take to kill that thing?" Jesse grumbled, dangling in the air.

"I don't know, but you're too much of a liability,

kid," Goldie said, dodging laser beams from two archangels. She lowered to the ground and released her cable, sending Jesse tumbling onto the steel floor.

"Fend for yourself," she said just before zipping to the other side of the factory. A convoy of archangels immediately zoomed after her.

"Fine, I don't need you anyway." Jesse unsheathed his plasma sword and dashed toward Motherboard's humongous left foot.

Jesse slashed away at Motherboard's ankle until the armored heel fell off. He then unlatched one of his last EMP grenades, shoved it inside her heel, and sprinted twenty yards in the opposite direction.

The grenade detonated seconds later, taking out a large chunk of Motherboard's foot. More importantly, the EMP blast short-circuited her entire left leg. Motherboard was now forced to drag her left foot whenever she tried to move.

Motherboard continued squawking like a wounded animal. Jesse almost felt bad for her. Well, he *would* have felt bad if she and her robotic children weren't trying to kill him and his siblings.

Jesse had just started to blast Motherboard with laser beams when Martin flew by and fired his grappling hook at her damaged knee. The hook imbedded into Motherboard's armor. Martin proceeded to fly around Motherboard in a large, elliptical orbit, essentially tying her legs together. Motherboard attempted to take a step forward and toppled face-first onto the floor, crushing several conveyor belts stacked with half-finished archangels. The entire factory shook, as if a massive earthquake had just shaken the entire island.

Jesse dashed over and continued bombarding Motherboard with lasers. Doc, Martin, Ororo, Journey, and Goldie hovered over her, blasting her with taser darts, laser beams, EMP grenades, and anything else they had. Giant pieces of Motherboard's armor began to crack and fall off. Still, it wasn't enough. Motherboard pushed herself off the grand and staggered to her feet.

One of the archangels shouted "Protect Motherboard at all costs."

All the remaining archangels flocked to Motherboard and circled around her head, creating a moving barrier. By Jesse's count there were about fifteen of them. The remaining mercenaries flew over as well.

Ororo swooped down and grabbed Jesse off the ground. They flew over to Doc, who had landed on the far side of the factory, and hopped off their hovercraft.

Journey and Martin flew over and landed, too. Goldie hovered over all of them, laser blasters sticking out all over her body. Jesse and his family stood on one side of the massive factory while Motherboard and her army stood on the other. Both sides faced each other, as if they were getting ready to engage in a sci-fi duel.

Motherboard pointed toward Jesse and thundered, "Destroy the humans and bring me their severed heads. And bring me the robot's computer processor for recycling."

"Well, it's been nice knowing ya guys," Goldie said, her lights blinking like an out-of-control nuclear reactor. "And ta think I never kissed a computer."

"Didn't we just have a similar conversation a few minutes ago?" Ororo asked.

The archangels and mercenaries zoomed toward Jesse and the gang and circled them. They were now surrounded on all sides.

"What do we do, Doc?" Jesse asked, his eyes darting back and forth.

"Well, we can fight to the death, or surrender and die," Doc replied bluntly.

"Isn't there a third option?" Ororo asked.

Journey blew raspberries. "Come on, guys, don't be a bunch of wusses. Sure it'll be tough, but we can take these bozos."

Journey had barely finished her statement when a giant trap door opened up in the ceiling. A few mercenaries flew out of the trap door. Then a few more flew in, then a few more, then a *lot* more, then dozens and dozens. Soon there were over 100 mercenaries hovering around Jesse and the gang, in addition to the archangels and mercenaries already circling them.

Journey shrugged. "Okay, so the stakes have increased ever-so-slightly, but if we dig in and believe in ourselves, we can take these clowns."

The mercenaries were soon joined by dozens of other archangels.

Journey's mouth fell open in shock. "Um... okay, this may be a bit more difficult, but it's still manageable."

Then the floor opened up in the back of the war room and two more 100-foot tall Motherboard Archangels emerged on rising platforms. They stepped off their platforms and joined the other heavily damaged Motherboard.

Journey's face turned ghostly pale. "Okay, our odds aren't great, but..."

Then Aladdin appeared on a hovercraft, his viper cables wriggling in the air.

"Aw, come on!" Journey shouted. "This is so not fair!"

Jesse agreed; it wasn't fair.

He and his family were royally screwed.

Chapter Twenty-Nine: Aladdin Victorious

Aladdin smirked and floated toward Doctor Xander and his rag-tag army of teenagers and smart-alecky robots (well, *one* smart-alecky robot). The massive army of mercenaries and archangels moved away from Aladdin, allowing him to enter the impenetrable circle.

Aladdin clapped his armored hands. "Bravo, Doctor Xander. You infiltrated my 'impregnable' fortress and caused widespread destruction. I'm most impressed. Furious, but impressed. How did you find me?"

Doc explained how he placed tiny GPS devices inside all the kids' ear canals. He didn't do this to placate his arch-nemesis, of course. He was simply trying to buy himself time as he mentally formulated an escape plan.

Aladdin continued smiling. "Ingenious. I used a similar method to locate Beauty."

"I must say I find your floating island most impressive, Aladdin," Doc said, stalling for even more time. "It truly is a technological marvel."

"Are you kidding me, Doc?" Journey cried. "We're about to be murdered and you're yukking it up with the Merchant of Death?? I don't believe this! I---mmmmm!"

Jesse threw his hand over Journey's mouth. She may not have realized what Doc was up to, but he did. Their brilliant uncle was trying to sweet-talk Aladdin until the robotic locusts arrived. Doc had released them as soon as they arrived. They must have been well on their way to destroying the island from the inside-out, similar to what they did to Aladdin's airship over the Arctic.

"I mainly created this floating paradise so my followers would have a safe place to call home," Aladdin elaborated, oblivious to Doc's stall tactic. "We are all wanted fugitives, you know."

"What's up with all the animals?" Jesse asked casually, trying to play cool.

Doc discreetly winked at Jesse for buying them even more time.

"This island wasn't meant just for my followers," Aladdin explained. "I always intended it to become a sanctuary for endangered wildlife. Over the years I have rescued hundreds of animals from poachers and wildlife traffickers. I've liberated creatures all over the world, from Africa and Southeast Asia to the Amazon and Oceania. My ultimate goal is to create a contemporary Noah's Ark, a shelter for every endangered species on Earth. Of course, I had to domesticate them first, hence the reason I control them with electric collars. I can't very well have wild lions and jaguars roaming the island, free to devour all the other species. It may seem slightly barbaric, but it's better than the alternative... *extinction*."

"That's quite a noble endeavor," Doc said. He gestured toward the Motherboard Archangels, who towered over them like silent sentinels in the night. "I must say your army of robotic mercenaries is almost as impressive as your floating citadel. Your giant archangels are truly remarkable."

Aladdin nodded. "Indeed. My Motherboard Archangels are arguably my greatest creation. So far I've only built three, but I plan on creating many more. The three you see right now are about to be shipped to Iran, North Korea, and Myanmar. The dictators of those oppressive regimes are paying me a pretty penny for them. Terror groups in Africa and the Middle East have also expressed interest. Within five years I expect my archangels to be in operation all over the planet."

"You're making the world an extraordinarily dangerous place, Aladdin," Doc said.

"Perhaps for America and her corrupt allies, but not for me."

Aladdin floated even closer to Doc. His cables crackled with electricity.

"Why don't you just hand over the immortality vaccine, Xander? I'm a forgiving man. Give me your Fountain of Youth and I'll let you and your family leave here alive."

Doc narrowed his eyes. "Sorry, Aladdin. My country has a policy of not caving in to terrorist demands."

Aladdin growled. "I am no terrorist. I am a freedom fighter. The U.S. and the United Nations are the true terrorists, gobbling up all the world's natural resources at the expense of the rest of the impoverished world. All I'm doing is helping arm the poor and downtrodden. I'm building up a buffer against the environmentally annihilative policies of the western world. The West has already corrupted great Eastern nations like China, India, and Indonesia. It is up to me to save the planet, by any means necessary."

Doc clenched his fists. "Your mind has become poisoned by your senseless hate. In essence, you have become evil incarnate. And that is why you must be stopped at all costs."

Aladdin exhaled. "We could spend weeks having a philosophical discussion about who's right and who's wrong, but I don't have time. My son is literally at death's door. All I want is for him to live. Is that such a horrible request?"

Jesse watched Doc lower his head and sigh. He could tell it was killing his uncle that Aladdin was using his terminally ill son as a pawn.

Aladdin held out his armored hand. "You're going to give me your vaccine one way or the other, Professor. You can either give it to me now and be allowed to leave my island *alive* with your nieces and nephew, or you can watch as I slowly torture them. When you can no longer tolerate their agonizing screams, then you will hand it over. The end result will be the same. You *will* be giving me the vaccine. It's your choice on how we get there."

Jesse gulped. He wasn't too fond of the second option.

Before Doc could respond, Goldie shouted, "Shove it, Aladdin! You're just gonna have ta torture us, because we ain't givin' ya nothing'!"

"Shut up, Goldie!" Doc snapped.

He was too late. One of the Motherboard Archangels reached forward and grabbed Goldie with her massive hand. Goldie blinked her lights and cried, "Hey, lemme go ya big freak!"

The Motherboard Archangel started squeezing Goldie's body. Goldie squawked as her metallic exterior squished against her circuitry.

Five of Aladdin's viper cables shot forward and wrapped around Jesse, Doc, Martin, Journey, and Ororo. Two more vipers popped out and ripped off Jesse's and Martin's helmets. Everyone else had already lost theirs.

"I'm only going to ask for it one more time, Xander," Aladdin said in a voice completely void of emotion. "Give me your Fountain of Youth."

Doc clawed at the viper cable crushing his windpipe. Jesse couldn't even do that because his arms were tied up. Aladdin's 100-plus mercenaries revolved around him in a giant circle, cackling like blood-thirsty lunatics. The Motherboard Archangels and their smaller counterparts simply stared in eerie silence.

"Okay," Doc gagged, his face turning the darkest shade of purple. "Okay…"

Aladdin released his stranglehold, allowing Doc to crumple to the floor. But he kept his vipers wrapped firmly around everyone else. All Jesse could do was gag; he would be unconscious in a matter of seconds. And a few seconds after that, he would die.

Jesse gazed at Doc through blurred vision. His uncle stared at him in horror, his face as pale as an albino.

"Give it to me, Xander!" Aladdin barked. "There is a fine line between life and death, and I'm about to thrust these children over the edge!"

Without hesitation, Doc whipped out a small vial attached to his utility belt. He held it in the air, his hand trembling in fear.

"Here, Aladdin. Here's your blasted immortality vaccine. Now please, let my family go!"

Chapter Thirty: Mayday

Aladdin left Jesse, Martin, Ororo, and Journey hanging for a few more seconds before loosening his viper cables. They all collapsed in a rugged circle around Doc. Jesse gasped and rubbed his bruised neck.

Aladdin had just started to reach for the vaccine when the factory walls began quaking.

Aladdin glanced around and murmured, "What the devil?"

A column of locusts exploded out of the floor, knocking Aladdin backwards. Doc staggered back as well, still clutching the vaccine. Another column of locusts exploded out of the walls, then another, then another. Soon there were thousands of locusts attacking armored mercenaries, hovercrafts, archangels, the Motherboards, and the walls, floor, and ceiling of the factory. Several locusts latched onto Aladdin's armored suit and mechanical vipers.

"Curse you, Xander!" Aladdin exploded. The veins in his neck started pulsating like crazy. "You brought your plague of locusts to my home! You're destroying my life's work!"

"I know," Doc said with a grin. "Sucks, doesn't it?"

The locusts continued picking at Aladdin's exoskeleton and vipers. He swatted at the locusts and pressed a button on his arm. Two gleaming, metallic wings shot out of his back and he floated into the air.

"This is not over, Xander. Mark my words, I will not rest until I hover over your crumbling, decayed body."

Doc flapped his wrist. "Yeah, yeah, tons of people want me dead. Join the club!"

Aladdin growled and zoomed out of the factory, a column of locusts hot on his trail. Jesse assumed he was going to get Mikhail. The rest of Aladdin's mercenaries followed him. The archangels tried to flee, but they were quickly ripped to microscopic particles by the locusts. The three Motherboard Archangels had already collapsed into smoldering piles of scrap metal, which the locusts were now feasting upon.

"Let's go, people!" Doc shouted.

Goldie released an electrical current, short-circuiting the dozens of locusts attempting to burrow inside her body. She then unfurled five cables and snatched up Xander, Ororo, Journey, Jesse, and Martin. Goldie carried everyone through a gaping hole in the factory, down the hall, and out a large glass window overlooking the southern part of the island, shattering it into thousands of pieces as she burst through.

As Goldie flew high into the sky, Jesse glanced down at the chaos unfolding below. Aladdin's island was still floating over the South Pacific, but it was rapidly falling apart. The citadel was completely covered in locusts, as were the airships in the courtyard. Aladdin's mercenaries were attempting to flee on hovercrafts and planes. Most of the mercenaries managed to escape the locusts, but several of their planes and hovercrafts disintegrated in mid-air, sending them plunging into the churning sea below.

The anti-aircraft laser cannons had already been ripped to shreds. The propellers keeping the island afloat were in the process of being dismantled. Giant columns of locusts burst out of the sand, eating away at the metallic, computerized platform underneath.

Goldie carried Jesse and the gang several thousand feet into the sky, up to where the helicopter-plane was hovering. The hatch door swung open, and Goldie carried everyone inside. Goldie then shut the hatch door while Martin made his way into the cockpit.

Jesse and his siblings plopped down in the cabin, emotionally and physically exhausted.

Journey looked over at Ororo and said, "Next time you feel like going for a midnight stroll, do us all a favor and *don't*, okay?"

Everyone suddenly burst out in laugher, even Doc and Goldie. After surviving countless near-death experiences, even the corniest joke seemed hilarious.

Doc plopped down next to Jesse and sighed. "I am so proud of each and every one of you. You all are my heroes."

"Shucks, Doc, you're making me blush," Journey cracked.

"I just can't believe we escaped without any major injuries," Martin said from the cockpit.

"Speak for yourself. My foot is killing me," Jesse said, massaging his swollen right ankle. "I hope I didn't break anything."

While he continued rubbing his foot, Jesse gazed out the window. Aladdin's 'Death Island' was now in full melt-down mode. The last of the propellers had just been devoured by the locusts. The mammoth island began its freefalling descent toward Earth. Halfway down it completely disintegrated. Dozens of mercenaries and animals plunged into the frothing Pacific. The thousands of locusts sunk with the island to a watery grave.

Jesse was pleased to see the animals swimming to nearby sandbars and island atolls. All of the exotic birds took to the air. Aladdin's mercenaries clung to chunks of the island that managed to stay afloat.

Jesse did not see any sign of Aladdin or Mikhail. He couldn't care less about Aladdin, but he hoped Mikhail managed to escape.

Jesse turned around when Doc shouted, "Hey Goldie, send out a distress signal to any nearby ships! I may hate my former student, but that doesn't mean I want all of his minions to drown. Hopefully they can save some of the animals, too."

"I'm on it, Doc," Goldie said, wheeling into the cockpit.

Jesse still couldn't get over how different Goldie looked without her fishbowl head. He hoped Doc would eventually replace it.

Jesse leaned back in his chair and closed his heavy eyelids. He heard Doc rush into the cockpit and tell Martin to head for New York. Jesse didn't care where they went, he was just thankful their arduous ordeal was over.

At least, he *thought* it was over. He realized he was wrong moments later when a thunderous *BOOM* jolted him out of his seat.

"Aw come on!" Journey hollered, buckling her seatbelt. "Can't we ever catch a break?"

Doc rushed into the cabin and shouted, "Everyone strap in! We're being atta----"

BOOM!!!

A laser smashed a massive hole through the back of the plane. Jesse and Doc were both sucked out of the plane and sent hurtling toward the ocean below. Jesse screamed as he plummeted toward his death.

Jesse looked up at the plane, which dove toward an island atoll off in the distance. Smoke billowed from the rear. Some sort of aircraft flew after it. He assumed that was the plane that shot them out of the sky.

Jesse then glanced over at Doc, who was a little higher up than he was. He could hear Doc screaming even with all the wind blasting his eardrums.

Jesse finally gazed down at the deep, blue ocean zooming toward him. They had fallen from 10,000 feet up and still had a ways to go. He knew he would never survive a fall from so high up. Even though they were going to land in the ocean, it would still be like hitting concrete.

Jesse closed his eyes and continued screaming. He just hoped his death would be painless.

Jesse was only in free-fall for a few more seconds before something wrapped around his waist and jerked him upward.

Jesse opened his eyes. Goldie's headless body hovered over him. Her propellers cut through the air, and a cable dangled from her side. Jesse looked down and realized the cable was wrapped firmly around his waist. Doc dangled ten feet below him.

Doc threw his hands in the air and cried, "Can you believe it, kid?! We're alive! ALIVE!!!"

Jesse burst out in hysterical laughter. He was ecstatic over not splattering against the surface of the ocean.

"You cried like a baby, Doc!" Jesse shouted to his still screaming uncle.

"So did you!" Doc cackled.

"I'm embarrassed for both of you," Goldie grumbled.

Jesse suddenly turned deadly serious.

"Are Ororo and Journey okay?"

"Everyone was strapped in but you two boneheads," Goldie said. "But I think the plane just crashed."

"No!"

Jesse stared off toward the horizon. He could see Doc's plane sitting on the beach of a deserted island. Black smoke billowed into the sky.

"Hurry up, Goldie, we've gotta help them!"

"I know, kid, I'm flying as fast as I can!"

The island grew closer and closer with each passing second. Soon Jesse could see Martin and his sisters crawling out of the wreckage of the plane. He expected to see nothing but flaming pieces of scrap metal, but Docs's plane looked to be in surprisingly remarkable condition.

Doc breathed a sigh of relief. "Thank goodness. I created my planes to withstand even the most horrific crash. It would appear my designs worked perfectly."

Goldie finally reached the island and hovered over the beach. She released her cables, sending Jesse and Doc tumbling into the sand. Jesse and his uncle immediately clambered to their feet and dashed toward the smoldering plane. Ororo, Journey, and Martin walked toward them, looking stunned but miraculously unharmed.

Jesse sprinted toward his sisters and enveloped them in suffocating bearhugs. "I'm so glad you guys are okay."

Doc joined in on the bearhug, as did Martin. Even Goldie wheeled over and patted everyone on the back. Jesse couldn't help but chuckle at her hilarious attempt to convey compassion.

Doc walked over to his plane, which was still smoldering. There was a gaping hole in the back.

Doc groaned. "We won't be flying home in this."

Jesse joined his uncle. "Who, or *what*, shot us down?"

Jesse's question was answered seconds later when one of Aladdin's hi-tech planes hovered over them. The plane looked similar to Doc's, except a lot larger. The plane landed on the beach, blowing sand into the sky.

"Everyone get ready," Doc growled as he unsheathed his plasma sword.

Jesse whipped out his sword, too, as did Journey and Martin. Jesse glanced over at Ororo and noticed she had no weapons. He tossed her his laser-blaster, which she caught in mid-air. Goldie hovered over them; laser-blasters poked out all over her headless body.

Jesse spun back around and held his plasma sword in front of his face. The hatch door to the plane suddenly opened. Jesse gasped as a 20-foot tall, cerulean blue robot stepped out of the plane and landed on the beach with a thud. The entire beach shook, causing several palm trees to drop coconuts. The coconuts rolled onto the beach, near the water's edge. The robot was so heavy its feet sunk into the sand.

The robot had bulky arms with two large cables protruding from the elbows. The cables connected to the robot's back. The robot did not have a head. In its place was a gleaming glass dome. Inside the dome sat Aladdin Salazar, pressing buttons and yanking on controls. His mouth was contorted into a hideous snarl.

Jesse gulped. "Looks like this is it, guys. Us versus the Merchant of Death... to the death... in sudden-death overtime."

"We get it, Jess," Ororo grumbled. "Jeez."

Jesse, Ororo, Journey, Doctor Xander, Martin, and Goldie prepared for all-out war against the deadliest man on Earth.

Chapter Thirty-One: Armageddon

Aladdin's voice blared from speakers on the robot's chest. "You have destroyed my life's work, Xander. Now I will destroy those you hold dearest to your heart."

Aladdin marched toward Jesse and his family and friends. A rocket flew out of his robotic arm and streaked toward Goldie. Goldie tried to out-fly the rocket, but she was far too slow. The rocket slammed into her side and detonated, exploding Goldie into thousands of pieces. Shards of her body rained down all over the island.

"NOOOOO!!! GOLDIE!!!!"

Doc snarled and raced toward his hated student. He was just about to thrust his plasma sword into the robot's massive right leg when a cable shot out of the robot's chest. The cable wrapped around Doc's waist and spun him around in circles before flinging him into the sky. Doc plunged into the sea, about 100 yards off the coast of the atoll.

Aladdin's robot proceeded to unleash a dozen heat-seeking, electrified darts. Three of the darts imbedded into Jesse's neck. Jesse cried out in agony as electricity coursed throughout his entire body. He crumpled to the beach in a smoking heap.

Jesse yanked the electric darts out of his neck and cried out in pain. He watched through blurred vision as Ororo, Journey, and Martin were all zapped with the darts. They all collapsed to the ground, their bodies smoking from the mild electrocution.

Jesse clutched the back of his neck and gazed up

just in time to see Aladdin marching toward him. The island shook every time he took a step. Jesse's vision was still blurry, causing him to see three giant robots spinning around in a circle.

Aladdin raised his monstrous robotic arm. "Die, Baxters, die!"

Aladdin tried to smash Jesse with his giant fist, but he rolled out of the way at the last possible second. The fist created a crater in the sand.

Aladdin spun around and attempted to smash Journey. Journey rolled out of the way and blasted the robot's domed head. The laser bounced off and shot into the sky.

Aladdin continued trying to smash Jesse and his siblings, all the while shouting, "Die, die, die!"

"This guy has major anger management issues," Jesse grumbled, dodging Aladdin's robot's razor-lined foot.

Jesse glanced over at Martin, who was still lying on the ground. Aladdin's darts were still protruding out of his neck.

Aladdin stormed over to Martin and raised his fist. Jesse dashed over and grabbed Martin's arm. He tried to pull him out of the way, but he was too late. Aladdin brought his fist smashing down on top of Martin's right leg. Martin cried out in agonizing pain.

Ororo and Journey dashed over, blasting Aladdin with lasers. Aladdin raised his fist off of Martin's leg and spun around to chase them.

Jesse knelt beside Martin, who gritted his teeth and blinked away tears. Jesse gasped at the sight of Martin's bloodied, mangled leg.

Jesse held Martin's hand. Martin squeezed it tight and muttered, "Go get morphine please…"

"Morphine? Where?"

"It's in the first-aid kit," Martin grunted. He squeezed Jesse's hand so tight that it was beginning to hurt. "In the cockpit…"

Jesse jumped up and started dashing toward

Doc's plane. Aladdin reached down and grabbed him with his monstrous, robotic fist. Jesse cried out as the fist tightened around his waist.

Aladdin brought Jesse up to his dome-protected face. "I'm especially going to enjoy squeezing the life out of you, Jesse Baxter."

"You're... mad...." Jesse grunted, banging on Aladdin's robot fist.

"Of course I'm mad," Aladdin snarled. "Wouldn't you be furious if a bunch of snot-nosed punks destroyed your arms-trafficking empire, costing you hundreds of billions of dollars?"

"No... I'd... forgive... them... and... let... them... go...," Jesse grunted, still banging away at Aladdin's fist.

Aladdin cackled. "Well, you're a better man than I. So long, Jesse Baxter. See you in the afterlife."

A sudden explosion rocked Aladdin to his knees. Aladdin released Jesse, sending him toppling to the ground. Jesse rolled out of the way and looked up at the sight of Journey lobbing her last EMP grenade at Aladdin's robot. The robot tried to climb back to its feet, but Ororo dashed over and bombarded the robot with her laser blaster. Journey whipped out her plasma sword and slashed away at the robot, exposing wires and gears. Jesse staggered over and unsheathed his own plasma sword. He joined Journey and the two of them took turns eviscerating Aladdin's robot.

"Do you have any more grenades?" Journey asked, still stabbing the robot in the back.

Jesse unlatched his last EMP grenade and pulled the pin. "Yep. Everyone move!"

Ororo and Journey ran over to Martin while Jesse jammed the grenade into the robot's mangled back. Aladdin glared at Jesse from inside his protective dome.

"When I get out of here I'm going to strangle you with your own intestines!"

Jesse made a face. "That's disgusting. You must watch too much *Walking Dead*."

Jesse spun around and dashed to the other side of the beach. The grenade exploded, slicing the robot in half. The top half plummeted face-first into the sand, with Aladdin trapped inside.

Jesse made his way over to Martin, who was still moaning in pain. Ororo and Journey hovered over him, looking terribly concerned.

Journey knelt down and cradled Martin's head in her lap. Choking back sobs, she murmured, "Don't leave me, Martin. Who am I going to marry?"

"Oh lord," Ororo grumbled, massaging her head.

Martin looked up at Jesse and groaned, "Did you get the..."

Jesse smacked his head. "Right, the morphine!"

Jesse ran over to the plane. He jumped inside the giant hole in the cabin, swung open the medical closet in the cockpit, and yanked out the first-aid kit. He then jumped out of the cabin and dashed back over to Martin.

Without saying a word, Jesse whipped out a vial of morphine, sucked some of it out with a syringe, attached a needle, and grabbed Martin's right arm. Once he found a vein, he plunged the needle inside. Martin stopped groaning almost instantly.

"Oh yeah... that's the stuff...."

"This stuff seems to work pretty quick," Ororo observed.

"Yeah, Doc engineered it to work several times faster than normal morphine," Jesse explained, withdrawing the needle from Martin's arm. "Heck, I'm tempted to use it. My entire body feels like it's on fire."

Ororo gasped. "Wait a minute, where's Doc?"

Jesse's face turned ghostly pale. He felt terrible for forgetting about his uncle.

Journey pointed toward the shore. "There he is!"

Jesse spun around and watched as Doc trudged out of the ocean. Jesse and Ororo ran over to check on him while Journey stayed with Martin.

Doc spit out a bunch of sea water and wiped his eyes. "What'd I miss?"

Jesse gestured toward Aladdin's demolished robot. "We totally kicked Aladdin's butt."

Doc made his way over to Martin, who was smiling and looking at his hand.

"What's wrong with him?" Doc asked.

"He's hopped up on morphine," Jesse replied.

Doc gasped at the sight of Martin's mangled leg. "Jumping Jupiter! We need to get him to a hospital!"

"How are we going to do that?" Jesse asked. "Our plane is totaled and Goldie is…"

Jesse trailed off. He noticed a lump forming in Doc's face.

Doc glanced over at Goldie's shattered body. A pile of smoldering metal and wires sat under a palm tree. Tiny pieces of her body were scattered all over the beach.

"Will you be able to rebuild her, Uncle?" Journey asked, still cradling Martin's head. She ran her fingers through his shaggy blonde hair.

"I don't know, dear. I…"

Aladdin's vipers suddenly burst through his robot's domed head, pulverizing it. Aladdin stepped out of the shattered dome and hopped onto the beach. Just like in Jesse's dream from the night before, his feet sunk into the sand. Ten glowing, writhing vipers whipped around over his head.

Jesse instinctively reached for his plasma sword, but he wasn't fast enough. Aladdin pointed his glowing right hand at Jesse and fired five laser beams. The lasers slammed into Jesse's chest, sending him flying into a tree. His head slammed into a trunk, nearly knocking him out. Stars floated across his eyes, followed by a stabbing sensation in his brain. He pushed himself up out of the sand, fighting to stay conscious.

Jesse watched through blurred vision as Ororo, Journey, and Doc ran toward Aladdin, firing their laser blasters. The lasers bounced off Aladdin's exoskeleton, but they did cause him to stagger back a bit. Aladdin sent six of his vipers shooting toward Ororo, Journey and Doc. Three of the vipers snatched their weapons while the other three wrapped around their bodies and lifted them into the air.

Aladdin sent three more vipers zipping cross the beach. One viper grabbed Jesse, another snatched his plasma sword, and the last one ensnarled Martin.

"How the tables have turned," Aladdin cackled, dangling Jesse and the gang over his head. He brought Doctor Xander right in front of his snarling face and snatched the immortality vaccine off of his utility belt.

Aladdin twirled the vial of the vaccine around in his gloved hands. "This is all I wanted, Xander. All I wanted was for you to help me save my son. And what did you do? You annihilated my empire."

Aladdin's face contorted into a hideous mask of rage. "You've taught me everything I know, Xander. But I cannot allow this grievous act of treachery to go unpunished."

"Please, Aladdin... don't..." Doc gagged, struggling to breathe from the viper wrapped around his throat.

"The time for mercy has long passed, Doctor Xander."

Aladdin stared at the vaccine in awe, like he couldn't believe it was finally in his possession.

"You know, Xander, I had originally planned on simply giving this to my son. But you've given me an even better idea. You and I both know there are far too many people on this planet. That's the main reason the world is falling apart. The best cure for global warming... the best way to stop the deforestation of the rainforests, the meltdown of the ice caps, the acidification of the oceans, and the pending mass extinction of all the world's wildlife... is to drastically *decrease* the human population."

Doc's eyes widened in horror, as did Jesse's.

"Aladdin... no... I beg of you...."

"SILENCE, XANDER!!!" Aladdin snapped, spraying spit all over Doc's face. "I'm going to use half of this to cure my son. The other half will be used to create a pathological weapon... a 'Fountain of Death', if you will. I will then unleash it on the human populace, wiping out the greatest disease the world has ever known... man."

"You're insane, Aladdin!" Jesse shouted. "The virus would kill you, too!"

Aladdin waved his hand. The cable around Jesse's neck tightened, choking off his air supply.

"Foolish child, do you not think I have taken that into consideration? I'll simply inject myself with the immortality vaccine. The nano-bots will fight off the virus. I'll inject my followers with it as well. It can't be too difficult to mass-produce the nano-bots, especially since I hold the blue-print in the palm of my hand."

Aladdin brought Doc so close that they were almost nose-to-nose. "Thanks to you, Professor, we have found a solution to our climate change problem. Too bad you won't be around to see it."

Aladdin waved his hand. His viper shot outward, until Doc dangled 20 feet away.

"Before I kill you, I want you to watch your family's execution."

"Aladdin... please...," Doc pleaded, tears streaking down his cheeks.

Aladdin held out his arms, and a wave of electricity washed over Jesse, Ororo, Journey, and Martin. They all cried out in gut-wrenching agony as electricity crackled all over them. Smoke emanated from their smoldering clothes.

Jesse was in such horrific pain that he couldn't even breathe. He had been zapped by Aladdin's electric vipers before, but that pain paled in comparison to this. This time Aladdin was *really* trying to kill them. Every single cell in Jesse's body felt like it was on fire. He would have actually preferred being submerged in the icy Arctic. Anything but this.

"ALADDIN! STOP IT! STOP!!" Doc screamed, writhing around in the air.

After what felt like hours, but was actually only seconds, the electrocution blissfully, mercifully stopped. But Jesse's body continued the throb in agony. He tried to act brave, but tears streamed down his cheeks. Journey and Ororo quietly sobbed. Even Martin groaned, and he had morphine coursing through his veins. They all continued dangling in the air.

Aladdin pursed his lips. "How does that feel, Doctor Xander ? How does it feel to watch the ones you love most slowly fade away?"

"Aladdin... please..."

"It feels horrible doesn't it? Now you know what I've been going through... watching my son fade to nothing. You could've eased my pain. You could've helped my son. But you didn't. And now you must pay the ultimate price. Say farewell to the ones you love, Xander. This time I won't stop until they're dead."

Aladdin was just about to unleash another wave of electricity, this time with enough voltage to kill his captives, when a meek voice shouted, "Stop it, Dad!"

Aladdin spun around and gasped. Mikhail floated toward him on a hovercraft, clutching an energy gun. He looked near death.

"Mikhail... wha... what are you doing? Get back on the ship!"

"No, Dad." Mikhail paused a moment to cough, then said, "This ends now."

Mikhail flew overtop Aladdin and lowered to the beach. He stepped off the hovercraft and cocked his energy blaster.

Aladdin's eyes widened in a combination of horror and incredulity.

"Son, don't----"

Aladdin was cut off by a crackling ball of electricity slamming into his chest. Jesse and the gang slipped through Aladdin's viper cables and collapsed to the sand in crumpled heaps. Aladdin flew out to sea and splashed into the frothing ocean. His vipers wriggled in the air before they, too, disappeared beneath the foaming waves.

Chapter Thirty-Two: The Fall Of A Tyrant

Jesse lay sprawled out on the beach, gasping for precious air. He finally lifted his head to make sure everyone else was okay.

Jesse watched as Mikhail trudged over to Ororo. Mikhail dropped to the sand and cradled Ororo's head in his lap.

"Are you okay, Beauty?"

"I am now," she murmured.

Jesse crawled over to Journey and helped her sit up. Out of the corner of his eye he watched Aladdin stagger to shore, his drenched hair hanging over his snarling face. He looked just like he did when Alex shot him out to sea all those days ago, in Jesse's dream. How prophetic that dream turned out to be.

As Aladdin drew closer, he shook his head, spraying water everywhere. "You too, Mikhail? You have turned on me as well?"

Mikhail aimed his energy blaster at his father. In between coughs, he said, "You've gone crazy, Dad. I heard everything you said about using that virus to kill people. I… I don't know you anymore. It's like you're a different person."

Aladdin narrowed his eyes into hateful slits. "So that's it? After everything I've done for you? This is how you repay me?"

Tears streaked down Mikhail's cheeks. "You haven't done anything for me, Dad. You cause death and destruction everywhere you go."

"This is all your fault, Xander!" Aladdin screamed. "You've turned Mikhail against me! You've destroyed my entire world, and now you've taken my only son!"

Jesse grabbed his plasma sword off the ground and held the gleaming blade in front of his face. "What should we do, Uncle Xander?"

"Take him down," Doc growled.

Jesse, Ororo, Journey, and Doc all barged toward Aladdin, wielding plasma swords and energy blasters. Martin was forced to stay back because of his leg. Mikhail stood next to him, his blaster still aimed at his father.

Aladdin sent five electric viper cables zooming toward his attackers. This time Jesse and his family were ready. Jesse hacked off one of the viper cables as it tried to wrap around his legs. Sparks flew out of the severed end as the viper cable flopped around on the sand like a real headless snake.

Journey sliced the viper wrapping around her legs. She then twirled around and hacked off the viper spiraling around Ororo.

Doc decapitated the last two vipers. Aladdin looked on in horror as his severed viper cables wagged around in the air, sparks spraying out of the ends.

Jesse whipped out his dazzler gun and blasted Aladdin in the face. Aladdin staggered back, clutching his eyes.

Ororo ran up to Aladdin and punched him in the gut with her robotic arm. Aladdin keeled over and gagged. Ororo then spun around and kicked him in the throat. Aladdin fell flat on his back.

Doc was just about to thrust his plasma sword into Aladdin's chest when another viper cable shot out of his suit. The cable lifted Doc into the air and hurled him to the other side of the beach. Two more viper cables popped out and smacked Ororo and Journey in their faces. Jesse spun around in circles, hacking all of the vipers in half.

By now Aladdin had regained his sight and hearing. He spun around and punched Jesse, Ororo, and

Journey in rapid succession. All three Baxter kids crumpled to the ground.

"You jerk!" Journey cried, clutching her bleeding nose. "You better pay for my plastic surgery!"

Aladdin raised his glowing hands. He was just about to blast Ororo when Mikhail ran forward and zapped him with an energy blast. Aladdin fell onto his side, holding his stomach. Mikhail hovered over his fallen father and pointed his blaster at his head.

"Give it up, Dad. It's over."

Aladdin growled and sent another viper wrapping around Mikhail's body. Mikhail gagged as the viper tightened around his neck.

"Dad... stop..." Mikhail grunted, dangling in the air.

Aladdin blinked away tears. "I'm sorry, son, but this betrayal is too much for me to bear. If I can't have you, then no one will."

Mikhail cried out in pain as Aladdin sent electricity coursing through his weak body.

"No! Let him go!"

Jesse jumped up and started racing toward Aladdin. He immediately slipped and fell face-first onto the beach. A coconut rolled in front of him. Jesse instantly flashed back to the dream he had in New York. Without thinking, he picked up the coconut, jumped to his feet, and hurled it at Aladdin's head.

The coconut smashed into Aladdin's temple. His eyes fluttered and he fell to his knee. His viper unraveled around Mikhail, causing him to plummet onto the beach. But unlike in Jesse's dream, Aladdin did not fall unconscious.

"Foolish... child," Aladdin muttered. He raised his arms and sent two of his crackling vipers wriggling toward Jesse. Jesse swung his plasma sword at one of the robotic snakes, but the blade didn't connect. The viper wrapped around Jesse's body and pulled him toward Aladdin.

"I'm going to choke you with my own hands,"

Aladdin cackled. There was a demonic gleam in his eyes, like he had officially gone over the deep end.

But Jesse had no intention of giving up just yet. In his haste to commit murder, Aladdin had forgotten to make sure Jesse's hands were fully constrained. Jesse raised his plasma sword and hacked Aladdin's left arm off, right at the shoulder.

Aladdin looked down in horror as his severed arm collapsed into the sand. He then unleashed an ungodly shriek of excruciating pain. Jesse slipped through the unraveling viper and rolled away from the genocidal madman.

Aladdin continued to cry out in pain. Jesse had expected there to be a lot of blood, but there was very little. The scorching heat from the plasma blade had cauterized the wound. It was just like when Darth Vader hacked off Luke Skywalker's hand in *The Empire Strikes Back* (one of the greatest movies ever made, in Jesse's humble opinion). But that did little to numb Aladdin's pain, as evident by his animalistic howls of agony and fury.

Jesse picked up another coconut and hurled it at Aladdin's head. This one sent him sprawling flat on his back. Aladdin's shrieks downed down. He was now on the verge of unconsciousness.

Ororo rushed over to Jesse and gave her brother a hug. Jesse returned the embrace.

Blinking back tears, Jesse said, "I... I didn't want to hurt him like that. But I had to, he wasn't going to stop. He wasn't..."

Ororo placed her robotic index finger against Jesse's quivering lips and whispered, "Shhh. You did what you had to, brother. Aladdin brought his ghoulish fate upon himself."

Ororo then ran over to check on Mikhail.

Doc wandered over to Goldie's smoldering, shattered body and dug through the wreckage. A few seconds later he stood up, clutching a tiny black box.

Jesse hurried over and asked, "Is that Goldie's

computer processer?"

"It sure is," Doc replied with a grim smile. "I was afraid something like this would happen, so I incased it in a black box, similar to the ones on airplanes. All we have to do is upload this processor into a new body and she'll be as good as new."

"That's great, Doc," Jesse said. "I really like Goldie. She's like the crazy aunt I never had."

Doc stuck out his tongue in disgust. "Please don't ever say that again. People will think Goldie and I are married."

"What about Mikhail?" Ororo asked, cradling his limp head in her arms.

Mikhail gazed up at Ororo and smiled weakly. "Don't worry about me, Beauty. I've lived a good life." He then turned his head and coughed. Blood splattered on the sand.

"And you're going to continue living a good life," Doc said warmly. He grabbed the vial Aladdin dropped on the beach and sucked out the vaccine with the syringe Jesse used to give Martin morphine. He then attached a needle and grabbed Mikhail's wrist. Aladdin lifted his head, watching the entire thing.

Mikhail widened his eyes in surprise. "Doctor Xander... is that your..."

"Yes, Mikhail, it's my Fountain of Youth. It should start attacking your tumors immediately. Within two weeks, all the cancerous cells in your body should be eradicated."

Doc stuck the needle into Mikhail's arm. Mikhail closed his eyes and winced in pain. After Doc removed the needle, Mikhail's eyes flickered open.

"Thank you, Doctor."

"Don't mention it, kiddo." Doc leaned forward and kissed Mikhail on the forehead. He then climbed to his feet.

"Thank you, Professor," Aladdin grumbled, pushing himself off the beach. His face was ghostly white and his teeth were clenched shut as he fought against the cascading waves of pain wracking his body. His severed arm still lay by his feet.

Doc stormed over to Aladdin and said, "You're welcome." He then punched his former student in the face, knocking him flat on his back. Jesse and his siblings stared at Doc in awe.

Doc straddled Aladdin's body and pulled him up by his hair. He clutched a small pistol of knock-out gas in his left hand.

"W... what are you doing?" Aladdin sputtered.

"Making a citizen's arrest," Doc barked.

"What?! You can't..."

"You're under arrest for crimes against humanity," Doc snapped, cutting him off. "You have the right to shut your stupid face."

Aladdin fell silent.

Lowering his voice so dramatically that it was almost eerie, Doc said, "You have aided and abetted countless genocides. You have allied yourself with the most evil and vile scum on the face of the Earth. My biggest regret is teaching you everything I know. You will be tried by the United Nations for your campaign of death and destruction. You will be forced to confront your victims, hear their stories, know their loss. Maybe then you'll realize just how far you've fallen."

Aladdin narrowed his eyes and growled. Jesse noticed one of his vipers beginning to lift into the air.

Jesse held out his hand and shouted, "Doc, watch out!"

The viper wrapped around Doc's waist. But Doc was ready. He instantly pulled the trigger of his pistol. A cloud of green gas enveloped Aladdin's face. His eyes rolled into the back of his head and he slumped backwards into the sand. The viper unraveled off of Doc and collapsed to the beach.

Doc faced Jesse and his siblings. "It's over, kids. Let's go home."

"But how?" Jesse asked. "Our plane is totaled."

"We can take Aladdin's plane," Doc replied.

"Right," Jesse said, slapping his head. He felt dumb for not figuring that out himself.

Doc and Jesse dragged Aladdin's unconscious body aboard the plane and tossed him into the cabin. They then came back out to retrieve Martin, who continued staring at his hand and giggling. Doc grumbled something about needing to dilute his extra-strength morphine. Once Ororo and Journey helped Mikhail climb into the plane, the hatch door slammed shut.

Jesse and Doc immediately stripped Aladdin out of his exoskeleton and tied him up with a grappling hook. Doc also wrapped a bandage around Aladdin's gruesome shoulder wound. Once the most dangerous man on Earth was completely disarmed, Jesse and the gang began to relax.

Doc flipped on the plane's turbo engines and blasted off toward America. Jesse and his sisters tended to Martin's leg wound, cleaning it out and wrapping it with bandages. Once they were done, Jesse collapsed into a chair. Within seconds he was fast asleep. And unlike last time, nothing woke him up.

Chapter Thirty-Three: Family Reunion

Jesse, Ororo, and the gang arrived back in New York several hours after leaving the South Pacific. It turned out Aladdin's plane was even faster than Doc's. They landed in the parking lot of the hospital Mr. and Mrs. Baxter were staying at and rushed inside. Paramedics met them at the door and placed Aladdin on a stretcher. When the paramedics realized their patient was the Merchant of Death, they nearly hyperventilated. Aladdin was intimidating even while unconscious and without an arm. Several police officers rushed out to stand guard while the paramedics stabilized the mass-murderer and rushed him into a room for emergency surgery. His cauterized wound had prevented a significant amount of blood loss, but it was still a serious, life-threatening injury. The risk of infection alone was enough to thrust him into critical condition.

Mikhail and Martin were placed on stretchers as well. In Mikhail's case it was mainly as a safety precaution. He actually looked healthier than he had in months.

Jesse, Ororo, Journey, and Doc were all checked out, too. Except for a few superficial cuts and bruises, they were miraculously okay.

Afterwards, Jesse and his siblings were taken back to see their parents. Mr. and Mrs. Baxter jumped out of their beds as soon as Jesse, Ororo, and Journey entered the room. They swallowed all three of them up in an asphyxiating bear-hug. Jesse's face was shoved up against his father's hairy chest. When he finally slipped through the group-hug, he hacked up a hairball.

Jesse and his siblings were in the middle of regaling their parents with their enthralling tale when President Robinson burst into the room, his tie flipped over his shoulder. As soon as he caught sight of Doc, he narrowed his eyes and clenched his fists.

Secretary of Defense Paternus barged in with several secret service agents and smirked. "You're in deep doo-doo, Xander."

The president raised his hand, prompting Paternus to shut up.

Doc gulped and twiddled his thumbs. "Um, hi Mr. President. I'm sorry I snuck away again... but I... well.. um..."

The president stormed over and jabbed his finger in Doc's chest.

"I have a couple choice words to say to you, Doctor Xander."

Doc closed his eyes and flinched.

President Robinson took a deep breath, then exhaled and blurted out, "Thank you."

"WHAT?" Paternus hollered.

Doc opened his eyes and stared at the president in shock. President Robinson held out his hand and smiled like he had just secured a Middle East peace deal.

Doc shook the president's hand and stammered, "You're welcome... I think."

The president laughed and slapped Doc on the back. "I got a call just a little while ago from one of our commanders out in the Pacific. Apparently you dismantled Aladdin Salazar's secret headquarters single-handedly."

"We helped a little," Ororo said.

"Oh please, we helped a lot!" Journey shouted.

The president chuckled. "One of our aircraft carriers received your distress signal and rescued Aladdin's soldiers from the Pacific. They also found a bunch of rare and endangered animals wandering around a couple nearby sandbars."

"Aladdin was trying to build a zoo," Ororo

explained.

The president nodded. "Well, several major wildlife organizations are en route to those sandbars and island atolls to rescue the poor creatures. They will be taken to wildlife sanctuaries in Africa to receive medical treatment."

"That's good to hear," Jesse said.

"On top of all that, I just received word you apprehended the Merchant of Death and brought him here to New York," the president said gleefully, unable to hide his excitement. He smiled like he had just hit the jackpot. "Rumor has it you guys, er, hacked off his arm."

Jesse's face turned red. He knew most people would congratulate him for severing the arm of a genocidal lunatic, but it was not something he was proud of. He simply did what he had to do to save his uncle and sisters from certain death.

Doc noticed Jesse's embarrassment and quickly said, "Aladdin will be fine. What do you need two arms for anyway?"

"You need them for a lot of things, Doc," Journey interjected. "You need them to tie your shoes, drive a car, go to—mmmmm!"

Ororo clamped her robotic hand over Journey's arm, a gesture Jesse truly appreciated.

Doc cleared his throat and said, "Anyway, as soon as Salazar's medical condition improves, you can toss him in prison and throw away the key. I think a life sentence would be justified"

The president's grin widened. "God bless all of you. Your heroic efforts have made this world a better place."

"What about the meeting at the United Nations, sir?" Doc asked. Jesse was grateful for the change of subject. "Wasn't that today?"

"Yes it was, and we had to postpone, seeing as how our star speaker went MIA."

Doc went back to twiddling his thumbs. "Er, sorry about that, sir. I had to go and save the planet."

"Don't worry, Doc, I already announced to the world that your vaccine has caused severe side effects in quite a few of your patients. There have already been reports of a drastic reduction in kidnappings and terrorist plots. And when word spreads that Aladdin has been incarcerated, the attacks should plummet even further."

Doc breathed a sigh of relief. "That's terrific news, sir."

Paternus marched over and sputtered, "Wait a minute, aren't you gonna reprimand Xander for disobeying our direct orders and---"

"You know, Robert, Xander wouldn't have had to disobey our orders if *you* had done your job and nabbed Aladdin years ago," the president interjected, cutting off his bitter secretary of defense.

"Ohhh, you just got burned by the president!" Journey shouted.

Paternus' mouth fell open in shock. "But Mr. President, you know my number one priority has always been capturing Aladdin Salazar! I... I..."

The president placed his hand on Paternus' shoulder. "Robert, you seriously need a vacation. Why don't you go home and spend some time with your family?"

"I hate my family," Paternus growled.

The president pointed toward the door. "Go, Robert. I don't want to see you for at least a few days. And for goodness sake, come back in a better mood."

Paternus grumbled how he hated everyone and stormed out of the hospital.

The president turned back toward Jesse and the gang and rolled his eyes. "That man's one of the main reasons I have so many gray hairs."

"Oh, I didn't even notice you were graying, Mr. President," Jesse lied.

The president glanced at his watch. "Well, I'm heading back to D.C. for a meeting with some foreign dignitaries. I booked your room at the hotel through the end of the week, so feel free to spend a few more days in

New York."

"Awesome!" Jesse exclaimed.

The president shook everyone's hands before exiting the room. Two secret service agents stayed behind. Unlike back at the hotel, Doc did not object. Jesse figured Doc appreciated the added protection. Now that Aladdin was incarcerated and his arms trafficking empire was in shambles, Doc was a marked man... even more so than before. Every criminal organization on Earth would want his head on a proverbial platter. They would also want revenge against Jesse and his family. But Jesse didn't care about that at the moment. He was just happy his family had survived their harrowing ordeal.

Jesse and his sisters proceeded to re-enact their improbable invasion of Aladdin's floating fortress. When they were finished, Ororo started rambling on about her wild chase through the skies of Manhattan. Jesse got slightly bored by this, mostly because he wasn't involved in the action, so he walked over to the window overlooking the city.

After they had escaped Aladdin's airship in the Arctic, Jesse thought about how much better life would be if he had a 'normal' life, with a 'normal' family. Jesse now realized how incredibly selfish he had been.

Jesse was truly lucky to have such an amazing family. Sure they were wacky, but they all had huge hearts. They cared about people, they cared about the world, and they cared about him. So many kids didn't have loved ones to care for them. Jesse did. And for that alone he was one of the luckiest kids on Earth.

Jesse's family wasn't too frightened to fight for what they believed in, for what they knew was right. So many people just sat around and watched the world burn. They may have had good hearts, but they did not have courage. His parents and siblings had good hearts *AND* lots of courage. His mom and dad were freedom fighters, extinguishing the flames of injustice. And they were cool enough to share their heroic lifestyle with him and his sisters... sisters his parents had saved from unspeakable horrors.

Yes, Jesse finally realized just how lucky he truly was. There was just one thing missing.

"Jesse?"

Jesse twirled around in shock. Alex Rodriguez stood in the doorway of the hospital room, her eyes welled up with tears.

Jesse broke into a giant grin and dashed toward Alex. She met him halfway and they embraced in the middle of the room.

"Thank god you're okay," she sobbed, burying her head in his chest.

Jesse ran his fingers through Alex's shimmering black hair and exhaled. The missing piece was now in place.

After hugging for what felt like hours (but was actually only a minute or so), Jesse and Alex stepped back, tears trickling down their cheeks.

"How did you get here?" Jesse asked, still struggling to overcome his shock that Alex was in New York.

"Everyone on the cruise ship was taken to Miami," Alex explained, wiping her eyes with her sleeve. "My parents then booked us a flight to New York. We live here part of the year. We heard on the news that you guys were staying here. We came as soon as we could."

Jesse and Alex stopped talking and hugged each other again. They did not break their embrace for a long, long time. When they finally did, Alex's parents and little brother walked in and exchanged pleasantries with Doctor Xander and the Baxters.

Jimmy rushed over to Journey and blurted out, "Hey gorgeous!"

Journey sighed and rolled her eyes, but Jesse noticed the faintest hint of a smile tugging at her lips.

Jimmy rubbed the back of his head and awkwardly said, "Sooooo... I was wondering, did you wanna hang out? My mom has coupons for Chuck E Cheese. We get fifty free tokens if we buy a large pizza."

Jesse expected Journey to tell Jimmy to buzz off. He was therefore astonished when she said, "If you promise to stop bothering me, then fine, we can go to stupid, lame Chuck E Cheese."

Jimmy's mouth dropped open in shock. Jesse's mouth dropped open as well.

Jimmy jumped up and down like a maniac. "Mom, I've found my soul mate! I can't wait to marry Journey and have a family!"

Journey slapped her head and groaned.

Alex nudged Jesse in the side. "Would you like to go to Chuck E Cheese, too? I'll probably have to babysit. I'd love to have someone my age to hang out with."

Jesse cracked a smile. "Are you asking me out?"

Alex returned the smile. "I suppose I am, although I would prefer our first date were somewhere a bit more classy... like McDonalds."

Jesse chuckled. "Chuck E Cheese will be our warm-up date, then we can have a real one later on. Burger King has a deal on Whoppers, I heard."

Mrs. Baxter cleared her throat. "I think you kids will need adult chaperones."

"I agree," Mr. Baxter replied.

Jesse smirked. He found it hilarious how protective his mom and dad were when it came to dating, and yet they allowed him to travel to the most dangerous places on Earth. It was one of the things he loved about his parents. They weren't normal by any stretch of the imagination, but they loved him... and he loved them.

As Jesse and his family and friends excitedly talked about their amazing adventures over the past several days, he couldn't help but feel happy and content. For the first time in days he was able to relax.

Jesse just hoped the good times lasted longer than a few hours this time. He knew they probably wouldn't, but he could still dream.

Epilogue: Black Phoenix Rising

Christmas Day, at the North Pole...

A polar bear and her two cubs scurried across the Arctic ice. They were on the hunt for a Christmas Day meal.

The mother skidded toward a crack in the ice. Her cubs tumbled over and started goofing around, biting each other and smacking each other in the face. The mother ignored her unruly children. She was busy peering through the ice, searching for a blubbery supper.

The mother bear had just started clawing at the fissure in the ice cap when a triangular-shaped flying object hovered directly above her. The bear stood on her hind legs and peered upwards. The object appeared to be some sort of golden flying pyramid, about thirty feet wide at the base. The metallic exterior of the pyramid glistened under the Arctic star-light. The mysterious flying object was the brightest object the polar bear had seen since the sun set back in October.

A thunderous cracking noise caused the polar bear and her cubs to topple backwards. The crack beneath her feet widened rapidly. The polar bear dashed away as fast as she could, her cubs trailing far behind. They had moved just in the nick of time. The ice sheet ruptured and collapsed into the freezing sea. Emerging from the monstrous fissure was an even larger pyramid.

Pretty soon the crack in the ice was nearly half a mile long. The base of the pyramid finally lifted out of the frigid sea and levitated into the sky. From top-to-bottom the pyramid was over 2,000-feet tall. The much smaller pyramid flew toward the larger one and entered a hatch door near the base. Once the smaller pyramid disappeared, the hatch door slammed shut and the giant pyramid submerged back into the sea. The fissure began to re-freeze almost instantly.

The smaller pyramid flew through a massive hangar and landed beside several other triangular-shaped aircrafts. Six half-naked men approached the pyramid. All six men wore white linen kilts and clutched gleaming, double-edged spears. They all had on black eyeliner and green and blue eye shadow. They resembled ancient Egyptians.

A small door at the base of the pyramid slid open, and out walked two more shirtless men. They carried a small, frail scientist and tossed him to the floor. The scientist peered up through his cracked glasses and gasped. The eight men were soon joined by dozens of others. All of the men were dressed like ancient Egyptians, Mayans, Greeks, Romans, and other extinct civilizations.

"Wha... what is this all about?" barked the scientist.

A cold, deep voice said, "Hello, Xing Lee. It has been a long time. Too long, I dare say."

Xing Lee staggered to his feet and peered into the shadows. Two fiery red eyes stared back at him. A muscular, 7-foot tall man suddenly emerged from the darkness. The red eyes belonged to him.

The man wore a kilt like the other Egyptians, but his was black, with blue and green stripes. An elaborate, similarly designed headdress adorned his bald head. A gleaming amulet hung from his neck, and his monstrous hands clutched a golden spear adorned with gleaming emeralds and rubies. The man's body made a clanking noise every time he took a step.

Xing's face turned pure white. He grabbed his chest in an attempt to control his rapidly beating heart.

The man smiled, revealing brilliant white teeth.

"What's wrong, Xing? You look like you've just

seen a ghost."

Xing stepped back, nearly impaling himself on a spear. In a hoarse whisper, he stammered, "My god... K.. Kelvin? But... you're dead!"

An Egyptian stepped forward and whacked Xing across the back of his neck. "You will refer to the Pharaoh as Lord Kelvin, you sniveling..."

Kelvin raised his hand, silencing the Egyptian. The Egyptian bowed his head and stepped back.

Kelvin walked over to Xing, his body making a 'whirring' noise every time he moved. He helped Xing to his feet and patted him on the back. Xing nearly fell back to the floor. Kelvin's hand felt like solid steel.

"I... I must be dreaming," said Xing, removing his glasses and rubbing his eyes. "Yeah, that's it. Kelvin is dead. This can't be real. I must have had bad sushi last night."

"You are not dreaming, Xing. Your sushi was just fine."

Xing shook his head in disbelief. "But... how can this be? Doctor Xander, Aladdin Salazar, and the Viper Squad killed you two decades ago when they..."

"Do not EVER mention Xander and Salazar in my presence," Kelvin snarled. "Nor shall you ever utter the name of that insidious special-forces group. They destroyed my empire... they destroyed my pyramid... they destroyed my body... they nearly destroyed my very soul."

"Your... your body?" Xing stammered.

"Yes. My old body was set afire by missiles. But unbeknownst to you peons, my mind had been scanned into a super-computer months before my death, making me nearly immortal. All I needed was a vessel to contain my genius... *this* glorious, indestructible vessel."

Kelvin stepped back and held out his arms. Xing looked up at his towering old friend in awe.

"On the outside I look remarkably human. But on the inside I am an imperishable cyborg. For the past twenty years I have remained in hiding...slowly yet surely rebuilding my empire... biding my time to strike. And that time is *now*."

Xing shook his head, struggling to wrap his head around what Kelvin was telling him. "But... what do you need me for?"

Kelvin snapped his fingers. Two Egyptians grabbed Xing by his arms and pulled him into an adjoining room. Kelvin and his dozens of followers walked in after them

Kelvin marched over to a towering warhead sitting inside a transparent container. "You're a nuclear scientist. I need you to help me activate this weapon."

"What?! No... I can't! I..."

Xing trailed off as he noticed a large screen in the back of the room. The screen showed a digital map of the world. Red dots blinked all over the place. Beneath the dots were names he recognized. They were the names of some of the most brilliant scientists on the planet. A lot of them were his friends. Some of the scientists were astrophysicists, others were geneticists, a few were experts in renewable energy, several were quantum physicists.... There were biologists, chemists, mathematicians.... Every scientific field a person could dream of was represented by the flashing map.

Four dots over Manhattan especially caught Xing's eye. The names under the dots read Hank Baxter, Ariel Baxter, Zachary Xander, and Aladdin Salazar.

Kelvin smiled as he noticed Xing staring at the names.

"You were only the first target. You are about to be joined by dozens of others."

"But why?" stammered Xing.

"After I destroy the civilized world, I need the smartest people on Earth to help me rebuild it," Kelvin said. His eyes glowed so bright that Xing was forced to look away.

"Destroy the world?! You expect to do that with one nuclear warhead?"

"My plan will make sense soon enough, Xing. Now can I count on you to help me, or do I need to wipe out your family?"

Xing's face turned even whiter than it already was. "My family?! No... leave them alone...."

"Good, so you'll cooperate. My men will show you to your quarters."

"But... I..."

Xing was carried off by the two Egyptians.

Kelvin turned back to his flashing map. He glanced at all the names. When his gaze fell over Manhattan, his lips curled into a hideous scowl.

"I can't wait until we reunite, Doctor Xander. I want you to see with your own eyes how I have rebuilt my empire... the empire you nearly destroyed."

Kelvin crossed his bulging arms over his strapping chest. His eyes glowed as bright as spotlights.

"The Phoenix Society had a catastrophic fall and went up in flames. But like the mythical bird we are named after, the Phoenix Society has risen from the ashes of its own destruction. And I, the Black Phoenix, will lead us to glory.

Kelvin clenched his fist and waved it in front of the map. "Enjoy your last few days of peace, Xander. Soon I will burn your world to a *crisp*."

To be continued in...

ADVENTURES OF A MAD SCIENTIST 2: THE FUTURE IS CALLING

Made in the USA
San Bernardino, CA
05 December 2017